THE SHADOWS BEHIND

KRISTI PETERSEN SCHOONOVER

Books & Boos Press

Hebron, CT

"Jarring Lucas" first appeared in *Canopic Jars: Tales of Mummies and Mummification* (Great Old Ones Publishing, Nov. 2013)

"Down in the Green" first appeared in *Sinfully Twisted* (Feb. 2006)

"Candle Garden" first appeared in *The Taj Mahal Review* (June 2007)

"Under the Kudzu" first appeared in *Behind Locked Doors* (Pill Hill Press, March 2012)

"Mujina" first appeared in *Dark Passages II* (Skinwalker Press, Fall 2016)

"Doors" first appeared in *Carpe Articulum Literary Review* (Vol. 3, Issue 3, Fall 2010)

"Roots" first appeared in *Pernicious Invaders* (Great Old Ones Publishing, Nov. 2016)

"The Thing Inside" first appeared in *Unnatural Tales of the Jackalope* (Western Legends Press, June 2012)

"Deconstructing Fireflies" (with Nathan D. Schoonover) first appeared in *The Illuminata* (Dec. 2006)

"How I Learned to Stop Complaining and Love the Bunny" first appeared in *Citizen Culture Magazine* (Feb. 2005)

Front cover image from pxhere.com, design by A. L. Cortez

Edited by S & L Editing (www.slediting.com)

First printing edition 2019.

Books & Boos Press
PO Box 772
Hebron, CT 06248
www.booksandboospress.com

ISBN: 978-0-9979329-6-6

For Manzino, who knew the shadows, but never let them crush
his spirit, and was always there when I needed him.
I love you.

. . . and miles to go before we sleep.

CONTENTS

FOREWORD

I ONCE WROTE that whenever you look behind a ghost story, what you will find is eternal love, unbearable loss, and unconquerable fear. To this list Kristi Petersen Schoonover adds regret, and mistakes that can never be set right.

These are the things that haunt us, creating, as Schoonover tells us in one of her stories, the shadows that "ghosts, or God knew what else" move into. The characters in her new collection, *The Shadows Behind*, occupy haunted, complicated worlds, where things go terribly wrong, and there is no easy way forward. People die, people hurt each other, people screw up, creating yet another monster to lurk in those dark corners we try so desperately to avoid. You can fight them, or you can surrender, but you cannot make them go entirely away. Sometimes the monsters win, sometimes you can even forge a truce, but they will always be there, and as long as you live, there will always be more to join the growing crowd inhabiting the shadows. The characters who do best in Schoonover's stories are the ones who embrace their shadows, and try to see them differently.

This doesn't necessarily lead to a happy ending, and this is what makes Schoonover's stories so satisfying. How can a life in which death and loss are inescapable, a life in which we make devastating irreversible mistakes, ever be truly happy? Acceptance isn't happy. It's peaceful—and it is a worthy and realistic goal. There is truth in the shadows, even if it isn't pretty, and you will find all your friends there. By the end of *The Shadows Behind*, Kristi Petersen Schoonover has masterfully illuminated a path to a liberating peace, in a poignant and deliciously scary way: look directly into the shadows, listen to your heart, identify what you are grasping so tightly and let go. Otherwise, like some of Schoonover's chilling characters, *you* will become the scariest—and deadliest—monster lurking in the darkness.

Stacy Horn
Author of Damnation Island *and*
Imperfect Harmony

January 5, 2019

IMMOLATION

I'M USED TO going to far-flung places and the various dangerous means of travel usually involved in getting there: dynamite-packed trucks that leak gas, planes with bellies so rotted I can see through to the open sky, elephants with sour attitudes.

Sumbawa was a different story: after a twenty-five-hour-plus flight from New York to Bali, every ferry, truck, minibus, and finally boat was not only unreliable, it didn't seem to come with a set price: I had to *negotiate, my friend, negotiate* much more than I ever had anywhere else. What got scary was that I had to know my Indonesian currency pretty well, or I was just plain screwed.

The leathery captain of the speedboat I hired for the last leg of the journey doubled his price and shoved a crude puppet—a flat, jointed thing with a hideous face (for protection, he said)— in my hand when he learned I was going to the mountain. He next cited vanishing tourists in an effort to change my mind, even as he drove like James Bond to get me there in a hurry.

When, at last, after forty grueling hours, I arrived—seasick and unnerved—at the port of Calabai, there was only one thing on my mind: a cot, or even a patch of ground covered in fronds.

Then, there stood Rosalia: a silhouette in a white sarong against a row of palm trees.

And I forgot everything.

⁂

When Rosalia had called me from her sat phone and asked if I could come to Sumbawa to help excavate a structure buried in Tambora's 1815 eruption, I was more than willing. "There are lots of eager kids around, Thompson, but this thing—this project needs you, your incredible instinct . . . *this could be* what's left of one of the cultures that was wiped out . . . but there's—"

The reception burbled into a choppy mess, like a badly scratched record. "Rosie? Hello?"

Suddenly she was clear again: ". . . need to know, are you happy?"

I looked around the only bar in Wilkeson, which at one in the afternoon was empty save for me. The question was a punch in the gut. The geese had flown south on my last relationship; Kelly had left me in my sea of papers and boots mucked with the dirt of perhaps twenty digs, including Pompeii, claiming I had no love for anything except my work. Rosalia didn't know this, and she didn't need to—we'd been out of touch, except for the occasional e-mail asking permission to quote one another's reports for a submission to some academic journal—for nearly a decade. Perhaps she was asking me this for other reasons: Did she want to get back together? "Why?"

Despite the terrible connection, I heard that frustrated sigh she always made when she had to clarify something she felt should've been obvious. "It's important." *Crackle, crackle.* "Just . . . just answer the question."

Well, that didn't sound too hard. "I'm on solid ground, Rosie. No worries."

Crackle, crackle. "I'll send you details. Come as soon as you can."

Rosalia is no longer that willowy, carefree girl in jeans, her sunburned cheeks spattered with ancient volcanic ash. She seems shrunken, and looks older than she should; she even has crow's feet. In my mind's eye, though, she's no different, and when she lends her slight hand to help me out of the boat, her pull is so strong I nearly crash into her.

"Thom." She hugs me; she smells like apples and sweat. "You look exactly the same."

"So do you." I peer beyond her shoulder. Because of the poor condition of the dock, I'm expecting a rundown huddle of shacks; what I'm treated to is a cheery neighborhood of vibrant cabins—yellow and aqua, pink and green, purple and orange—with colored glass windows. Palm trees sway lazily, and a thrashed-together bridge plunges deep into a jungle laced with pops of jasmine. The air smells of salt and lemons.

It's hard to envision that only two hundred years ago this place was a seething cauldron of hell that took the lives of thousands in an instant.

"I've rented a really nice place, but it's a ways outside of town." She leads me from the dock.

I'd heard this island never really recovered from Tambora's eruption—entire *kingdoms* were buried, lost forever—yet it doesn't seem entirely true. There's no shortage of guides to take trekkers up the mountain, and as we walk through the village, the scents change. There are the smells of fresh-baked bread, and cooking fish in a spice I don't recognize but is reminiscent of burnt shallots and cinnamon. The residents of this shoreside village are in shorts, T-shirts, and other modern clothes—except, it seems, for one.

The shoeless young woman in an orange dress has jet black hair—like Rosalia, who wears hers in a bun—down to her waist. She seems aware I'm staring and returns an alluring smile, one that makes me realize I *am* lonely.

"Did you hear what I said?" Rosalia sets her hand on my arm.

Prickles of excitement course through me. I realize I've been staring down an alley.

The young woman is gone.

"Is everything okay, Thom?"

"Oh—yeah. I'm fine." I look into Rosalia's eyes and understand, that, yes. *I want her back.* "Just anxious to get started."

"That." She sighs. "Could be a while, actually." She approaches a motorbike propped against the side of a pineapple-colored building and stands it up, motioning for me to put my pack in the basket behind the double seat. "Get on."

We navigate the bumpy roads. For some reason, not even Rosalia's closeness wipes the image of Orange Dress from my mind.

❧

It's difficult to pinpoint the reason for the split between us. It isn't like there was shit tossed on the lawn or that the bed grew cold; Rosalia and I didn't even live together. While we'd focused on getting assigned to the same projects and digs, we were separated for four in a row. The conversations and calls dwindled during those months; I was in the middle of leading an excavation in Akrotiri when suddenly I realized we hadn't communicated in almost eight weeks. We just sort of . . . well, lost track of each other after that. Things died in the volcanic fallout of new discoveries, you might say.

I never stopped thinking about her, though; she was almost like an excavation herself. When the loneliness eventually got to me, I started dating Kelly, one of my students. At first, she seemed so much like Rosalia; passionate and excitable, ready to travel the world and solve its Plinian mysteries. After the first few months, it was clear she preferred staying home. She eventually shifted her focus to developing new ways of bringing excavations to life virtually, for students who couldn't have those experiences. It didn't mean she wasn't brilliant. It just meant she didn't want to play in the dirt, sweat like a boar and worry about where the next drink of clean water was coming from, and it caused friction between us that, in the end, we couldn't overcome.

Now, in the sprawl of Rosalia's coconut timber house nearly an hour outside of the village, I'm struck by how Kelly pales in comparison. Rosalia seems taller and more agile than she did this afternoon as she works in the open-air kitchen, cooking a dish that fills the night with the smell of turmeric and garlic.

Two bottles of Balinese wine sit in front of me. I choose one calling itself White Velvet, twist off the yellow top, and pour some into her glass. "I read about your collaboration at Sunset Crater a while back. Great work."

"Yes, well, I'm always working on someone else's baby." She pats something dry inside a towel and sets it aside. "I've never made that one discovery that's going to make me *National Geographic*'s darling."

"So what? I didn't." I set her glass on the counter and return to my seat. "Lots of us don't."

"That's not what I'm about, Thom." She grinds spices using a mortar and pestle. "I want the stability to stay in the field. I don't want to end up curating at a museum or consulting at an engineering firm, but that's where I'm headed. I've put in the work. It's time I get what I deserve." Sipping her wine, she turns to face me. "But I think what I just found may be it."

She tells me about the trip she took that's resulted in my being here. "It can take a couple of grueling days to reach Tambora's summit." She leaves the inset grill and seizes a skillet. "About ten hours into the hike, my right leg was in a massive amount of pain. When I rolled up my pants, I found leeches. A few, in fact. Rimbo—my guide—told me to stay still and plunged into the jungle."

"We know that's never good." I sip my wine. It's lighter than I like, with a hint of an almost cantaloupe-but-not-quite fruit I can't identify.

"He came back with something to cut off the leeches." She wipes her hands on a cloth and reaches into a small box on her counter. "Look." She drops an object in my hand.

It's a pie-shaped piece of quartz a little smaller than my palm, and it's clear it's been worked. "There's evidence of percussion flaking here. This was part of a tool. No, wait." The rounded bottom betrays it. "It was maybe part of a carrying vessel of some kind. Possibly a bowl, maybe for gathering."

She's beaming. "Turn it over."

On the side that isn't carved, a blood-colored but indecipherable design reminds me of a primitive cave drawing.

She folds her arms. "It's not like the pieces that were discovered in the lost kingdom that was found on the opposite side of the mountain . . . I've actually handled those, and they're like ceramic." She sips her wine. "I made Rimbo take me to where he'd found it. There's a crack in a pumice deposit, spilling stuff just like this." She takes the rock from me and puts it back in its box. "I think what I've found is yet another buried village that, instead of having ties to Vietnam and China, has ties to somewhere else . . . *southe*ast."

I envision the globe in my head. "Australia."

She smiles. "I'm willing to bet that color on there is ochre."

There is the *hish* of food sizzling in the frying pan.

"Jesus."

She returns to the skillet. "Which might mean yet another culture was completely erased, one influenced by a country that was even more difficult to get to. I mean, we know of at least one language that was wiped out. This could be a second." She sets our dinner before us, seats herself, and reaches for more wine. "This is it, Thom. This is what I've been waiting for my entire life. Mmmm." She chews. "Looks like I finally got the balance right."

I look at the plate. A fish stares at me through clouded, dead eyes. "What is this?"

"Ikan bakar," she says. "It's in a soy and chili-based sauce."

I've eaten plenty of off-the-wall stuff: steamed silkworms, giant ditch frog, candied grasshoppers—even tuna eyeballs. This dish, for some reason, is disturbing; I feel like I'm being watched. I pick at the jumble of unidentifiable vegetable bits that serves as a garnish. "When do we dig?"

"Would you do anything for me?"

I stop chewing the hard vegetables, which are like spicy grains of sand gritting against my teeth. "I'm here, aren't I?"

"We have to obtain a permit."

I try to hide my disappointment: Is *this* really why she asked me to come? Because I have stronger credentials? "Of *course* I'll secure one for you."

"It's not like that. This is a requirement for a bit of a different reason." She sips her wine. "We have to show we're strong enough not to fall prey to the ghosts of the eruption."

I almost choke. "What?"

She sighs. "There have been disappearances on the mountain. The locals claim the angry spirits tempt the victims with illusions of grandeur, leading them farther and farther up the slopes. No one knows what happens, but they never come back."

I think of the crude puppet my sun-parched captain, babbling away, had forced on me, and now it makes sense. I've heard my fair share of eruption-related ghost stories. Residents of Naples say they hear the screams of the dying in the ruins of Pompeii; Hawaiians believe the goddess Pele knocks on doors asking for water; people in Katibung insist the burnt apparitions of refugees from Krakatoa's wrath wander the nearby mountains. I took these stories as fictions, but Rosalia didn't. She grew up on

Martinique, and claimed that every morning she'd be awakened precisely at 7:52 a.m. by the final, hysterical prayers of the victims of Mt. Pelée. She fervently believed. It was part of her.

Because she believes, I always pretend to. "So how's a permit going to protect us from the supernatural? I don't get it."

She picks at her fish. "These people don't want trouble—in their language, Tambora means 'gone.' They don't want to be under scrutiny if a tourist or visitor disappears. Anyone who wants a permit has to go before a council and prove he's impervious to any temptation. That he wants for nothing. If he wants for nothing, the spirits have nothing to use against him. A lonely soul, apparently, is the biggest risk." She looks at me.

In those eyes I see so many things. Her face nearly touching mine as we extracted pottery shards from the dirt. Her old mattress, practically new because she was so busy shovel-bumming she was hardly home. Her leap into my arms when she got the assistantship at the ruins near Hekla. Her thrill when we finished touring Pompeii and cruised Naples in search of the world's best *torta caprese*. Her awe at the imposing loom of Mt. Paektu; her sadness at the ash-thronged landscapes beneath Mount Aso and the Soufrière Hills. Our pushpin-spangled wall map . . . we'd marked every volcano. Green meant we'd been there. Red meant we hadn't.

We had a lot of greens and only a few reds when things broke down.

"I tried to secure a permit myself, but they made it clear they don't want an unaccompanied woman going up there." She reaches for the wine, tops off both of our glasses.

"What do I need to do?"

"I told them you were my husband and you were on your way. We have money, we have each other, we have passionate careers. We are fulfilled and there is *nothing* the mountain can take away from us."

I can't believe I've just heard those words. *Husband.* I can almost feel the small of her back beneath my fingers, and my mind goes other places, and I remember something she said: *You know that poem, rage, rage against the dying of the light? What was it like in those last hours in Pompeii? What were people doing? Were they holed up in their homes making love to take their minds off the terror? Were they hoping that, if they insisted on living life, it would never end? What did the air smell like, was it—*

"... with a fork?" she asks.

I'm jarred. "What?"

"I said, 'Wouldn't you rather eat that with a fork?' You're sitting there squishing the chilis between your fingers."

"Oh! Oh, yeah." My cheeks flush with embarrassment as I reach for the cloth napkin.

She watches me intently over the rim of her glass, but when I meet her gaze she looks down at her food. "I wouldn't want to ruin your happiness with . . . whomever . . . it is you have back home. We'll keep this between us."

I harrumph out of nervousness. *There's something there, isn't there?* The candle on the table flickers. "I . . . I don't, actually."

I fail to get the pleased response I'm expecting.

Instead, she stiffens her back—much as she would when she'd open a letter and discover she'd been denied whatever residency or grant to which she'd applied—and her brow furrows. "No?"

I shake my head.

The only sounds are the far-off cries of unfamiliar birds and a low rumble.

"There was someone for a while, but . . . it didn't work out."

She drains her wine. "I'm sorry." She gets up from the table, takes her dish, and sets it in the wash basin.

"Hey, no, it's fine, really, I—I'm good."

Her only response is turning on the tap and furiously rubbing a cloth against her plate.

I push back my chair, relieved to be away from the judgmental glare of the fish, but having a hard time quelling the need to go to her and set my hands on her arms. Instead, I stop short of the counter. "Rosie."

"I've changed my mind." She shuts off the spigot and fixes her gaze on the small box for a moment, then faces me. "I think it's best that you go. We'll arrange for your travel in the morning."

"Rosie—"

"Your room is across the way." She motions with her head. "Good night."

In the bowels of night, I sweat awake to the taste of scorched paper and a rumble in the distance. I'm not sure where I am.

Rain spattering into my room grounds me in Sumbawa, at Rosalia's, after a painful conversation. I feel exposed; interior rooms are wall-less and border a courtyard. Although I can't see her room from mine—it's obscured behind the wall of the formal dining room—I can see into the now-dark kitchen, and beyond that, the front door.

The rectangular swimming pool, its surface shimmering in the moonlit rain, beckons.

I flip back the sheet and listen, straining in vain to hear her snore that I know would lull me back to sleep.

Didn't she say she needed *me*, specifically?

Yes. That there were plenty of eager kids, but that she needed *my* instincts.

Me. She needed *me.* So why this sudden shift?

I hear a noise in the kitchen. A petite shadow moves in its depths.

"Rosie?"

There's no response, and I remember that often, when renting in these remote places, Rosalia would hire a local to keep the place clean so we could concentrate on the work; sometimes they came at strange hours. Still, if that were the case, wouldn't she have said something? Why is this person working in the dark?

The figure steps onto the grass and pads toward me. She appears to be the young woman I'd seen in town—Orange Dress. She seems undisturbed by the rain, except to cup her delicate hand over the flower in her hair.

When she reaches the threshold of my room, I can see it isn't Orange Dress at all.

It's Rosalia.

My breath catches in my throat as she glides into the room and approaches the bed, her fire-red batik robe—open and exposing her slender, slip-clad form—caressing my thigh as she settles close.

I find my voice. "I thought you wanted me to leave."

She presses a finger to her lips, traces a delicate line down my cheek. Her touch is strangely cool.

Things are stirring.

You know what you really want, Thompson.

Her hair coils around me like a silk curtain, and as her mouth blossoms on mine, I close my eyes and taste all notes familiar but one: piquant and reminiscent of an extinguished match.

"I just haven't seen you in a very long time." She smiles in an almost coy manner. "I need you here."

The sky opens up, thunder roars, and lightning electrifies the night.

⁕⁓⁕

At the furthest reach of my consciousness is Rosalia's voice, and I become aware of a burning sensation in my throat. I open my eyes and it feels as though someone has smeared mud on my eyelids.

The world is filmed in gray.

Rosalia is over me. "Get up, Thom." She coughs. Her breath smells like brown sugar. "Get up."

I wheeze and feel like I can't get enough air. "What—was there an eruption?"

"No, just ash. Permit or no permit, we're going up the mountain."

"*What?*" I set my hands on her arms. Her skin is coated in grit.

She's not wearing the robe or slip I'd removed when we made love last night. She's in a silk tank with no bra. Aware that I'm staring, she moves her violet kimono over her chest.

It's odd, but there are more imperative matters.

"But you said—"

She leaps off the bed and seizes my bag from a nearby chair. "We know Tambora ashed for months before the disaster." She unzips the bag and rummages through it. "It won't be long before scientists arrive. If we're headed toward another eruption, my disc—*our find*—could be buried even deeper. It will be inaccessible for a long time." She tosses jeans, jacket, and socks on a carved chest in the corner. "We have to travel light."

I sit up. "Did you mean what you said last night?"

She straightens her back and doesn't turn to face me. "Circumstances have changed."

"Then I'm here."

She pivots to give me a sad expression that vanishes so quickly I'm not sure it was even there. "Hurry up. Rimbo will guide us. He's not afraid."

She moves across the room and stops on the courtyard grass, a brilliant butterfly of purple against the gray that coats our world. "Thom."

"Yeah?"

Her hands are clasped so tightly her knuckles are white. "I'm sorry."

It's true that the last twenty-four hours have been emotionally confusing, but I know where I stand now. We'll get up on that mountain. We'll get back to that kaleidoscopic world of passion-work-thrill. We're not far from a new wall of pushpins . . . I can feel it.

"It's okay." I get on my feet. "It's fine."

✳✳✳

It was bread-oven hot yesterday, but there's an almost greasy humidity that accompanies an ash fall that even the breeze while riding the motorbike doesn't alleviate.

We reach a plantation on which the main building is a palette-rendered shack. On its sagging porch, Rosalia makes arrangements with a little man, whom she introduces as Rimbo; he's hunched over, like a chili, but she assures me he's the most nimble guide on the island.

A dozen sweaty hours later, after switchbacking through car-sized boulders, parched fields of tall grasses and near-impenetrable tropical forests, it's evening. We're camped not far from Rosalia's discovery. She was right about Rimbo not fearing the ancient devils, but he grouses plenty about the rotten-flesh stench of rafflesia—corpse flower—as he makes us a meal of mutton.

Rosalia contemplates the cooking fire, which only adds feverishness to an already steaming jungle, over the rim of a tin cup of coffee. She looks more youthful than yesterday; it seems even her crow's feet have faded.

"What do you think is there?" She sips. "A house? A barn? A temple? Was there anyone inside? If there was, what was he doing?"

The fire snaps, hisses. A drop of sweat runs down my chest.

"Did he even understand what was going on?"

There's a distant rumble.

She looks up, her brow furrowed in worry. "I wish we could start now. I just want to get up there."

For a moment there's only the sound of the fire and the echoing, fervent chatter of animals, the crashes of them moving through the undergrowth. Rimbo, who's sleeping on a bed of fronds on the other side of the fire, pulls at his damp shirt in his sleep.

I have an insistent, burgeoning need to kiss her, and begin to close the distance between us.

She stands up, empties her cup on the fire. A *hish* of steam rises into the night. "Well, I'm going to turn in. Or try to, anyway."

"Rosie?" I look over my shoulder.

"Yes?"

Her expression isn't one that gives me any indication she wants me to join her. "Never mind."

She frowns and holds my gaze a moment. Then she says, "I'd stay up longer, but . . . I've been waiting for a day like tomorrow for a very long time."

I wipe my forehead with my sleeve. "I know."

She ducks into her tent, and I can't help thinking that last night didn't mean what I thought it would. There's no breeze, but the faint whiff of sulfur in the air strangely makes me wish I hadn't left the puppet the captain gave me back at Rosalia's.

❧❀❧

I only half descend into sleep.

I'm haunted by the rumbling ground, the waft of corpse flower, the sting of sulfur and Rosalia: the rise of her stomach beneath my hands as we motorbiked to her rented place, the smell of apples on her skin and brown sugar on her breath. Her untethered breasts. The sound of her voice: *Are you happy?*

Someone's near my tent.

I wake to the salt of my own sweat on my tongue; it seems as though the air has gotten hotter and thicker in the past few hours. There's a silhouette in the pale light from our camp's lantern: the petite shadow of Orange Dress; there's no mistaking the shape of the flower in her hair.

Stop it, you're delirious in this heat. What would she be doing out here?

I open my eyes and see Rosalia—carnal gaze, sullen mouth, damp halter top, tangy scent. "I can't sleep," she purrs. She crawls toward me and straddles my legs. I touch her cool skin.

The noise of the mountain and the brutal heat. The stink of rafflesia. The smart of sulfur in my eyes and nose.

I forget it all.

⁂

At dawn, there's an empty spot where Rosalia had curled up next to me. I drag myself into the sweltering day. The land is dusted in more ash. There's a rustle in the underbrush.

"Rosie?"

It's Rimbo who steps clear of the wild grasses at the edge of the woods. He beckons me to follow him.

The path is narrow, and I curse when a stinging nettle gets me. I steel myself to the pain, trying to forget his warning about nettles resulting in instant infection.

We reach a clearing. Rosalia, taking photographs, is dwarfed before a towering embankment where layers of eruptive material are exposed: ash, pumice, pyroclastic matter. Stones similar to the piece she showed me litter the ground.

"It's quite a sight, isn't it?" She's sheened in sweat and blots her brow with her forearm. "We should plan on getting equipment, maybe even some ground-penetrating radar. We'll have to hire extra guides, porters, students to help us dig. Right now, I'm thinking I want to follow some of this back up toward the summit. See if there are clues to how big this settlement may have been."

She stands before me and my breath hitches in my chest: she's as stunning as she was in youth, and I'm back in that glorious past, watching her scrutinize an ancient grape seed unearthed in the ruins of Pompeii, photograph the buried city of Plymouth on Montserrat, flick a brush around the edges of a ten-thousand-year-old tool up on Nabro.

I kiss her, hard and full of fire.

She pushes me away. "What the hell are you *doing*?"

My cheeks burn. "What do you mean? We've . . . we've been together the last two nights."

She furrows her brow. "What are you talking about?"

I detail. The stormy night in my room. The sultry night in the tent.

She pales. She covers her mouth with her hand and turns from me.

I watch her back rise and fall with every breath.

Finally, she says, "Listen to me. You were dreaming."

The humid air sits heavy between us.

"You were as real as you are now." I settle my hands on her shoulders, kiss her neck. "I love you."

"No you don't." She smacks me away. Shrugs me off. "You can't love me. You *can't*."

I'm confused. "I *do*."

She pivots and gives me a smoldering stare. "How was I supposed to know that? What was I supposed to think?"

I'm stunned. "What?"

"You made your choice. Your work over me. You stopped calling." Her voice breaks. "You decided to make your big discovery at Akrotiri and leave me behind. Like everything we'd shared wasn't important. Like I didn't matter to you at all."

It's as though someone's stolen the air. "What? No. We just . . . we were both busy. Work always came first."

"No. Mine never did until now." She swipes a tear from her cheek.

The jungle comes alive with noise as birds take to the sky.

I'm dizzy, but I'm not sure if it's because of the heat or because somewhere in my gut I think something terrible is about to happen. "What is going *on?*"

"Nothing. Just go." She returns to the formation, presses her hand against it, and bows her head as her shoulders sag. "Just go."

I make my way back to camp amid an eerie quiet, laboring to breathe in the steamy air.

⁂

The inside of my tent is broiling and reeks of sulfur and melting vinyl as I shove gear into my pack: *socks. Towel. Bandages. She needs me. She doesn't. She doesn't love me. She does.*

Rosalia ducks inside the tent.

"What do you want, Rosie?"

She hangs her head. "I'm sorry."

Khakis. "You call me from halfway around the world to play your husband. You're upset when you find out I'm not with anyone. You want me to leave. You want me to stay." *Last night's shirt.* "You make love to me. You say I can't love you."

I feel her arms settle about my waist. The press of her cheek on my back. I'm about to push her away when she murmurs, "Do you remember the pushpins?"

No, no. Don't let her do this to you again.

Her grip tightens around my middle.

I close my eyes and heave a sigh. "Yes. Yes I do."

"Come with me. To the summit."

I put down my pack and turn to face her. "Rosie. We need to—"

God she's beautiful. I wipe the smear of dirt from her cheek. *I want to go anywhere with her.*

No.

A feverish wind ripples the tent. "Do you hear that?"

She shakes her head.

"Exactly. Nothing." I brush a strand of hair off her forehead. "No birds, no animals. I think it's not safe. I think we should leave."

She gives me a tight-lipped smile. She reaches into the pocket of her jeans and presses a green pushpin into my hand.

In her eyes, I see the *us* that hasn't happened yet. Her hair beneath a kerchief as she's piecing together the objects from the lost culture she's just discovered. Her beckon to a hot spring to soothe my sore muscles. The press of her lips on a champagne glass after she's cut the ribbon on our exhibit in a marbled museum. Her beauty even in age, her face wrinkled but still kind, her hair gray but still soft.

I forget everything, and I follow her straight up.

⁂

As we near the crater, the heat is molten. The changing landscape is a paradox the farther we go; steam rises from cracks in black barren earth, but a stream trickles lazily down the side of a lush embankment. Dead birds dot a patch of wilted plants, but dwarf trees, their fruitful, thick branches gnarled like arthritic hands, riddle the pathway. When we are at last just a few feet from Tambora's rim, the clouds are too thick to see anything. Rosalia guides me across a patch of red sand, and everything clears. Before us stretches the caldera, a four-mile wide hole ringed by centuries-old scree, a scalding lake of acid, patches of boiling mud and spewing fumaroles. It's like standing near a blast furnace. Sweat runs into my eyes.

Rosalia grips my hand. "Would you do anything for me?"

The air sears my throat and lungs. *Water. What am I doing up here? Why didn't we bring water?* I take a step back, but she pulls me toward her.

"Would you?"

We are precariously close to the edge.

My face burns. Sulfur squeezes my lungs.

The ground rumbles beneath our feet and my legs turn to jelly. Rosalia falls forward and over the cliff.

"No!" I dive to the ground, scraping my chin on the jagged ledge. I manage to grasp her right wrist. My mouth is full of the foul taste of iron and dirt.

She's dangling over a drop into the seething pit.

My sweaty hand is slippery. "I can't hold you long! Give me your other hand!"

There's another rumble and a belch of steam from below.

"Hurry!"

Her fingers grope for mine, and finally, I feel her palm.

It's strangely cool to the touch.

There's a voice from nearby: "Thom! Stop! *That's not me!*"

Barely able to move, I strain my neck to look.

Behind me, standing firmly on the smoking earth. It's Rosalia.

What?

"That's not me! Let her go!"

No, you're seeing things. The heat is playing tricks on you.

I look at my hands below. Rosalia is still there. Begging me.

The mirage screams, "That's. Not. Me! Please, Thom!"

"Help me!" Comes the urgent cry from beneath the crater lip. "Don't let me die!"

A pop from inside the basin results in a hissing column of steam.

The mirage doesn't stop. "Do you remember the story about the ghosts tempting you with your strongest desire? That's what happened, Thom! They made you think you were with me!"

There's a flash of lightning. A clap of thunder.

"Help me! I'm slipping!"

I fervently face the suspended beauty at the end of my grasp: *she's real. She's desperate and real and that thing behind you telling you to let go is a delusion. You're overheated and breathing in fumes. You're delirious.* "I've got you!"

"Let go of her!" The mirage shouts. "She's here to take your soul! I . . . I traded you for the mountain's deepest secret but I've changed my mind!"

The Rosalia below me has sheer panic on her face. "I thought you said you loved me! Pull me up!"

The mirage thrusts out her hand. "I'm giving it up! I'll go work in an office, I don't care, just come with me!"

The tug on my arm is insistent. "Help me!"

The mirage yells, "I'll prove it! Do you remember the dying of the light? Do you remember that?"

Rosalia?

No. "Go away! You're in my head!"

"Do you remember when we went to Naples and I hated *torta caprese*?" The mirage says. "You had it planned out. Every restaurant. Every taste. And I hated it. And you were so angry!"

Yes, yes I do . . . and I forgave her . . . Rosalia!

Then whose hand am I holding?

I peer into the crater.

Orange Dress gives me a chilling smile.

She yanks on my hands with what feels like the force of a hundred men, pitching me into the igneous pit.

The last thing I see is Rosalia. Her hand outstretched. Her face contorted.

Once, we wanted to see every volcano in the world.

Not like this.

THIRTY-SEVEN BIRDS

VERA'S FRONT STOOP was littered with dead sparrows. She hugged her silk robe against the December bite and stood, transfixed by the desperate gazes that seemed to betray their last thoughts: *Oh God I'm falling.*

Breathless, she flung shut her white colonial's front door and braced against it.

When they'd first moved in, Vera had seen a meteor shower, and was certain it had meant the world was ending (which, of course, it hadn't—the only world that had ended was the one in which her new friends invited her to their parties). Six months ago, she had gone to a wedding at which the altar flowers were wilting. When she'd tried to warn the bride's mother that this certainly was a bad omen, she had found herself escorted out before the organist had begun the prelude.

But this time, these pathetic little thirty-seven birds on her stoop—this time she was certain it meant something. She told her husband Richard as much: "Don't you think that's odd?"

He chewed the ice from his emptied rocks glass. "Not really." He headed to the bar and gave himself another generous pour. "Animals die all the time. Birds probably hit the windows. You know, *glass kills,* they call 'em. One's big enough, lots of birds, it makes the news."

She stirred the rice she was cooking to accompany their quail a bit faster. "That's when they fly into skyscrapers. We live in the middle of nowhere."

He leaned against the doorjamb, gulped more scotch, and shoved a hand in his pants pocket. "Please, Vera, it's not the end of the world and no one's marriage is doomed. If you're that worried, call the BOCES or the university or something. I'm sure they'll tell you it's exactly what I just said. Or some wacky disease brought over from God knows where." He wandered back into the living room and turned on the television.

Vera knew he was probably right: *be rational; don't embarrass yourself by calling in experts to tell you what you should already accept.* So she didn't call the BOCES or the university. Instead, she took a pair of tongs into the indigo dark and deposited the feather bombs into a garbage bag, which she sealed and dropped in the trash receptacle at the head of her driveway.

✳✷✺✷✳

Millfoil had always been a quiet little community, an enclave for 2.4 kids, ten a.m. coffee hour, and five o'clock pot roast nestled among sparkling lakes and apple orchards. It was not at all like the place in which Vera had grown up. She was used to car horns, not the *hisht* of falling snow. She adored the smells of spices and fresh-baked black-and-whites, not necessarily those of spring mud and chimney creosote. Her pulse quickened at the sight of neon, not at a single porch light in a five mile stretch. She was comfortable with being anonymous: not with her neighbors attending the same church, shopping the same stores, and checking books out of the library where she worked.

But mostly, where there had been parking lots there were woods, huddles of gargantuan trees whose winter limbs seemed hungry. What was worse was that any unpredictable beast could be lurking there. Wolves or bears or owls or even creatures she couldn't envision, ones with gnashing teeth and piercing chartreuse eyes. She much preferred the denizens of the city, because they were human—perhaps desperately poor, oppressed, strung out, or lonely, but human, with the ability to choose.

⁂

It had snowed during the night, a light dusting. She thought they might have a white Christmas, then realized with regret the holiday was a little more than a week away and she hadn't put out any decorations.

More than that, there was something else having to do with Christmas, something she was supposed to do, but she couldn't remember what. She looked at the clock—an hour before she needed to go to work.

It was Saturday—the day the library held Story Morning, which meant that from ten to noon she essentially entertained children whose parents needed a little downtime. It was the part of her job she loved most; she had never been able to have children, which Richard hadn't seemed to mind, but it had left her wholly unsatisfied, burdened by the constant feeling that no matter how many times she read *Why Mosquitoes Buzz in People's Ears* or helped them make colored paper turkeys by tracing their little hands or filled their cups with apple juice, there would always be something . . . unfinished.

Ann, a short, dark-haired woman who always wore paisley scarves and worked behind the front desk, smiled warmly. "They're waiting on you, Vera."

Vera hurried past the children's section's half-height water fountains and walls painted with leering suns and jocular moons.

The six-year-olds were restless. Annalisa tugged at her Barbie's hair, Carlos and Mike whacked each other with Nerf bats, Sylvia picked at a string on her kitty applique's eye. The other children were in various fits of giggles and yells.

She sat in her usual chair. "I'm here now, everyone! Time to settle down!"

A few seconds and a repeat badger later, they were quiet, all eyes attentive and blinking.

All except Alan. "Alan, come on now, it's time for—"

He turned around. A trickle of blood frothed from his ear onto his *Phineas and Ferb* T-shirt, a splotch of red covering the blue platypus's pursed lips. A chunk of Alan's head was missing, the wound's liquid glistening under the fluorescent lights.

Vera clapped a hand over her mouth to suppress a scream and closed her eyes. *Help, get help—*

"What's wrong, Miss Vera?"

She took a cautious peek.

Alan was normal.

"Nothing. I'm . . ." she quelled the bile coming up her throat. "I'm fine."

The children just looked at her curiously.

Vera took a deep breath, opened the cover of *Why Mosquitoes Buzz in People's Ears*, and began to read.

⚜

Richard would be out at the country club most of the night. While she normally filled the hours with housecleaning and craft projects, she thought that after what she'd seen, she deserved an evening off. She could read a book and drink some tea.

The only problem was she was out of her favorite. She'd have to go to the store to get it.

Yannity's parking lot was busy. She wedged her Volkswagen into the small space between an SUV that had overshot the white lines and a shiny Volvo wagon. Suddenly feeling drained and wondering whether or not she should go in at all (couldn't she just make do with the hot apple cider K-Cups she had at home?) and deciding the answer was no, she climbed from the car, grabbed her bag, and trudged to the building.

The smell of bananas, grapes, and deli meat assaulted her as she set her handbag inside a red shopping basket.

A woman's voice. "Hi, Vera! How are you?"

Patty. Patty also worked in the library's children section. But she had a bloody hole in her chest and her face was half-burned. Clear liquid ran down her neck.

Vera's basket hit the floor with a *clack*.

"Oh my God! Are you okay?" Patty was back to her chemically tanned tennis-playing self.

Catching her breath, she awkwardly bent to pick up the basket, tucked a loosed strand of hair behind her ear. "I'm fine, I'm . . . just . . . so busy this time of year, you know?"

"I hear you," Patty said. "I've barely started my shopping and now I'm hating myself that we have the Christmas party tomorrow. What are you bringing?"

"Christmas party?"

"Yes. At the library. For the kids and their parents."

Vera cursed herself. *That* was what she had been trying to remember this morning!

Patty's expression changed to concern. "Are you sure you're okay?"

Vera barely heard her. She was looking at the brightly colored display of pre-baked holiday cookies, a chaos of sugars and chocolates and reds and greens. "Cookies."

"What?"

"Oh—cookies." Vera smoothed her coat. "Cookies. I'm bringing cookies."

Patty was slow to respond. "Okay."

There was silence between them, nothing except the soft Muzak version of "Do You Hear What I Hear?"

Patty smiled nervously. "Well, see you tomorrow."

"Yes. Tomorrow."

She watched Patty venture off into the produce section.

You're tired. You're tired and those stupid birds just spooked you, that's all. The hell with tea. You need something stronger.

She paid for the cookies, drove home, and fixed herself a scotch on the rocks.

❧❀❦

When she awoke, daylight was at the window. The bottle of scotch, on the coffee table, was empty, alongside a crusty bowl; she couldn't remember eating at all, let alone what.

Her head throbbed, and she sat up. There was a note on the table. *We missed church, but didn't want to wake you. Went to the gym, see you later. – R.*

She vaguely recalled now: Richard had come in, kissed her on the forehead, and turned out the living room light.

What the hell time was it? She looked at the clock; it was past noon. She went into the kitchen and saw the package of cookies. The party was today, in an hour. Half the kids in town would be there. *See, yesterday is over. It's time for you to get up, go to the library, and do your job.*

She went into the kitchen, popped a Donut Shop K-Cup into the Keurig, waited the minute for the machine to heat up and another to brew. When it was done, she took the mug into the bathroom and set it on the marble vanity.

Just after she turned on the shower, she caught a glimpse of herself in the mirror.

She was bleeding. Badly. Blood burbled down her chin, her hair was matted in it, and her ear . . . her right ear was missing—

—she jumped and nearly fell into the shower, popping the curtain from its hooks on the way down. Coolish water stung her eyes.

She touched herself. Her hair, her ear . . . her ear was still there.

She clambered to her feet. *It's nothing, it's nothing, it's nothing. Open your eyes and look in that mirror.*

She was fine. Her chin was clean, her ears were intact, and her hair was only wet.

Doctor. You're calling a doctor, and you're doing it right now.

Today was Sunday. She'd have to wait until tomorrow.

Her back ached and her right arm throbbed. *That's it, you're not going to work today. To hell with the party. You're going to lie down, take some aspirin, and get some rest.*

She turned off the shower, shrugged back into her robe, grabbed her coffee, and went to call the library to tell them she wouldn't be in.

✻❦✻

It was just past three. Vera stared at the ceiling and listened to the sounds around her, nothing but ticking clocks, out of sync with each other, *tich-tach, tich-tach.* And something else—a distant beep.

Her cell phone.

She climbed out of bed and went to her purse. Six missed calls. All from Richard.

She frowned and dialed his number. "Richard?"

He was panting, nerve-wracked, wavering. "Oh, thank God. I've been trying to reach you. You're alive? Are you hurt? Where are you?"

"Richard, what's the matter?"

"I'm outside. I'm outside but they won't let us near the building."

She frowned. "What are you talking about?"

"You're okay, though, right?"

"Yes, I'm fine. Why wouldn't I be?"

There was a long silence. In the background, she could hear a distant siren, men yelling.

"Richard, what the hell is going on?"

"You're not at the library?"

"No, I didn't go in today, I felt . . . oh, baby there's

something I need to tell you about, something awful and I have to go to the doctor . . ."

"There was a shooting. At the library. Some guy burst in and just—shot everybody up—they don't know how many are dead yet, but little kids, maybe, these guys down here are saying—there's just ambulances and cops and reporters and . . ."

The news hit her full in the stomach. She staggered backward, stopping only when she hit the half-wall between their kitchen and dining room.

"Are you there?" He was moving; running, it sounded like.

"I'm here, I—"

She could hear clearly that he was crying. "God, it's so awful. Fucking animal. What the hell makes somebody do that? What?"

She swallowed, and when she spoke her voice was nary a whisper. "I don't know."

"Lock the door," he said. "Lock the door. I'm right around the corner. I'm coming home. Right now."

Dead air.

Her robe flew open as she rushed to the television and turned it on to the absurd scene of cartoon elves cavorting around a Christmas tree. News. She needed news. CNN. The ticker on the bottom of the screen: BREAKING STORY: SHOOTING AT MILLFOIL, CT LIBRARY. SOURCE: THIRTY-SIX SUSPECTED DEAD.

She sank to her knees in front of the television. Thirty-six. Thirty-six people. In her mind flashed the gory images she'd seen: little Alan would have been there today. Patty would have been there today. And she . . . *those birds—those birds had meant something . . .*

There was a sound at the front door.

"Richard?"

No answer.

"Richard, is that you?"

She climbed to her feet, toed to the door, and listened.

"Richard?" She set her hand on the knob.

You were supposed to be thirty-seven.

HOURGLASS

I WAS ON page 298 in Clive Cussler's *Raise the Titanic!* when the first kid in our neighborhood disappeared.

It was Vinny Dolorosa from number thirty-eight across the street. He was, basically, the neighborhood bully: on Halloween, he'd swipe your plastic pumpkin and brain you with his full pillowcase. You weren't exactly safe the rest of the year, either. If he decided you annoyed him, he'd take off his belt, which had a big western buckle, and use that instead. Not that he ever beat up on me or my six-year-old sister Kimmie; we were girls. But he loved to call me Dent-face Denise.

The half-mile walk up the hill to the bus stop was too much for his chunk, so he'd take a shortcut up our driveway to the cave path. He wasn't allowed in our sandbox, but nobody in our neighborhood didn't know about it. It was a kingdom of riches. Dad had gone out of his way to fill it with bones, shells, shark teeth and other treasures—probably things he'd pilfered from his office; he was a geologist for the state—and sometimes, we even found nickels and the occasional dime.

Not that there weren't plenty of popular hangouts; it was the seventies. The swing set at the bus stop, the caves in the woods where Vinny and the older boys stashed their *Playboys*, and a stream that was a fine choice when you were too lazy to walk to the lake. But a day at the sandbox was a day that a kid could strike it rich, and everyone came; even, sometimes, when we weren't home. Twice a year, on Easter and Halloween, Mom and Dad made sure there were some treats—candy buttons, chocolate cigarettes, wax bottles—hidden too. Sometimes I swore I saw Vinny out there at night, rummaging.

Mrs. Dolorosa was a comfortable woman who ate a lot of pasta and rarely came out of her house. The day Vinny disappeared she at first thought he was up in the caves with his "hooligan friends." Then the police came and started asking questions. Then she thought maybe he'd gone down to the lake and drowned. Then everyone searched the woods.

He was never found.

When Halloween came two weeks later, her porch light was off.

The whole thing scared the hell out of all of us.

❧❀❦

The first time I wondered about the closet in Dad's den, it was just after Labor Day—and it was the first time I remember feeling hunger.

Dad had lost his job several months before, but until the past week, it'd seemed as though nothing had changed: Mom was cheap and could make that buffalo scream. She'd go to Bantam Market, stock up on meat, put it into plastic bags she'd label with the item and date, and freeze it in an orange behemoth she called Bessie. Bessie lived in one of the *off limits* rooms of the house because Mom was afraid less-than-bright Kimmie would play in it and lock herself in, but I suspected our supply had run out, and there was no money to get more. The last few nights, we'd been living on canned kidney beans and generic cheese from Grand Union.

That day was rainy, and the house was dark: it was cut into the hillside, so the windows in the back rooms of the first floor sat at ground level. While they provided a convenient out when I wanted to meet Myron—the kid next door—in the woods after I was supposed to be in bed, they made the den a foreboding place crammed with yellowing books. Across from a shrink-wrapped Robert Frost poster that talked about the road less traveled was the knotty pine, padlocked closet.

A storm was rolling in. Thunderstorms were terrifying prospects; the house wasn't properly grounded, and it'd been hit a couple of times. Once, a fireball shot past my head. Twice, the electrical box, in the closet too close to the woodstove, got whacked. Because my bedroom was below grade, I felt like I'd be safest there—but sounds from Dad's den stopped me.

I heard banging and scraping, and there was a peculiar smell, like mud and wet metal; different from the usual smoky vanilla and old paper. I crept closer and pressed my ear to the door, but the only thing I clearly grasped was that he was doing something in the closet; I heard the unmistakable press of the doors and snap of the padlock.

I heard Dad drop into his leather-covered chair. Although I imagined all sorts of crazy things going on in there, when I had to interrupt him for something like "Mom has dinner ready" or "Mr. Leary's here"—there was never anything but him in the chair, a book on his lap, his loafered feet propped on his mahogany desk.

I raised my hand and knocked.

He always knew it was me. "Yes, Denise."

"Can I come in?"

"Just a minute." I heard the unmistakable *snap-thrush* of a match; he was lighting his pipe. "Okay."

I entered the room and I could see the crack of Dad's rear end through the open lower back of the chair. He was wiry and seemed to have no hips or butt. Even when he wore a belt, his pants wouldn't stay up. "Is dinner ready?"

"No, I . . . I just wanted to . . ."

"Are you bored?" He looked at me—with *one* of his gray eyes, anyway. His right one was lazy, and sometimes it wandered and I couldn't tell what he was looking at. It was unnerving right then, actually, because if I knew that if I said yes, he'd give me a crummy job to do. But he didn't wait for my answer. "You finished all your Nancy Drews, huh?"

I was a pretty advanced reader for ten years old, so the three Mom had given me just last week for my birthday I'd already read.

I thought I heard something shift in the closet, and eyed it.

"Never mind that. I was reorganizing. Tell you what." He got up off his chair and motioned around the room. "I think you're old enough. Any one of these books you see here—any one at all—you go ahead and choose and you can start reading that."

I was immediately distracted. Dad's library towered around and walled in the window, and there were all sorts of pretty hardcovers—*Sargasso, Telefon, Jaws*. I'd been down here when he wasn't and looked at them so many times in all their glorious covers, wondering if what was inside them was as good as the cover art itself. There was one I had my eye on in particular.

I stretched to place my middle and index finger on the top of Clive Cussler's *Raise the Titanic!* I'd learned about that ship in school and had been captivated by it.

"Just don't tell your mother, and if you have any questions about anything, you come to me—and *only* me." He puffed his pipe as he noted my choice. "It's got deep-sea submersibles and marine archaeologists and spies. You might like that one."

Just then, Mom called us for lunch. It was the usual slop can of cheap stuff smashed together to make a meal—one of the women at church, perhaps knowing our predicament, had given her a new Crock Pot, and she was digging it. The only uncool thing was that I knew we should've been eating nicer recipes—like Hungarian goulash, stuffed green peppers, and hamburger casserole—but instead, we were eating last week's leftover chicken in a tomato broth that tasted like watered-down ketchup.

We had a house they'd built themselves that was murder to maintain, and even if we lived in a nice neighborhood, it wasn't beyond me that they were always this far from losing it: my bedroom was directly under theirs, and I could hear them fighting at night, especially about Mom's faith. "We can't keep tithing to the church like this," Dad would say. "You just trust Jesus and everything will be rosy fucking fine, for sure! But is the church really going to help us when we're out on the street? How about Jesus? Is he going to descend and give us a place to live?"

Mom would never respond. I'd just hear the bathroom door slam.

✻

Myron's real name, Mom said, was Ronnie, but his mother would refer to him as "My Ron" so eventually all the kids started calling him Myron. He was a rough-and-tumble who covered his hands in socks instead of gloves, always wore a maroon, puffy, dirt-smeared coat, and when it was chilly or he had a cold, had a bright green caterpillar of snot crawling out of one or both of his nostrils. He pronounced the word *number* as *numper*, and when you got too close to him, he smelled like stale air freshener and matches.

The only thing he liked more than me, he confessed, was the sandbox.

There, we built castles as tall as we were and pitched rocks at each other in a game called Bury the Dead: Dad would always entomb chicken bones, so we'd dig them up, then split the pile so each one of us had an army. The idea was to pitch the ammo at the other one's army and knock the bones over. Whoever knocked over the most won, and there was usually some sort of "slave duty" at stake.

A late-September storm was threatening; bloated gray clouds trundled over the lake. "Let's go in!" I told Myron.

"Nope-a-dope!" He hurled another rock, but it missed. He ducked back down behind his fortress. "I'm winning!"

"Not for long!" I popped up from behind my castle and opened fire. I was trailing behind him, for sure. He still had twenty-one out of twenty-eight bones standing; I had only seven left between me and incurring the penalty of having to pull his toboggan up the hill all winter long.

He stood up and winged another rock. It knocked over not one, but two of my bones. "Numper twenty-one! Numper twenty-two! Your hands gonna be freezing when you towing my magic carpet through the snow!"

I popped up from behind my fortress. "Nope! I'll have real gloves!" I fired a rather large rock, confident it was going to wipe out maybe two or three of his bones. I was fighting a losing battle, but I wasn't about to give up.

I knocked him in the head. He fell backward, his shoes thrusting right through the front of his fortress, his wall crumbling like so much brown sugar.

When I got to him, he wasn't on his back. He was standing, with a hand over one eye, pointing at the ground where he'd fallen.

I went to grab his arm, then thought better of it when I saw the smear of an unidentified substance on the arm of his coat. "Are you okay, Myron?" His mom was going to kill me, and she was going to tell my mom, and this could very well mean spending next summer weeding that stupid pachysandra.

He shook his head and went white. "The ground moved."

I frowned. "What do you mean?"

"It. Moved!" His breath came is short gasps. Snot crawled down his upper lip. "I swear, man!"

Silence. There was the whine of the boats on the lake.

I started to laugh.

Myron looked horrified at first, but I just laughed harder.

He turned up the corners of his mouth in a nervous expression, and then he laughed, too.

❧❦❧

Two days after Vinny disappeared, Dad refilled the sandbox. He'd taken the Scout down to Lloyd Lumber, loaded it up with twenty-pound bags, and slashed them open with his Bowie knife. Whitish puffs clouded the Columbus Day breeze when he emptied the bags.

Myron and I started a new game of Bury the Dead almost immediately, but the thicker layer of sand made it harder to knock over the bones.

"Whaddaya think?" Myron hummed a rock at my line of bones, but it didn't hit—the pile of sand around it blocked the assault, and the rock just slid to a stop.

"About what?" I retaliated with equal force, but the same thing happened.

"You know—Vinny." He threw a rock again, to no effect. "You scared?"

I was. Halloween was coming up, so Channel 11 was showing scary movies on Saturdays. I thought maybe what happened to Vinny was the same thing that had happened to this woman in the *Three o'clock Thriller*: she was dragged into hell by monsters that lived in her fireplace. Maybe in those caves where Vinny kept his dirty magazines, there were monsters lying in wait. Not like I'd ever go up there, but what if they ran out of neighborhood baddies to eat?

"You are!" Myron razzed. "You *are* scared!"

My cheeks burned "Am not!"

"Are too!"

"Am not!" I lobbed another rock, and it, too, ploughed into a sand pile and failed to take down a soldier.

"This is a bummer." He came out from behind his fortress, and for a horrifying moment I thought he was going to wander out of the sandbox and back home.

He didn't. Instead, he flopped down between our castles. "Sit down, 'Nise."

He never put the *De* at the beginning of my name. Not that it bothered me; if anything, I felt this sort of special flutter in my stomach when he said it, except for right then, when it was irritating. "No. You're laughing at me!"

"Nope-a-dope."

"You *are!*" I watched another inchworm of snot crawl down his upper lip. "And you oughtta learn to wipe your snotty nose!"

He patted the sand. "Get your butt over here."

His eyes, the color of a blue jay's back, were honest. So I emerged from the depths of my granular castle and sat next to him, getting a whiff of stale air freshener.

"Vinny was a dumbass." He made little circles in the sand. "He prolly did sumpthin' stupid."

"How do you know?"

"'Cause I do. Besides"—he wiped his nose—"you shouldn't be scared. I'm gonna be Mark from *Battle of the Planets* for Halloween. So if sumpthin' bad was coming, I'd stop 'em."

I was giggly and blushy all at the same time, and when another snot worm started coming out of his nose, it didn't seem as gross.

⚜

Myron wasn't the only one who got defensive after Vinny disappeared; the whole town went crazy. In health class, puberty discussion was booted in favor of *Stranger Danger* education, which meant two things: filmstrips about kids getting kidnapped and assemblies with local policemen. By mid-November, we were all pros at rebuking candy-pushers in Chrysler Newports.

"I know this is, like, scary city for you kids, but you just need to be cool." Mom, who was cooking, took a slug of her usual pre-dinner bourbon. "Those boys were always in a tango with trouble." She lifted the lid off the Crock Pot and inhaled.

I thought about what Myron said. Maybe he was right.

"It's perfect!" She smiled the biggest smile I'd seen in a while, and I noticed she'd put on frosted melon lipstick. Mom had always been a manicured person who wore the latest fashions when Dad had had a job, but lately I'd noticed tiny indiscretions, like the absence of earrings, a necklace, or makeup. Today she had on all three. "*Smell* that bacony smell!"

"What is it?" I asked, interest in mealtime renewed.

"Authentic pepper pot soup." She ladled it into one of her harvest gold serving bowls.

I'd never heard of it. "What's that?"

"You promised this was gonna be far out, Mom!" my sister Kimmie whined, banging her spoon on her *Land of the Lost* placemat. "I don't like peppers!"

"Well." She set the bowl in front of her. "There are actually very few peppers in it."

Dad grabbed a beer from the fridge and cracked it open. Mom kissed him.

Mom set my bowl in front of me. The soup looked rich and smelled like bacon and onions, but there was something hot in it, because I could feel the sweat pop out on my cheeks. She plopped a platter of crusty bread and margarine in the middle of the table. "Eat up! It's the soup that won the American Revolution!"

Kimmie wasted no time gobbling it up, her eyes gleaming like a thief's, nodding and *yum-yumming* like a child actor on a bad sitcom.

I was a little more cautious.

Mom seated herself and spread her paper napkin across her lap. "Come on, now, Denise, didn't you know that George Washington's troops didn't even have shoes? They were leaving bloody footprints in the snow. And then the cook came up with this soup—"

"Good God, Adelaide," Dad grunted. "We don't know that's true."

Mom, clearly annoyed, eyed him. "It was in my cookbook."

The room grew heavy; the only sound was my sister, who had lifted the bowl and was slurping.

For as good as it smelled, it was horrendous—I swore I could taste turds in it someplace. I choked it down and found myself, although at least no longer hungry, desperate for diluted ketchup and crackers.

"So." Mom blew on her spoonful to cool it. "What are *your* plans after dinner?"

"TV!" Kimmie cried. "TV!"

"I'm going over to get Myron," I said. "We have to finish this week's battle."

"What battle?"

"In the sandbox." I fished three or four potatoes out of the soup; they were, at least, tolerable.

There was silence. My parents looked at each other.

Dad lifted his beer. "Why don't you read instead?"

The whole reason we had the sandbox was so that we could have friends over. "Why?"

Mom set her hand on mine. "Oh, you know, we've just turned the clocks back and it's a little darker now than usual. And it's cold. Don't you think it's cold?"

Kimmie slammed down her bowl. "More! I want *more!*"

I knew better than to argue with my parents, but that didn't mean I had to follow their instructions. So after I'd managed to hide at least half of the bits of meat in those flimsy napkins, I went over to Myron's.

His mother came to the door, wiping her hands on a muddied apron, a Benson & Hedges clenched between wine-colored lips. When she spoke, I could see her yellow teeth.

"My Ron! My Ron, baby, come here—it's your friend from next door!"

No response.

"My Ron?"

No answer.

"Ronnie?"

She turned and smiled at me sweetly, but I knew she was panicked.

"Wait. Just wait right here."

She searched the house, the basement, she cried out into the night air in the neighborhood. The police came; they dredged the lake.

Myron was never found.

He might have been grungy, half-illiterate, and stale smelling, but he was just about the only real friend I had. Every day after school I'd want to go out to the sandbox, then think better of it and sit in the window and look at it instead. The chicken bones and castles were still there from our last game of Bury the Dead. For once, I was about to beat him—I'd figured out a way around the too-high-pile problem, and he hadn't. So I had twelve left in front of my castle; he had three.

When an odd Thanksgiving snow fell, the little bones stood against the white like forlorn orphans.

Numper twenty-one, numper twenty-two echoed in my head. I never imagined I'd ever miss hearing that mispronunciation.

Sometimes when I went to bed, I could swear I heard Myron's voice, and I felt like there was no one else who could stop the bad from coming.

Me and Kimmie had been hoping for a turkey on Thanksgiving. We got something *like* a turkey—a turkey loaf, it was called, that Mom simmered in bourbon and green apples in the Crock Pot. Kimmie gobbled it up like it was her last meal.

"This is the best turkey *ever*, Mom!" She had so much gravy on her fork it ran down her arm. She licked it off her skin. "Tastes just like the real thing!"

"It *is* real, dear. It's just pressed together."

It didn't taste too much like turkey to me. Maybe it was all the Crock Pot fodder we'd been eating, but it tasted the same as everything else. I was okay with it until I bit into something hard that jammed itself painfully under one of my teeth. I pried it loose.

It was a fragment the size of a pebble, white with a nick in it. "Ew, Jesus!" I threw it next to the salad cruet and jumped up from the table.

"Language!" Mom snapped, her eyes wide. "What is the *problem?*"

"It's an icky hard thing!"

Dad examined it, holding it up between his fingers under the glare of the hideous daisy light fixture. "It's a bone."

A wave of nausea hit me. I ran for the sink and prepared, but nothing came.

From behind me at the table, there was only the sound of Kimmie's fork on her plate, the *glug-glug* of my mother pouring more bourbon.

"Look at me, Denise," Mom said.

I turned, but still braced myself against the sink in case I needed it. "To make these turkey loafs, you know, Land o' Lakes puts them in a big grinder. Sometimes pieces of the bone get missed." She took a sip of her bourbon. "It's just like eating around the buckshot in the pheasant. Remember when your cousin Anton brought us that pheasant?"

My stomach heaved at the mere mention of it, but I did remember. I couldn't eat that either.

"It can be a sandbox treasure, that's all." Dad set the bone on a napkin next to his beer.

We played with bones all the time, but for some reason, the thought of that one in the sandbox made me lose it altogether. I threw up in the sink.

Immediately after Christmas, Dad found a job, and all was right with the world again. Mom abandoned the Crock Pot in favor of steaks and Welsh rarebit and even fondue.

Still, Mom and Dad never truly seemed happy after that.

Mom died ten years ago. Dad died last month. I stand on the house's collapsing, moss-encrusted back porch and can hardly believe four decades have passed since that year the boys disappeared.

I can barely see the sandbox beyond out-of-control grasses and sumacs. I can, however, make out an impression in the ground, a square where the trees part. Dad didn't take care of anything toward the end—understandably so, he was an old, ill, curmudgeon—but I can guarantee you he never had to yell at the neighborhood kids to get off his lawn; no kid in his right mind would go near this house the way it's fallen into disrepair. I'm even willing to bet the only kids who ever visit are on Halloween dares: *go touch the door and see if a ghost grabs you!* I'm sure our house is now the local haunted one, the house with the eyes that watch you.

My first reaction is to burn it down and grab the insurance money; I'd be better off. Not that it wouldn't sell if it were cleaned up—it has beach rights—but there are things about it that are weird and will probably cost more to fix, things beyond a new roof and an update to the avocado kitchen. Dad built the place himself, but really hadn't the carpentry skills for anything much beyond stage sets. The electrical has never been wired right. There's the matter of the wood stove he put in himself that he never got a permit for, the makeshift Formica shower in the downstairs bathroom, the backward plumbing, and the colony of bats living in the attic.

I understand why Kimmie wants nothing to do with it.

The side door's lock is so rotted the door whines open with just a push. I stand in the foyer, wondering what disasters I might find on either floor.

I head down the stairs, past my old bedroom. The brown plaid wallpaper peels off the walls, and the metal bed frame has started to rust. The bathroom is in no better shape—there's a clot of mold on the shower ceiling as well as a gaping hole in the buttercup Formica, and the spigot is coming out of the wall.

Dad's den looms ahead.

The closet's padlock is broken.

I grip the edge of the knotty pine door and it comes off in my hand, nearly flattening me onto copies of *Sargasso* and *Ghost Boat* and *Jaws*—their bright covers speckled in mildew—and the Robert Frost poster, which long ago abandoned its post on the wall.

When my head clears, I peer into the closet. There aren't typical horizontal shelves or even a hanging bar for clothes. Instead, the shelves are tucked into the side walls, like wide ladders.

At the back of the closet is a door. It's typical of a crawl space door—if it even opened, I'd have to bend over to get through it.

I step into the closet, set my hand on the tiny door's knob, and turn.

I'm hit with a blast of cold air reeking of earthworms and mushrooms. Whatever this is—a room, root cellar or cold storage—it's pitch. I reach into my pocket for my cell phone and turn on the flashlight app.

It's a tunnel.

What the hell? How could this have been here and I never knew about it?

I step inside, feeling the squelch of the claylike mud beneath my feet. It appears it was used for *some* storage; to the right is a wall of shelves, obviously my father's handiwork, as they aren't evenly spaced and a few of them slant. On them are a couple of aging bottles of Seagram's 100 Pipers. A few rusted Budweiser cans litter the floor.

The tunnel extends a few feet and bangs a sharp left, and that's when it comes into view:

A mound of sand, as high as my neck.

I look up. There is a sliver of the gray sky above. A sheaf of sand falls into my eyes and some in my mouth. I gasp and spit it out.

The sandbox.

I'm under the sandbox.

❧⟡❧

When I'm coughed out and clear, I look again.

Above me are doors. They're metal doors that meet together in the middle, but over time, they've warped and separated.

I take a step forward and trip on something, falling on my chest in the dirt. More clouds of sand. More coughing.

Rolling over, I sit up, brush caches of sand out of the pockets and wrinkles in my red barn jacket. There's another smell in my nostrils, like mildew and rotted plywood, and a void of sound, as though I'm in a snow-covered field.

As my eyes better adjust to the dark, I see the tunnel extends several more feet toward a hulking form; emerging from the gloom, half buried like a wrecked ocean liner in the depths, is something large and square.

I take a deep breath, then hate myself when a lungful of fine dust makes me choke. I feel around for my cell phone, sift through the sand, grimace at the familiar coating on my hands.

Reengaging the flashlight app, I'm relieved to see it seems fine, save for some grains wedged between the phone and its Otterbox, but the light isn't far-reaching enough to distinguish what's out there. I struggle to my feet. I edge closer.

It's Bessie, Mom's big orange freezer. As I approach, so does the past: the Bantam Market and its refrigerator cases brimming with veal and beef, Kimmie banging her spoon on the table, the horrific thunderstorms and yellowing books, the lean times and Mom's inedible Crock Pot meals, the endless games of Bury the Dead that stretched across summers and falls until Myron was gone.

Myron—Myron and his maroon puffy coat. I suddenly miss him terribly. If we'd have parted ways, would he have gone into the world or stayed next door, so that today I could knock and find him there, the same old Myron, just older, less the caterpillar of snot and in a coat of a larger size?

Bessie, the one I remember, never had a lock; here, there's clear evidence that one existed—a hasp and staple, rusty but still viable, sit waiting for their padlock.

I shiver as though startled, feeling watched, and could swear I hear someone urging me to look inside. When I turn, there's no one there.

The last thing I want to do is let go of the flashlight app, so instead, I try to prop the phone on a nearby rock outcropping. It does little to dispel the stygian murk.

I pry open the freezer. It sticks at first, and when it pops open, out wafts the most ungodly smell, like mold and dirty sweat socks.

The lid rests against the back wall, and I grab the cell phone and peer inside.

It's a black hole, but, surprisingly, there are items inside—a disintegrating magazine, on the cover of which I can only make out a *P* and a *y*, what looks to be tinfoil, and some old clear plastic bags with marker hastily scrawled on them. I reach down and pick one up. It's filthy, and it sticks to my hands, but the marker is still visible:

M, Rump . . .

. . . and the date Myron disappeared. A sharp pain stabs my jaw—I get one there every once in a while, ever since the bone from the turkey loaf got wedged in my teeth.

I feel slightly nauseated, and reach for another bag.

M, Shoulder.

Rump. Shoulder.

The tickle of an unpleasant thought worms into my mind, creeps into my soul. I push it away. *These are cuts of beef.*

I dig a little deeper. There's a western belt buckle, there's another bag in Mom's handwriting, *V, Thigh . . .*

M is for Myron.

V is for Vinny.

The handwriting is Mom's.

A cold hand enwraps my heart.

I think of Kimmie's bright eyes. I can't breathe. I think of the bacon in the pepper pot soup. My mouth fills with the horrid taste of pennies. I think of the vomit in the sink. I sweat. I hyperventilate.

I retreat from the chest, stumble in the sand piles, end up on my back, beneath the sandbox. Trap doors. They were *trap doors.* The kids fell down here, and then Mom and Dad . . .

. . . then Mom and Dad . . .

I see Mom at the Crock Pot, telling us not to worry about the neighborhood kids. *I know this is, like, scary city for you kids, but you just need to be cool. Those boys were always in a tango with trouble.*

I struggle to my feet, plunging my hands deep into the pile for balance. My fingers tease a trove of thin, hard items—sticks? No, bones. The bones we used as pawns in Bury the Dead.

I pluck one from its grave, and see it's not a chicken bone at all, but a piece of human rib.

I kick myself clear of the pile and watch as the sand silts away, slowly uncovering a maroon puffy coat.

JARRING LUCAS

S OMETIMES ALL IT TAKES is a push. To be born. To kill your asshole father. To convince the parole board that you are, to your very *core*, remorseful for what you did. To assure the astonished realtor you're so desperate to put the past where it belongs that yes, *really,* this broken hulk of a mansion in Murrells Inlet lying just beyond a state preserve is *perfect.*

My childhood friend Leza's excitement that I'm back makes her even more beautiful than I remember, and I wish I'd taken the time to shave and look decent, although it seems she doesn't notice. She wrinkles up that cute little nose of hers, folds her arms across her form-fitting yellow sweater and says, "Really, Lucas? Why didn't you pick something in better shape?"

I'd hoped she'd instantly fall in love with it. "This was the most out-of-the-way place I could find." A ghost crab scuttles across a patch of sand in front of my car; they're nocturnal and beach-dwellers, so I take this as proof of its isolation. I survey the weather-beaten stones, the rotting door, the broken stained glass window overlooking the foyer. "Plus, the owner died, the family wanted nothing to do with it, and it's been sitting here like this for years. So I got it for practically jack. I can fix it up."

I'd always worked construction and had returned to the job I'd left, thanks to the company's being owned by a family friend. I have income and inexpensive access to materials. "Wait 'til you see the inside."

She moves next to me; I can smell her, a faint hint of cucumber and melon. That's when I see the scratches on her neck: five neat lines, like a claw mark. I reach out and brush back her hair to get a better look. "What's that?"

She shifts the collar of her sweater to obscure it. "You know me. Always getting into things."

Although I sense something's off, it's true. When I was in prison, she sent me a letter just about every week, chronicling her volunteer activities at Huntington Beach State Park, sharing hijinks at her for-fun job at Whales pushing $3 towels and sand art, and familiarizing me with the strays she feeds after her daily runs.

"It was just one of the cats." She moves across the arid, sea-grass-choked lawn and hesitates on the stone steps. The cicadas are so loud she almost has to shout: "Come on, I haven't got all day. My husband's done at five."

Kent is a pilot and inherited his dad's tourist-shuttling scenic flight business. He's always been possessive of her, and I notice she's nestled her red Miata beneath a cluster of palmettos, up against the untamed tangle of woods that separates us from a cliff overlooking a beach.

She's right. We don't have much time.

The massive door is padlocked. I fish the ancient, scroll-worked key from my pocket and work inside the rusty hole; when at last it pops open and the door gives way, it creaks like the grinding of worn brake pads.

There is the smell of camphor, mildew and wet stone, and the sound of the ocean echoes in the cathedral-ceilinged main hall.

"Jesus," she says. "How are you going to sleep? It's like being inside a conch shell."

"That's part of the charm." I reach for the light switch; the wrought-iron chandelier spits to life, shedding orange-gold shafts on a paling mural of a river and desert beyond gold columns and palm fronds; in front of that is a dusty—but solid—intricately carved Cleopatra-style sofa. The teak bannister along the stone stairs to the second floor is still in good shape, just gossamered with cobwebs. "See? Not too bad. A couple things, but, really, it's mostly cleanup and updating. She's structurally sound."

She frowns.

"Come on, I'll give you the tour."

We begin in the sitting room to our left, which, like most of the rooms, is full of ancient rattan and mahogany furniture, curiously none of it covered by sheets.

She points to the stenciling on the wall: a repeating rose-navy-amber series of large symbols. "What's with that? It looks Egyptian."

I regret not having made more accurate mental notes when I was with the realtor, but I remember a few things. "This place was built in the twenties, when the whole Egyptian revival was going on."

She steps forward, looks more closely. "I get the pyramid and the sphinx and all that, but what's with the vases with the heads on top?"

Every fourth symbol is crowned with a head wearing a smug countenance: a man. A monkey. A dog. A bird of prey . . . no, the monkey is a baboon, the dog is a jackal, and the bird of prey is a falcon. That's right. The realtor had explained it when she'd noted if I didn't like them I could remove them. "Those aren't vases. I think those are . . ." I dip into my memory, but can't pull up what they're called—only what they're used for. Embarrassed, I just say, "funeral jars."

"What?"

"When Egyptians made mummies, they took the innards out and put them in those."

"Why?"

"So the person could use them in the afterlife."

"Ew." She pauses. "They couldn't pick staffs or suns or something like that?"

"I think the last owner was like . . . he'd been to Egypt a bunch of times, studying burials or something. The same thing's in every room in the house."

"They're looking at me."

Actually, they hadn't bothered me when I looked at the place. "There's a way to get rid of them."

She considers me for a long moment, steps forward, and sets a hand on my arm. "I know you wanted to start over, but . . . at least consider staying at Pop's hotel until it's . . . restored to its former grandeur."

I flush at the feel of her hand, so I look at my feet. "Nah. I'll be fine."

She looks disappointed.

A furious beating noise surrounds us, drowning all else. Leza crouches, thrusting her hands over her ears, and out of instinct I pull her against me. Huddled together, I'm less focused on the ungodly pounding than on the thrill coursing through me.

The sound recedes, and I realize it was a helicopter passing overhead.

We don't move for what seems like several minutes. At last, she looks up at me. Something hangs between us.

"I . . . I have to go." She breaks our embrace, stands up. "It's late." She retreats to the rectangle of gray and palm trees that is the front doorway, and I follow. "You're *sure* you don't want me to get you a room."

I know I should say yes, but something tugs at me: *this is where I belong*. I shake my head.

"Well," she says. "I'm not crazy about it, but I guess I'll just have to visit you out here then."

She turns to go, and I watch as she fights the dense growth around where she's parked, gets into her convertible, and drives away.

In her absence, I am drawn once again to the wall stencils.

My mind gropes for the jars' proper name; I'm gravitating toward words that start with C, words I realize I'm making up: Canic? Conundric? No. Something *like* that, though. I stare at the falcon-shaped one a bit longer. Its eyes seem to pierce through me.

Canopic. That's what they're called. Canopic jars.

I wonder what Mom—the *queen* of jars—would have thought.

⁂

I grew up in a one-thousand square foot trailer on a permanent site in the KOA Campground in Myrtle Beach, and it was crammed with jars: buttons, change, safety pins, everything you could think of was stored in blue glass, pink marble, stoneware, metal; some shaped like chickens, fish, cottages. Mom combed estate sales and thrift shops on a regular basis to find more, and when she wasn't doing that, she was pickling, jamming, canning: Lemony Cauliflower, Spiced Plum Jam, Roasted Corn Salsa. She'd put everything in Ball jars, fleece them with gingham, and sell them anywhere she could, sometimes even at the state fair all the way in Columbia.

When I was in elementary school, my birthdays always fell during a themed week—Fire Prevention Week, Ecology Week, Dental Hygiene Week. In second grade, my day landed in the middle of Personal Safety Week, and it was so hot it felt like even our vinyl siding would melt. I was supposed to go to Leza's pool—her parents owned the Polynesian Golf and Beach Resort—but Mom wanted me home right away. Although we didn't have air conditioning, and the simmering menagerie of fruits on the stove made the kitchen a sticky, mango miasma, I was more disappointed I wasn't going to see Leza.

Mom sat me down at the table. "Now, honey, I know you've been learning at school about when to tell adults certain things that you see or hear." She slid me a honey-colored ceramic castle jar; the bottom was the building, the top a pagoda-like spire. Needless to say, I was a kid and would have rather been given a toy, so I just sat there, and saw what I swear was the slight sag of disappointment in her deep blue eyes. Still, she smiled. "Go ahead, now! Open it."

I wrapped my chubby hand around the spire and lifted the top. It was empty.

"Do you know why it's empty?"

I shook my head.

"Because it's meant to keep your secrets. See, we don't tell other people outside this house what goes on here. It's . . . private. So instead of telling someone at school, you come home, and you whisper into the jar, and then you put the lid back on, and no one will ever know. And if you want, you can keep your secrets about other things in there, too. Okay?"

There was the bang of the sunroom door, and I knew what that meant.

My father was home.

"Go, go." Mom shooed me to my room.

Jar against my chest, I was ear to wall for the usual: the insult ("Love those flowers you put out there. If only you were that pretty"), the reprimand ("It stinks like a whore's cheap perfume in here!"), the slap, the slam ("Jesus. I'm going out!"), the tears, and later, when I would alight the rickety spiral staircase leading to our sundeck atop the kitchen to find her, the excuse: *I fell, I cut myself on a broken jar, clumsy me, I burned my arm on a hot pan.*

That night, before bed, I whispered a secret into my jar. But I'm sure it wasn't the secret Mom'd had in mind.

The house *is* like a conch shell—the *hish-roar* of the sea permeates every nook, overwhelms every space. I'm successful in drowning it out only when I'm immersed in various renovating tasks: for now, covering the damaged stained glass window with thick plastic; ripping out the ancient cabinets in the kitchen; removing the stencils: pressure washing and using a solvent.

The rooms in the house are also oddly shaped. Most are hexagonal or octagonal, but in each there's one wall that has a closet-sized protrusion ruining the flow, like a buck tooth in an otherwise perfect smile. Since it's not stone—it's fake brickwork, in some places deteriorated enough I can see there's horsehair plaster underneath—I've assumed there are probably pipes and electric inside, but today, I feel like someone is standing in there, watching me.

Don't be a jackass, I tell myself. I rev up the pressure washer and move for a hose-down on one of the jackal-headed jars.

I swear he's leering at me.

⁂

My father rarely deigned to acknowledge my existence, so I wasn't afraid; I was, instead, angry. Which wasn't an issue when I was eight, but became one as I grew. Thanks to Mom's Hungarian heritage, I towered over that squat pepper-shaped Italian; the image of us abreast was a Sasquatch vs. Man illustration. By the time I was seventeen, my physical presence in the house was enough to keep things from being incendiary.

Until the night I came home to the violent sounds of shattering glass.

I rushed into the house and found Mom cowering in the corner on a bed of what amounted to her entire jar collection and its contents; my father was hurling them at her, and blood covered the refrigerator, the stove, the cabinets. She could do little more than duck and scream for him to stop.

Everything inside me boiled over. I clocked him, picked him up by his belt and his thick little arm that had swung at Mom for the final time, and made for the spiral staircase to the sundeck.

"Lucas, don't!" Mom yelled after me, but I was deaf to everything but the sound of his body landing on the crack-riddled shell-stone of our parking area; I wanted to hurt him the way he'd hurt her.

As it turned out, I killed him.

As a minor with no priors and the mitigating factor that I was under duress, I was given half the normal sentence and released early for good behavior. But every night I spent in J. Reuben, I thought of Mom, and her last words to me before she died of her injuries: "We could've kept it a secret."

❧❦❧

Sweat pours into my eyes as I chip away at the stencils; the sitting room is almost completely clear of them, and although the pressure washer stage drowns the noise of the ocean, the solvent-and-brush stage doesn't, so I buy a cheap radio and work to whatever's spinning on 94.9 The Surf. When I was a kid it played beachside oldies most of the time, but now it's a mix of everything, not all of it worth hearing.

As far as stencil removal's concerned, it's the falcon-headed jar's eyes that are particularly difficult; it's like someone used tar. After I've wiped out the jar, the beak, and the feathers on the head, I'm always left with the eyes. I'm about to tackle a pair when the radio turns to static.

Dammit, that's what I get for buying a five-dollar special. I put down my brush and crouch to play with the antennae. I bend it left and there's a high-pitched sound; I bend it right, and hear something that curdles my blood.

Voices. Gutteral, sinister, low.

Who would listen to this crap? I think, but I can't help feeling there's something not right about this. There's no melody. It's spooky. Frantically, I spin the dial both ways, trying to get another station to come in. Nothing. I try to turn the volume down. Nothing.

There's a loud knock at the door, and I jump.

The radio pops to the 4 Jacks's "Bobcat Woman."

More knocking. "Coming!" I switch the radio off, wipe my hands, and tuck the rag into the back pocket of my shorts.

Leza stands on the front steps, haloed by the afternoon sun and in a peony-patterned dress—appropriate for the heat, although she's wearing an olive-colored sweater that completely covers her arms.

She holds up a reedy basket laced with green gingham. "My husband's at work, I have the day off, and I thought we might . . . celebrate? Champagne? I brought your favorite. Or at least it used to be. Cold lime chicken?"

As glad as I am to see her, I wish I'd had warning so I wouldn't have been a sweaty mess.

She blinks expectantly. "Well?"

I open the door wider. "Come in."

She does, peers into the sitting room, and I note she looks tired. Not sleep-tired. Done-with-life tired.

"Lucas? Did you hear what I said?"

"Oh . . . sorry. What?"

"I said, 'You've done a beautiful job erasing the stencils, but how come you left the jars?'"

I'm confused and follow her gaze. It's true. The other symbols—the pyramids, sphinxes, and scarab beetles—are gone. But the jars are back. It's as though I never touched them at all.

At first my stomach wrenches. Then I remember the nature of things like paint coverage jobs. Why would this be different? "They're . . . probably ghosting. They look like they're not there when they're still wet, but when they're dry . . . "

"Like a stain on a carpet?"

"Yes, that's it." They probably need a few more applications, I figure.

Another helicopter passes over the house, and although Leza reacts, I've gotten used to it. Still, I say, "Let's go eat in the courtyard."

✣❦✣

The jar Mom had given me held my secrets—most about Leza. Somehow, I'd always understood, from a first glimpse of her in kindergarten, that I *wasn't* just friends with her. That there was more than that.

But I also knew I wasn't good enough for her—not like that, anyway. My family didn't own a motel, restaurant, bar, or attraction. I was the son of a trucker who drank away his paycheck. She could never feel that way about me. And I remember the day Kent became all she talked about.

We were at our favorite spot on the beach, the sun a glowing red orb sinking into a swatch of fuchsia, violet, and tangerine.

"So what would you like, Lucas?" Leza dug her toes in the sand. I'd brought her an ice-cold Bud, and she sipped it even though I could tell she didn't savor the taste.

I wasn't sure what she was getting at. "What do you mean?"

She rooted her beer in the sand and leaned back, propping herself up on her elbows. "I mean, what do you want?"

I knew what I really wanted, but my jar carried that secret, so I just said, "Someday I'd like to live in an out-of-the-way place. Somewhere private where I don't have to deal with any arguments."

She laughed. "No, I mean, like, *now*. Like . . . something more."

I was confused, so I just shrugged. There was only the crashing of surf; in the blue-gray water, a dolphin leapt not far from a phosphorescent patch of plankton.

She shifted, looking away. "Well, Kent really loves me, you know. I've never had *anyone* care so much about where I'm going and who I'm with—I mean, not even my parents ever did!—and he even lets me take his dogs for walks. He's teaching me how to be more affectionate." She drained her beer. "He's really good for me."

"Leza."

"What?"

"Are you happy?"

A long silence. "Sure."

We stayed until the dark descended and the ghost crabs emerged. Then I went home and threw my father off the sundeck.

The day before I was carted off to prison, she came to say goodbye. I remember her sad expression as Kent, copping a satisfied look, stood behind her.

❧⟡❧

We're halfway through our meal in the weed-choked courtyard when a violent afternoon downpour moves in from the sea. Squealing like we used to when we were kids in her beachside pool, we toss everything into the basket and bolt for shelter.

"Come on!" She tugs me along. Her hand feels small and fragile.

In my back hall, she stands, staring at me, seeming expectant.

I let go of her hand and move toward the kitchen. "We can finish in here. It's dusty still, but doable."

She patters behind me. "Actually . . . I should go. With these storms I'm sure Kent'll be checking in."

"Are you sure?"

"I don't want to, but." She sighs. "Yes. I should. You know, I'm soaked, anyway. Don't want to catch a cold."

"Why don't you just take the sweater off? Let it dry?"

She rubs her arms. "No . . . I'll be fine."

I notice her shoulders seem a bit slumped as I show her out. Just before she steps across the threshold, she hugs me. And she holds on.

I let her, feeling things I know I shouldn't, a warmth in my extremities, an incredible calm.

At last she pulls away and looks up at me.

"You." My voice cracks. "You need to go."

Her lips part like she's about to say something; then, she nods.

After I secure the massive door behind her, I'm unsettled, but not sure why. I'm overwhelmed by the sounds of the crashing ocean waves, the thrum of the deluge, the rumble of thunder.

And something else.

The voices I heard before, like a group of old men having a conversation. But this time, the radio isn't on.

Is it possible there's someone in the house? "Hello?"

No response. Champagne wells up my throat, and I force it back down as I clamber for something to carry as a weapon. I settle for the broken base of a lamp in the shape of an Egyptian goddess.

I make my way from room to room. Through the kitchen with its water-damaged outer wall, the dining hall with its broken mahogany table, the sitting room with its web-canopied chandelier. I ascend the staircase, but there's nothing in any of the rooms, not the strangely painted nursery, the two guest chambers, my bedroom with its unusual brick floor. No matter which room I'm in, I'm goaded to the next.

A crack of thunder and a *smack-crash* makes the second floor buck beneath my feet. I fall backward, wrenching my knee.

What the hell was that?

I recover from the shock to find the voices have stopped. But it sounds as though it's pouring inside the house.

I limp downstairs and a moist breeze blows from behind the stairwell: the library. When I get there, I see that it *is* raining in the house. A palmetto has plunged through the glass ceiling.

The voices begin again. This time, though, they've melded into a single voice, and it's somewhere in this room.

Everything inside me screams *run*, but I'm strangely compelled to go inside. The rain pelting my eyes makes navigation over the broken glass and around the metal girders sticking up at precarious angles difficult.

I'm lured to the tree's fronds, and then I see it: the tooth wall, that odd chunk that juts into every room, has been compromised. Pieces of brick façade and plaster litter the area around the tree.

The voice is definitely inside that wall. Some kind of speaker, maybe? That doesn't seem likely, but I need to find out.

Ax. Get the ax.

The air is heavy with the smell of mud and palm as I work, and the voice continues. I hack off frond after frond, throw it aside. When I've got most of them gone, I'm still blocked by part of the trunk. Undaunted, I get my chainsaw.

Halfway through, the blade hits the tree's core and gets stuck. I try to force it, but the machine squeals and grinds, the smell of scorching metal and gas getting stronger. I stop and try to shift the tree. My arms burn, but I manage to make a wide enough gap to get close to the wall.

The storm is moving away; the thunder is trundling off in the distance. But in the voice, I can almost identify words now— almost. I wedge myself between the tree and the wall and press my ear against it.

Pain shoots through my right ear. I scream and cup my hand to it, feel a warm trickle, but glance in time to see the bas-relief of . . . a bird, that's a *beak*, fade back into the wall. My ear stings like someone has poured alcohol on the open wound.

What the hell is *that?*

Enraged, I throw everything I've got into rolling the tree away, and succeed. It feels like I can't get enough air, my arms throb and my ear pulses, but I'm too pissed off now to stop. I seize the ax and hack at the plaster. Eventually, I see the sand-colored curve of an object, a glint of gold, a hint of navy. I fling the ax aside and reach into the hole, dismantling carefully, not unaware of the scrapes and cuts I'm putting on my fingers. Piece after piece snaps off; white powder puffs into the air, sifting onto my boots, skinning the puddles. When I'm done, I take an abashed stumble back.

Leering from the gloom is a three-foot falcon-headed canopic jar. It stares right through me.

Not one of these weird spurs in the house is for pipes. These were put here to conceal the jars. And God knows what's in them.

No wonder the family wanted nothing to do with this place. "What do you *want?*" I ask.

Behind me, something skitters. Ghost crabs. Scurrying for cover.

A deep male voice says, "Open me."

It laughs.

"Open me."

I knot in fear, but I've come this far. I close my eyes to summon my strength, step forward, and reach.

"Oh my God, Lucas, what happened? Are you okay?"

It's Leza. Still soaked, still in her olive sweater.

"Jesus, your ear!" She takes a step forward, touching my cheek.

The deep male voice: *Open me open me open me open me.*

She has no reaction.

My God, she didn't hear that, I think. I pull away from her.

"What? What is it?"

"Leza, I have to tell you—"

She sets her hands on my shoulders. "I have to tell you something too."

"Something isn't right and—"

"Listen. When we were kids, did you think I didn't know what was going on in your house? Did you think I was blind?

Our moms shopped at the same Piggly Wiggly. I know you did what you had to do. You were protecting your mother." She puts her arms down, steps back, and unbuttons her sweater.

"Leez, please, just listen to me for a second—"

"And now you need to protect me." With one deep breath and a look of determination, she pulls back the cardigan.

I gasp. Both her upper arms are mottled with bright purple and blood red bruises ringed in sickly yellow, and now it all makes sense—scratches on her neck, sweaters in the heat, cloaking the car and how, how did I not see this? If there's anyone who should've known it was me. "He did that to you."

She is so quiet and tearful I almost don't hear her. "He has been. Since after you left."

Instant anger. "Why did you *stay?*"

She doesn't respond. Instead, her mouth, warm and tasting like champagne, is on mine. A surge courses through me. She pulls back, breathing the words. "I was just waiting for you to come home. I've *always* been waiting for you."

The voice: *Open me open me open me open me . . .*

The front door bangs open. "Leza? I know you're in here!"

Kent.

"Answer me!"

We separate. I help her back into her sweater even as she winces.

"I'm here!"

I feel ill. I follow her out to the hall. Kent was always a big man, built like a string bass. But who he is has, over the years, taken a toll on his body; he is lean, corded, wolf-like.

And he's brandishing a crowbar.

"I'm here, Kent," Leza says. "I was just . . . stopping by to see how—"

"My ass. You been here a couple of times—I seen it from the air."

Jesus, I think. *The helicopters.*

"Get over here."

"Honey," she says.

"Get. Over. Here."

It breaks my heart to see her head bow in obedience. She folds her hands in front of her and walks dutifully behind him.

"Go home, baby." Kent taps the crowbar against his palm. "Now."

She doesn't move.

"Do what I tell you!"

Her lower lip trembles. She looks like she's about to cry.

I'm having visions of what he's going to do to her later. "This isn't what it looks like—"

"Shut up."

I glance back into the library.

I could swear the falcon's expression is different: pleased.

"Look at me, coward!" Kent screams.

I look at Leza. She looks small. "It's okay, Leez. Go on home."

She hesitates, then pivots and flees.

Kent and I remain locked in quiet, seething opposition until the car engine fades.

The voice: *Open me open me open me open me.*

There is an awful burning inside me, as though someone's poured scalding water down my gullet. I have the sudden urge to get the hell out of the house. "Kent," I can barely talk. "Let's take this outside, man."

"So you can run, chicken?"

"No. This place is under construction. There's stuff around here that could get you hurt."

He laughs. "Oh, I'm not the one getting hurt. Somebody's gotta teach you not to come near my property."

My fingers tingle. My face gets hot. *She's not property,* I think. *She's a woman, dammit.*

Openmeopenmeopenmeopenme.

He's advancing, pushing us back toward the library.

"Listen, I swear to God, I will never talk to her again. Just don't come closer."

He comes at me with the crowbar and I duck. He ends up standing with his back to the library, and I notice the falcon-headed jar is not where it was a minute ago.

It's sitting in the doorway.

Openmeopenmeopenmeopenme!

"You really don't want to do this, Kent."

He leers at me. "I can do anything I want. She's the one with the problems, you know. She provokes me!"

It boils over in me then, the stuff I've kept inside. The things I should have told others. The things I should have said to my father's face. "You're a sissy little man, that's what you are, a fucking pansy-ass, picking on her! Now I'm gonna show *you* what it's like to be picked on!"

I lower my head and plow into his stomach. He falls back over the jar, the crowbar flying from his hand, and a spritz of blood peppers the air as he's impaled on one of the giant girders that used to cement my glass ceiling.

His legs spasm, his arm drops to his side, and his body goes limp. Then everything is still, and I'm numb.

Jesus. I killed him.

This can't be happening. It can't. I won't get such a lax punishment this time. I won't finish this house. I won't be with Leza.

I break down into tears.

For a while there is only the sound of my sobs and the surf. Then I hear the voice:

Open me open me open me open me.

I remember what Mom said. Her last words: *We could've kept it a secret.* I think of the jars in the walls all over this house, the jars that were made for holding human body parts, the jars no one will ever know are there if I do it right.

I know what Mom meant now, and I pick up the ax.

DOWN IN THE GREEN

SUMMER HAD PRESSED in early this year on a June first heat wave, shrouding the camel's-hump mountains in a blue-green haze, turning the lake into a gray expanse of razor-hot sparklers.

A fish nibbled at Melanie's toes, one of those damned bluegills. In the harsh light of the burning sun, when they writhed on the end of her fishing pole, their chartreuse bellies fat with peeled grapes she'd used as bait, they were silvery orange and rust, with a tip of blue on their gill covers. Beneath the green water, they were translucent brown slithers that hovered above the sand, converging on her feet.

She was treading her way to the wooden raft with the diving board— one of the few left on the lake. The owners of this beach didn't seem to care about insurance: *swim at your own risk, dive at your own risk*, the ancient yellow posted signs read, and if you cracked your head open, there would be no sympathy.

She was halfway there when a bobby pin sprung loose from its home in her thick curls. When a pin tumbled from your hair, it meant someone was thinking about you, and you were supposed to retrieve it and say that person's name three times; but she could not retrieve it now—it was floating down, past the tethering shoelaces of seaweed and darting ravenous bluegills. Cradling lazily to the depths like a falling leaf, landing in the sand not far from the gargantuan anchor at the base of the rusty chain which kept the raft from drifting away. But she could not resist the pull of the old wives' tale, and so she envisioned the bobby pin between her pruned fingers and murmured the name anyway: *Mom, Mom, Mom.*

Was this near the spot where they'd dumped her? Tied the boat anchor from their long-retired outboard around her feet and trundled her frail-as-driftwood body off the dock with a splash like the sound of vomit? She wasn't sure, even though she and her brother had had the balls to do it during a blazing August Sunday morning. But everyone who was holy had been in church, so the beach had been deserted. In the burning sun there had only been Melanie, her mother's body, and her brother's argument that maybe they should have wrapped her in the old sun-faded green canvas boat cover.

He'd lost the argument. They hadn't dumped her at night, because she'd told them, before they'd given her that last dose of morphine—the fatal one—she'd wanted to *see* her beloved beach one last time. Make sure her eyes were open when they threw her in, she'd said, and no, no, don't do it at night, because all she would see down there would be murk and the fish that came in to feed, and she didn't want to watch them peck out her eyes before she got to have a few moments of clarity.

The disease had kept Mom from her beach for eight years, and the doctors said she could live at least eight more, even if she could barely talk above a whisper and all she could mouth were soft egg salad sandwiches trimmed to the size of toast points; even if she were in pain and her waste products were filtered through a tube and into a bag at her side. Mom was tired. She was ready to go to that place where the road hopefully gave way to the Elysian Fields.

Melanie and her brother, too, had been tired. Tired of reading lips or asking Mom to repeat her raspy whisper-gasps; tired of burning their fingers on the slick skins of hot boiled eggs and the smell of mayonnaise; tired of turpentine-colored stains on the bed clothes. So when last August had come, the insidiousness of sciamachy had made her brother fill the hypodermic needle, had made Melanie tie a silk peacock-blue turban on her mother's balding head so she could have a proper burial, so that, perhaps, the bluegills would not be shocked by this lifeless mermaid's lack of a swirling mane.

Or, perhaps, Melanie had done this ceremonial tying so she would not have to endure the last sight of her mother's body as a sinking head, crowned by only a few sparse, kinky hairs, like fiddlehead ferns brittling in a summer's drought.

Yes, perhaps Mom was beneath her feet now. Perhaps the bobby pin had landed near her. The tots and moms that were here sometimes had no idea what lay beneath their fat little feet and fleshy jiggling bodies, burnt as desert buttes. Those mothers had their babies to prevent from eating sand, and those babies had their mothers to plug their open mouths with ice cream. They didn't give thought to the fish nests or the litter down in the green.

She reached the raft and set her hands on the ladder, its stairs slippery with the tendrils of young mosses just beginning to weave their annual carpet. She hauled herself up, glancing briefly at the rounded blocks of pale aqua foam that kept the structure buoyant, noticing they were pocked with black craters of mildew that reminded her of cancer-infested smokers' lungs. The water from her body dribbled onto the raft and she spread herself out facedown on the wood to drip-dry and peer down through the slats. The water was lime green, like the Chichen Itza sacred water hole she'd read about, which had been dredged to unearth fifty human skeletons. She winced, wondering if, just maybe, she could see to the bottom. Would she see her mother?

The tip of the anchor they'd bound her with? Her eyes, glassy and open or long ago ingested?

The idea spooked her. She rolled over onto her back, feeling the hot boards brand her skin and threaten her, if she shifted the wrong way, with a splinter. There was a faint smell of vegetation and fish and sand and motorboat gas—*ahhh, the familiar scent of summer*; on the far shore, a cluster of white and red boats bobbed like ducks, their merrymakers diving off transoms, sending thick white splashes and fountains of water into the air. She heard laughter, and the cigarette boats were revving their engines so high she envisioned herself not on a lake but at an air show. She closed her eyes and let that thought soothe her, and she fell asleep.

Hours later, the sun was low and weak as a soft white oven light in the thick gray sky. A breeze blew up and she chilled. A storm was coming; she could tell because the decades-old trees looming over the sandy slope of the distant beach had the pale underbellies of their leaves showing. The boats that had been full of revelers had moved on now, over to Down the Hatch for beers, probably.

She stood and stretched, felt the pin-prickle of sunburn on her chest. The water would feel cool on it, comfort until she could get to a vinegar bath at home. She stood at the edge of the raft and studied the water below, prepared to jump as she had done on so many summer afternoons growing up.

And she couldn't do it.

A volley of waves rocked the raft, droplets splashing on her feet and the boards. She tried not to imagine the *splash-gurgle* sounds were really from a pair of hands rising from the water to clutch at the boat-tie rings—

She sucked in a breath and turned. There was nothing there.

Just jump in, she told herself. Where was this irrational fear coming from? She had swum here, in this same cool dark water, every summer day since she'd been in diapers. Even after she and her brother had done *it*, she'd come on the loneliest of afternoons to assure herself her special place had not been warped in any way. That what was beneath the water had not turned it to poison, and the swimming she did in it blasphemy. She sat on the edge and dangled her feet. Big toe, in. *See? That wasn't so hard*, and the water was baby-bath warm.

She stood again and studied the surface, not lime green anymore but oily in her own shadow. She thought she saw movement, down there, and changed her mind again.

She rested her hand on the side of the ladder as though it were the shoulder of an old friend. She could climb down it, she supposed. Grip firmly onto the sides, turn her back to the enemy, slip down, and butterfly back as quickly as possible, concentrating on her lonely tropical fish-spattered beach towel, looking now like the sad remnant of someone who'd gone for a dip and drowned. It was the only item on the beach.

She grabbed hold of the ladder, and then pulled her hand away.

Jump in, just do it, quit being a baby.

She closed her eyes and pinched her nose and down she went, the blub-blub low rush of water roaring past her ears. Underwater she popped open her lids. A curtain of white bubbles parted to reveal green murk and a bright yellow-rust whip of seaweed—

Something shot past her. *A fish*, she told herself, a fish, but the panic made her clamber for the surface as though she were drowning, and she reached for the sky as though it were a tangible thing to grab, as concrete as a rock ledge, and she gasped at the air and then—

It hit her, *thud*, on the bottom of her foot, and she didn't want to look down but start swimming instead and then it was in front of her, her mother's *head*. The bright blue turban mottled, a feather of seaweed jammed in it in queenly fashion.

The head bobbed and rolled and she saw one eye, pink and bulging like a grapefruit, the tattered remnants of a lid winking.

Melanie screamed as a fountain of water spewed from the head's mouth, puckered as an angel in a gothic garden, pelting her in burbling, thick drops.

The next morning it was her brother who found Melanie. She was washed up on the shore, not far from her favorite towel, a dead bluegill near her empty eyes.

SNAKE IN THE GRASS

WENTY-ONE YEARS after I was the first girl to get boobs in fifth grade, I woke up with a penis.

The first thing I noticed was an unusual weight, like a lump of mud was pressing on my pubis. I thought the cat was sleeping on my lower half, but when I sat up, there was nothing there—just a bump, poking up beneath the wine and cognac plaid of my quilt.

Jesus, what *was* that?

The room was shrouded in January's pre-dawn ink, making it tough to see. I sat up, slid back, and groped for the lamp switch. Everything went awash in a forty-watt shade of ivory.

Cautiously, I lifted the quilt and looked. And there it was. At attention, erect, and with one thick vein running up the middle. If I didn't know better, I'd swear it was giving me a single sloe-eyed stare. I closed my eyes and took a deep breath. I peeked again.

Still there.

It was not a product of the five apple martinis I'd imbibed the night before.

I rolled over to the other nightstand and grabbed my charging phone: *Google it. Surely somebody in the world knows something!*

All that came up was a *Daily News* article entitled "Rise 'n' Shine! Why a Morning Erection is a Sign of Good Health" (I guess I should've been relieved by that) and a tidbit in *Cosmopolitan* heralding the "5 Things You Need to Know About Morning Wood." Frantic, I changed my search criterion to *what should i do if i suddenly wake up with a penis?* I felt hope when the top result was "I Woke Up with a Penis Today (Part 1)" from *Journal Frankfurt* in Germany, but hope was dashed when it turned out to be a humor column. I scrolled a few pages, but there was nothing more.

Clearly, I was alone in this.

I could call my gynecologist—maybe he'd heard of such a thing! I looked at the clock—my alarm hadn't even gone off yet, so his office wouldn't open for a few hours.

Great.

It wasn't like I'd never seen a penis, of course—in fact, I'd beheld a mighty member just recently. Yesterday. Just before I'd dumped my . . . weekly bang? Weekend hookup? After our fight earlier in the week I'd finally realized Jim clearly wasn't the one. He was really cagey about where he was when he wasn't spending time with me, we rarely went out in public, and after four years I'd never met his parents. He wasn't a boyfriend, as badly as I wanted him to be. He was, however, the hottest fuck on the planet.

"There's no woman on Earth who can keep up with me the way you do," he'd always say after either a five-hour stint (yes, really) or sticking it in me while I was asleep (something I enjoy, although I understand most women find this violating).

"Why are you doing this?" He'd looked hurt. A slushy Waterbury rain fell on the windshield and made little rivers down the glass. "Don't leave," he said. "You're everything. You're so beautiful."

"That's right," I'd said. "I know. And someone else is really going to appreciate it."

"But I do appreciate it!"

"No," I said, "you don't. Now get out of my car so I can go find him."

Then I'd gone home and cried it out, fallen asleep, and awakened with a penis.

My cell phone buzzed—a text. From him. *Lets talk come over after work.*

I half thought, *Maybe I should make a date with him and wave my new club in his face.*

I didn't respond.

I tried to assess this thing I was looking at; I had a strange urge to try and figure out if it was better than Jim's. And what did *better* mean, exactly? Bigger? Longer? Thicker? Sure, I was aware that men compared themselves this way and slung insults at each other about it when they were pissed, wielding barbs like light sabers about overcompensating; I'd heard the girls at work laugh about our office manager Mr. Pancefoot's package, claiming that's why he was so anal about things like the tape dispensers: they had to be perfectly cocked at a forty-five degree angle to the magnetic paper clip holders. But mine was slim and a strange shade of ivory, not quite the darker color that another ex-boyfriend's had been, and definitely not the flesh tone Jim's was. It was somehow feminine, with clean, crisp folds. And yes, it had been circumcised. So where did that fall on the spectrum?

Trembling, I reached out to touch it.

It was all the hot and hard, smooth and veiny, silk and muscle that I expected—but it was also weird, because *I could feel my own fingers on it.* I worked them down to the base, then felt farther underneath, wondering if there were—

—balls. They felt like warm, damp tea bags.

I had to pee.

I hauled myself up out of bed and set my feet on the floor, then slowly stood, which didn't seem to feel too odd; walking was a different challenge. It was like having a third leg.

I went into the bathroom and stared at the toilet. Okay, guys aimed, right? How hard could this be?

I held it at its base, like I'd seen Jim and a cavalcade of ex-boyfriends do. Then I pushed.

Pee went everywhere. It sprinkled the toilet seat (which I'd forgotten to lift). It splashed the white walls and spit on the black tiles; it sprayed the mirror, soaked the toilet paper, and fountained into the bowl brush holder.

When I was done I needed a shower and a gallon of bleach.

I considered calling out of work, just until I figured this peeing thing out—although after my cup of coffee, sitting down and doing the tuck thing was much easier (and at least I didn't have to have a second bout with harsh bathroom chemicals). But then I remembered today was the last day of the month, and my partner was out on appointments. Which meant I had no choice but to go in.

Which also meant I had to find something to wear so it wouldn't be obvious.

Underwear first—and all I owned were thongs, because Mom always said *you'll never have to worry about your panty lines showing* before swiping my frillies to cut the cheeks out of them. That was back in the 1980s, before thongs had paraded out of the dirty corner at Victoria's Secret and became acceptable for not just sex kittens and women trying to put the spark back into their bedrooms.

Well, this was one of those little things in life Mom had failed to prepare me for. I rooted through the stretched-out collection—sage polka dots, goldenrod stripes, lavender lace— none of them had a crotch area that was, in my opinion, large enough to rein in the johnson.

There *was* the period stash—that ratty collection of full briefs I kept just for that time of the month.

Oh, God . . . I'd be excited if I didn't because it's a pain in the ass, but would I ever get my period again? Was my vagina still even *there*?

Carefully, I bent and reached past the dangly bits. Sure enough, behind them, there was a hole.

Damn.

Definitely a question for the gynecologist.

I looked at the clock . . . they still weren't open yet.

The period stash yielded a host of possibilities, but I had to squash the old man down into a lump in order for it to stay in place. It probably didn't help that the panties were decades old and stretched to California.

Clothing that kept the todger out of sight was also going to be a hurdle—mostly what I wore to work were three piece suits with pencil skirts, which stretched flat across the lap; there wasn't exactly room to hide much. At the back of my closet was a Hot Topic two-piece Halloween costume, the skirt of which had an attached crinoline. Perfect! Okay . . . maybe not *totally* perfect; it was brocade with gold thread and patterned with the No-Face character from *Spirited Away* . . . but it would have to do. I paired it with a white blouse and a black sweater. It didn't look half bad.

I tried not to think about what I was going to do if this thing didn't go away. I couldn't keep wearing the same skirt to work.

At last, my gynecologist's office was open. I called and got the usual *If this is a medical emergency, please hang up and dial 911* message over a bad Muzak version of Def Leppard's "Animal," then was on hold for a solid ten minutes before a nasal woman named Joan thanked me for holding and asked for my name, date of birth, and what I wanted.

"I need to see Doctor Laron."

"Is this for a checkup?" She tapped the keys on her keyboard. "Let's see . . . I have . . . Thursday, October 20 at 3 p.m."

Three weeks away.

"I need something—soon. Like today or tomorrow."

"Is there a problem?"

"It's . . . I just noticed this morning there's an unusual growth . . . on my . . ."

What the hell do I say?

". . . labia."

There was a moment of silence. Joan was probably wondering who the hell felt up her labia every day.

"Hang on, Marietta."

I hated when people called me by my given name.

"I'm going to have the nurse call you back."

"No, I just . . . I just need to see the doctor as soon as possible."

"I'll have the nurse call you. Is this 7569 number the best way to reach you?"

I gave up. "Yes." I pulled my briefcase off the chair in the corner and tossed it on the bed. "Yes, that's finc." Nothing said I had to answer the phone.

"Okay, just hang in there, Marietta. She's going to go over these notes and look at your chart and she'll give you a call."

Wonderful.

I finished pulling myself together and made the somewhat challenging—I drove a stick, so it felt like a lump was moving around every time I put in the clutch—drive to work.

At a stoplight, I pulled up in front of a Honda sporting the bumper sticker NICE TRUCK—SORRY ABOUT YOUR SMALL PENIS.

I instinctively looked down. Pecker was still present, and I wondered for a second if I'd measure up to the bumper sticker's standards.

My cell phone buzzed again. Jim: *lets just talk if u won't come over pls call.*

I ignored it, but the more horrifying thing was that I knew I *would* call him. I had to admit that Jim, as much of a failure as he was as a good boyfriend, wasn't all bad. There was familiarity in him, something I recognized—my dad had left us when I was eight. I had always wanted to please him, but no A+ essay about lobsters, winning a medal during PE week, or baking him his favorite hermit cookies (even if they did come out looking like freakish amoebas, they still tasted good) was going to do it. But Jim: Jim I could get a second shot at. If I worked hard enough, if I kept trying to please him, I could make him into the boyfriend I wanted and needed.

The marble-floored office lobby was its hustle of well-dressed go-getters rushing to the elevators to ensure they were early to their desks.

Zig, the tall, lion-maned Derring-Do Donut guy who sold more Kona blend coffee than he did chocolate frosteds, hoisted my morning black-two-sugars in the air.

The captain went to full-on attention.

Is that Zig or the coffee doing that? I didn't even think of anything!

I fumbled to shift the briefcase over my skirt.

"Hi, MJ." He was always bashful with me. This time he looked surprised and eyed me up and down.

I pulled a five out of my blazer pocket and tried to take the coffee, but he swooped it out of reach. "Something's *different* about you!"

Oh, no.

"Come on, Zig, I gotta go." I did, actually. I had to pee again.

"I got it!" He grinned, showing his shockingly perfect teeth for someone who owned a donut cart. "Your skirt! Studio Ghibli!"

I nodded politely and he handed me the cup. I hurried away.

Upstairs, no one noticed as I walked down the cubicle-buttressed hall to my office, wondering what I should do with the pictures of Jim living there. I felt a twinge of sadness: there were pictures of us camping, hiking, whale watching. I didn't want to toss them yet, but I wasn't sure I wanted to look at them all day, either.

It was amazing how things could change over a weekend.

Ginny, Mr. Pancefoot's secretary who hailed from somewhere in Texas, sipped her coffee and stared at her computer screen, perusing barbecue recipes. She held up a delicate hand to stop me. "Well, don't you look nervous as a fly in the glue pot."

I held my breath.

She got up out of her chair and set her hand on my arm. "What's goin' on?"

I heaved a deep sigh. "Jim and I, we—broke up."

She cocked her head to the side; her bell-shaped bob didn't move. "Well." She smiled. "At last. He was crooked as a dog's hind leg and if that ain't a fact God's a possum. You just come right over here and sit with me and have some tea." She tugged on my arm, the delicate silk of her pink blouse shimmering in the harsh fluorescent light.

"No, really, Ginny. I have coffee."

"We have time! Pussyfoot won't be out for a little while. He's chawin' away on a conference call."

Just then, Mr. Pancefoot's door opened to reveal my sweaty-shirted boss, a flame-haired, bedraggled Barney Rubble who looked like he'd slept on the faux leather couch in his certificate-spackled office.

I couldn't help it. I wondered what his wang looked like. My eyes strayed to his crotch.

Then I shuddered at the thought.

He eyed me. "What are you looking at, MJ?"

I jerked away and stared at the corner of Ginny's desk. I hated to throw her under the bus, but . . .

"Nothing." I straightened up and smoothed my hair. "I need to get back to work."

"Wait." He crept up to Ginny's desk. "Wait, what did you see on Ginny's desk?"

Ginny gave me a dirty look.

I shrugged, turned, went into my office and closed the door.

When I picked up a framed photo of Jim and me camping up at Lake Waramaug last summer, him trying to shove a marshmallow in my mouth, I got a boner.

❦❦❦

Jim's texting was relentless. *Pls call me* devolved into *this isn't over* and *I just bought lobsters and champagne for 2nite.*

My heart was starting to soften. I'd put three years into this relationship. I shouldn't just throw it away, should I?

Clearly, my new peen wasn't having any less confusing of a day. It rose when the numbers on my reports added up and fell when Ginny brought me a cup of coffee; it shriveled when the afternoon lunch cart rolled by and hardened every time I thought of Jim and lobster and champagne and butter . . . *butter* . . .

I couldn't stand it. I picked up my phone to text Jim: *yes, yes, I'll be over at seven and we'll talk* when one of my coworkers—Mike—stopped in. I'd always liked and confided in him, and we'd even knocked back a few at The Thirsty Goat on several occasions (maybe he was the guy waiting in the wings). My office flooded with the scent of his cologne—wood and musky oranges, and his maroon-striped tie was slightly crooked. At six foot one and broad in the chest, Mike was the opposite of Jim, who was just about my height and wiry. "What's up, MJ? How's your day?"

My face flushed and my cock swelled. I grabbed a file and pretended to flip through it.

"Last day of the month, so, you know, very busy," I said. "*Very* busy. How about you?"

"Just crap," he said. "Filing from last year I need to take care of."

The way he'd motioned with the manila folders when he'd said *crap* turned me on; the way he'd just admitted that he was a total rebel—my God, filing stuff from last *year?*—turned me on.

My crotch throbbed.

He winked. "You know how it is."

I shifted uncomfortably, the period panties stretching to accommodate the bulge. "I do."

"Well," he stood up.

I could swear I saw his muscles flex beneath his shirt.

"Y'know, back to the grind." He rested his hand on the doorknob. "You want this door open or closed?"

My dick pulsed so badly it hurt, and there was only one way to take care of that.

"Closed is fine."

At last he was gone, but there was a bigger problem—where was I going to go? My office wasn't at all private; it had pane glass windows that overlooked the bustling cubicle floor. Anyone could walk into the bathroom, and somebody was always rummaging in the supply closet.

The file room had no windows and needed a key. It wasn't the most romantic place in the world and reeked of aging paper and printer toner, but I'd have plenty of warning.

I barely had the room's door closed behind me before it happened. Warm and wet seeped into my panties. I lifted my skirt to survey the damage.

A drawer slammed.

Oh, God! Had somebody been in here the whole time?

Mike literally stared at my crotch and dumped the contents of his paper coffee cup on the floor.

"Holy *shit*, MJ!"

My mouth hung open.

"Really? Reduced to masturbating in the file closet?"

"No!" I shouted, then lowered my voice. "I mean, yes . . . but it's not like that . . . it's—"

Suddenly it occurred to me that I should just tell him everything. He was a guy, after all. Maybe he could help me. "Come here."

I took his arm and led him deeper into the crevice between the file cabinets full of W-9s and fingerprint cards going back at least twenty years, and into a corner by the emergency exit that dumped into the parking lot. "If I show you this," I said, "you can't laugh."

He looked pale.

"Swear," I said.

He glanced back around the corner, toward the entrance. Then he looked at me again. "Okay."

I shut my eyes and lifted my skirt.

"Holy *shit*!"

"Shhh! Someone'll hear!"

He paled and looked down at the floor. "Have you been a *guy* all along?"

"No—it's—"

"You got a sex change? When you said you and Jim were on vacation in Bermuda last year—"

"No—"

His face sagged. "I knew it. I *knew* you guys were into weirdness."

"No! Stop!"

There was a suspended breath and the hum of the fluorescent lights between us.

He heaved a sigh and set his hands on his hips. "What the fuck? Why didn't you tell me?"

"I—I woke up with it this morning."

"You what?"

"I woke *up* with it this morning! I broke up with Jim last night—"

"Oh crap, it happened to you *too*?"

I was confused. I didn't think he had anyone in his life; most of our talks revolved around asking him for guy advice about Jim, office politics, what was happening on *The Last Man on Earth*, his nieces, and what we did on our weekends. When we were drunk at happy hour, we got deep—about things like perception and death and would you take a one-way ticket to a Mars colony—deeper than any conversation I'd ever had with Jim in between all that banging, now that I thought about it. But none of that deep stuff had ever been about *his* relationship. "You broke up with somebody?"

"No. No!" His face lit up. "I woke up with a vagina last week!"

My mouth fell open. "What?" A hundred questions. "What did you do? Did you talk to a doctor?" I eyed his crotch. "Did it go away, did it—"

"I'm living with it. It's not too bad, actually. Except for the strange chocolate cravings." He rubbed his chin and looked me right in the eye. "But I did some reading."

"I don't understand."

He ran a hand through his hair. "Okay. So, in the animal kingdom, right? There are animals that change gender. Clownfish start off male, but if the female dies they become female. Male garter snakes can mimic females, copy their behavior exactly. Cuttlefish can appear female on one side and male on the other, depending on who's around."

"That doesn't happen to humans."

"How else do you explain this? I made a decision, I woke up with a vagina. You made a decision, you woke up with a penis." He grabbed my hands. "We're changing. Because our environment is about to change."

It was out of my mouth before I could stop it. "I haven't made a decision yet. I'm thinking I should maybe get back together with Jim."

He stared at me.

His hands were warm and encompassing; meaty and strong. My first instinct would've been to pull mine away, but I was strangely compelled to keep them where they were. "What was your decision?"

He looked sheepish and let me go. "After we went to The Thirsty Goat last Sunday. I realized."

The words hung in the air.

"What?"

He hesitated.

"Tell me."

More hesitation. Then he said, "I wanted to ask you out. If you were really serious with Jim or not. If you were willing to break up with him—to go out with me."

I felt the pressure down there again. I had a thing for Jim, I did. The romance was awesome. The sex was awesome. But could he ever be the boyfriend I needed? Was it worth the time? And Mike . . . well, he was more like a friend, and was I attracted to him in that way, *really*?

My cell phone, in my sweater pocket, chimed Jim's familiar ring.

"That's him." Mike nodded at my pocket. "Isn't it."

I sighed. "Yes."

"Listen, I can see this was a dumb idea." He went to the door.

"Mike, wait—"

He let himself out of the room, and the door slammed. There was an eerie echo.

I felt the lump between my legs and thought about all the trouble it had given me that morning, but at the moment, it felt like an old friend. I thought about waking up out of a dead sleep to being fucked, how hurt Jim had looked in the icy rain, roasted marshmallows and champagne and lobster and butter. I thought about The Thirsty Goat and tossing back a few and *The Last Man on Earth* and one-way tickets to Mars.

I thought about the fact that it was four o'clock and the nurse from the gynecologist's office hadn't called me back yet.

When I only had the vagina and Mike only had the penis, it would never have worked out between us.

But now that we had both, it just might.

CANDLE GARDEN

I T USED TO BE that in each of Lilly's candle gardens she had a favorite, one that melted slower or had milkier wax; since the fire, she found she loved each one equally, as one might love multiple children.

In the bedroom, a trio was lit: silver, gold, and forest pillars set in a bowl of glass stones. Flames jitterbugged on the pineapple wallpaper. The pattern was incongruous, and the paper peeled in the corners where she'd matched the seams. Wickford had approved the repairs rather than lose the structure altogether, and so, long after she'd scrubbed the smoke-damaged beams and replaced the rugs, she had spent torpid afternoons mixing paste and listening to appeals regarding the removal of fungus from the colonial-era stones in the yard. "Take the money and improve the grounds, too," her pregnant friend Iris, who still had *her* two other children, said one afternoon.

"The house is on the historic registry. I don't want things to change," Lilly answered, climbing down off her ladder. "Why don't we have some tea?"

The pineapples flickered: dark and light then dark again, and one of them blinked at her; she could see a face if she looked hard enough. The psychiatrist told her that she merely did something called pareidolia, mentally arranging leaves, smoke, coffee grounds, and patterns into faces. But she didn't believe that. She believed the pineapples pulsed with the spirits of her dead girls: Lucy had been four, Edna had been six, and Amarinthe had just turned seven. They had begged to sleep with the gardens lit because they believed the candles kept away the ghost of a man who shredded the wallpaper with his squiggled nails. "He tears faces so we can see what people look like on the other side," Amarinthe had said.

She wondered if the man had burned like her girls, the night they had cried from that very room where they couldn't break the window with glass so old it warped the yard's lilies into lavender smears. Her husband had gone back in to get them and had never emerged; by the time the firemen had arrived there was only her, a cotton bathrobe, a dash of soot on her cheek. What remained of her family was charred swaddling.

She didn't believe her beloved candle gardens caused the fire. That night three summers ago, the lightning had lit up the very back teeth of her defenseless girls—yes, it had—and she wondered what arrow she had shot at God to make him so angry.

She was going to take something back from God. And Jeremy was going to help her.

In Jeremy's hands, wax was flesh. He crafted candles in shapes for the shops in town: glittering pale blue sea shells for Operculum; goddesses for the Grateful Heart; apples for the outdoor tables at Wickford Gourmet; flowers for Newport's mansion weddings. Yes, Jeremy did amazing things with wax. He was twenty years her junior but seemed older because of his shock of skunk-stripe hair. "My dad, he went gray by the time he was thirty," he said. "You'd think my older brothers' would'a popped first, but they didn't." She secretly wondered if all that melting and burning, all that paraffin and dye, had made him old.

She and Jeremy had met at Rose Books. That day, she was in the crafts section, examining volumes on the fashioning of candles, what equipment she'd need, how long it would take, what the flashpoint was for paraffin. She thought of Edna, sitting in her Three Bears rocking chair, watching the flames. *What makes wax burn, Mohma?* she'd asked. *And why is it hot?*

"I make candles," a man said. "That isn't really the book you want."

She turned, startled from her examination of *Waxwork Basics*. Before her was Jeremy and his white flame of hair. In his hands, he cradled a biography of Mucha and a black Moleskine with scraps thrusting from it like tongues.

"What you really want," he reached for a book on a shelf above her head, "is this one." He presented her with copy of *Candlemaster's Bible*. "It's more expensive, but you'll get more burn for your buck."

She clutched both of them, wishing she'd washed her hair and brushed her teeth; that morning had been too nauseous with sorrow. "All of this is so expensive."

"It depends on what you're going to make. What you're planning on doing." There was a mole on his upper lip, a squished heart on its side, like the ones Lucy had squeezed from the frosting tubes when she'd made her special Valentine's Day cookies. *Mohma, I'm making hearts.* "I have lots of molds," he said. "Nice ones. Special-ordered ones. But now, I make candles in my own shapes. I . . . make my own molds."

Her gaze fell to his belt buckle, which was in the shape of the state of Rhode Island. "I was looking for faces," she said, blinking back up at him, at the swath of freckles across the bridge of his nose.

He rested the books in his hands on his waist, covering the buckle. "You know, I might have some older molds I don't use anymore."

"Oh, I don't know if you'd have what I need."

"I might."

She looked nervously toward the door of Rose Books, into the intense silver of rain, and then down at her feet, shocked to see she'd worn her black velvet slippers that were only meant as house-shoes. She was sweating. "It's like a veil out there."

He motioned with the book. "I just live upstairs."

She opened her mouth, prepared to say no, she had to be getting back, and then she remembered there was no one home to miss her.

She left her unpurchased books on a table that identified itself as an *Unwanted Potentials Depository* and followed him up the flight of worn stairs. His door bore a burn hole, and despite her horror she touched it and felt the splintered wood as he stuck a key into the lock.

"Wax fire. It hit its flash point." He looked up at her, jiggling the key, then pushed on the door; it didn't move. "It's—it's only happened to me"—he worked the glass knob—"one other time." He shoved with his shoulder, and the door banged open.

The room beyond opened up in a canyon of cornflower walls. The kitchen stove was shimmed crooked, and spattered with yellow and pink wax; small appliances, pots and pans, and metal thermometers littered the countertops. Against one wall, a mail holder had been converted into a dispenser for three spools of string, and a pair of scissors hung under a grimy light switch. The couch and recliner, the coffee table were buried under rainbow piles of candles; birds, fish, flowers, and seashells, moose, deer, Bibles and wreaths tumbled to the floor like colored stones.

"Sorry there's nowhere to sit. You can have one of those candles from that mess, if you want." He disappeared down a hallway. Somewhere, she heard a clock ticking, but it seemed to be stuck, because a buzz like the hornets in her yard kicked in every few seconds. She plucked a wax bird from the pile and stroked its milky back.

Jeremy emerged from the room with a box, one side of it smeared black. "You might find what you're looking for in here. They're still good—I'm pretty sure I didn't use them as many times as possible before they recommend you get rid of 'em. Want to see my latest work? Come on." He went over to the bathroom. "I just keep this in the shower so it's out of the way."

The bathroom window was shrouded with a wax-speckled sheet, but when he flipped a switch, work lights made up for the lack of sunlight. What was most strange were the walls, plaqued with thumb-tacked photos of young women and old men, of children hugging stuffed toys.

When he swept back the shower curtain, she gasped: a six-foot wax mermaid cast her eyes to the ceiling. She remembered Amarinthe, who had once taken a trash bag, glued glitter on it, tied it around her waist and romped about the house. *I'm a mermaid, Mohma!*

"I recognize her," she said.

"Yes, you would. Her face is Elsa, owner of Rose Books."

She touched the brown-sugar dollops on the figure's breasts. "It's beautiful."

"I study the face, and then I craft a mold." He reached up to the face and picked at something on the wax cheek. "I do these in metal because I like to smith, and I find metal molds produce better detail. I shop for women's garments and fashion body parts from those, and then I make each piece and melt the seams together, then smooth them over. Here." He reached out to her, cupped her trembling fingers, pressed them lightly on the wax creature's breastbone. "You can't even feel it there."

The warmth of his hand was such an unfamiliar thing, as alien to her as a smile, and the tickle of corn silk hair, and the chirrup of giggles. He moved her fingers across the wax as deftly as the hand of a blind man might hover over braille; she was behind the ear and down the hair, across the waist and circling the shoulder: he was showing her the seams, the places where she could be taken apart.

He stopped at the crease of the mermaid's eye, let go of her hand, and exhaled. "It's the second one I've done that emerged as a good likeness."

"Who came through before?" she asked.

"Mom." He pulled the shower curtain closed, and she withdrew her hand as though stung. "It was her birthday present." He strode into the living room, lifted her box of molds onto a table, brought them back toward her, and pulled them out, one by one; like mismatched shoes, they landed on the counter, abreast of a stack of newspaper clippings and photo albums. "You know, she never brought herself to burn it? She said it would be a bad omen. I told her *nothing* was a bad omen. If bad things are going to happen, they'll happen. You can't create trouble for yourself. At least, that was what I thought." He stopped cradling one of the molds, holding it up in the darkening light from the windows. He ran his finger along its chin, its drawn, thin-lipped expression. "I was teaching her how to melt wax when it happened," he said. "It just—everything went up so fast. It was my fault. I should've been watching."

"I'm sorry," she said.

"I'm sorry too." He offered her the mold, his hand over his mother's eyes. "About your girls. I was living here. I watched the fire engines."

She pulled the face against her breasts as he wiped his hands on his jeans, frosted with melted wax. He brushed past her, his words suddenly urgent. "I'm going to give you my card"—he was mining a pile of magazines and papers on the counter—"and if you have any questions about making candles or where to go to get wax—Waximillion up in Providence carries the highest quality stuff—or you could order it on the internet, but I don't always trust what I'm buying—"

Her feet were cold, suddenly. "I want you to do it," she said.

He ceased and looked up at her, and the stack on the counter toppled to the floor like a cascading waterfall. "Uh . . . my people are . . . they're not for sale. I just do that as a project, really; it was therapy, kind of."

She nodded toward his refrigerator, where several bills with threatening red stripes were pinioned beneath kitchen magnets. "A gift, then. I'll make a donation."

Outside, there was a timpani of thunder, and the lamp on his corner table dimmed.

⁂

It rained an angry deluge with a sound like a horde of frogs slapping the roof, and up in the room with the pineapple wallpaper, she extinguished the flames and waited for Jeremy; she pressed her nose against that omnipresent thick glass, brushing aside the drapes that were stitched in Revolutionary War silhouettes.

He drove up in his sky blue truck; rust spots gnawed at its back wheel well. In the bed a tarp shrouded four lumps.

She watched him leap up the steps, and when she pulled open the front door, she found his weathered hand curled in a fist, about to knock. "They're here," he said.

She frowned, not at him, but at the burn swath down the front of his jacket. She touched it, rubbed the cracker-crisp leather under her fingers.

He pulled her hand away. "This is . . . what I was wearing. The day she burned."

There was nothing between them until the boards above their heads creaked.

"I'll, uh . . . help you put them in the garden," he said.

"No," she said. "Just set them on the rocks over there. I can move them myself."

He nodded and turned back to the truck, and she pulled her checkbook from the letter table drawer, thinking she could not put a price on what he'd given her. She thought of the hospital bills from when she'd given birth to her girls and wrote him a check for the balance of what she had left in her account.

The next day, she set blue-wax Lucy, whom Jeremy had fashioned sporting a smear of glitter and a blush of chocolate cake as on her second birthday, among the tiger lilies. And she set lavender Edna, cross-legged and reaching for a butterfly as in the photo of her romping through a corn maze, in the patch of her garden populated with dead sunflower stalks. And yellow Amarinthe, who was fixing her hair and pulling down the brim of a floppy hat she'd stolen from Mohma's closet on Halloween, Amarinthe she set down by the stream that burbled behind the leaning shed. And because she herself did not have a favorite spot or a favorite child, she set the likeness of herself where it could see them all.

It poured, and when the last raindrop rolled off the tiger lily petals and a shaft of April sun parted the pigeon gray, she pulled a key from her bra. She unlocked the steel box on her fireplace mantel and held the matches in her palm. Then she went out to the lawn, and she lit her girls, and she watched them burn, and she wept that she was sorry, but that she would see them soon.

HAIRLESS GIRL DOES THE HULA

A WOMAN DROWNED in the Kahiki Moon Resort's Volcano Pool this morning.

This means the waitresses—like me—and performers at the resort's nightly luau can revel in a paid day off. Since central Florida's rocking a serious heat wave, I'm gonna splash through it in my apartment complex's pool.

Some of us aren't so lucky. Like Toke—his real name is Tokala, or something else no one wants to pronounce—whose pool is undergoing refurbishment.

Speaking of hot—Toke, the show's senior fire knife dancer, is muscled, tan, and carries himself so the one missing tooth in the corner of his mouth is actually *sexy*. All the waitresses and hula girls pine for him, but since the heat wave's cusp he's been winking at me, even going out of his way to talk to me.

So you can imagine how psyched I was when he actually *called* and asked if he could come over to my place and swim in *my* pool. And better, could I come pick him up, his car's radiator cracked and it's at the shop.

"She's got nice legs, Hailey. But her spring's showing." Toke chucks a toweled bundle in my Toyota's back seat.

"What?" Then I realize he's referring to the wobbling hula dancer figurine tacked to my dashboard. Her red grass skirt has come unglued at the seam.

"She's only got legs up to her thighs. There's a spring where her gut should be. You should Krazy Glue her."

I look more closely. I'd envisioned a full body under there—in fact, I'd even been curious about how they'd handled her you-know-what—but never checked. "Oh, shit." I key the ignition and twist my body to back up the car. "I bought that at the Kahiki and paid like fifteen bucks for it."

"Fifteen bucks? Christ. Coulda got one down at Eli's Orange World for two."

"Yeah, they had chintzy tourist stuff. I really liked this one. There was something about her."

"Looks like you, maybe?"

I blush as we turn onto Route 192. Truth is, she looks like I *wish* I did. My long black hair, unbeknownst to everybody, is a wig. I have alopecia universalis, which means I'm bald and have no hair anywhere on my body. I learned how to draw pretty good eyebrows, wear fake eyelashes, and have worn a wig my whole life. Nowadays, there are permanent hair implants, and I've saved whenever I can so someday I *will* look like her, for *real*. But I'm still a ways off—my piggy bank, just like everyone's, gets the change punched out of it now and then. "She does, you know. Look like you." He fingers my cheek.

Holy crap, is he really touching me? I think of the huge balls of fire he passes between his legs and whips around his torso. "Really?"

"Sure." He pulls a cigarette from his pocket, rams it in his mouth, and lights it. His fingers feather the tips of my hair.

Please, dear God, let the wig hold . . .

If guys find out I have no hair, they won't want me—this I know.

My last year at junior high, there was this guy Peter in my geology class. We'd flirted for weeks, and on a quarry field trip, I'd just uncovered a rare trilobite when he asked me to the eighth grade dance.

That night, I was dancing with my head on his shoulder and my wig shifted and came off. Back then wigs—even expensive ones—just weren't as well made as they are today. Consequently, my dreamboat in the blue tuxedo ran out. I stood in the middle of the floor, the circling spotlight beaming off my bald head.

No boy came near me after that. I'm still a virgin.

So I'm sure Toke'll turn off if he finds out. He'll never wink at me again, and the highlight of my work shift—where pretty much all I do is restock all-you-can-eat platters of pineapple bread and Polynesian rice—will be collecting my tips at the end of the night.

We pass the Chick-fil-A. Toke flips on the radio and out blasts a reggae version of "Slave to Love." The hula dancer bobbles away—I swear, for just one second, her eyes flash red.

Probably just a weird effect of the sun.

⁂

I call the Augustus Apartments—a garden-style community done in reds, golds, marble, and fountains—home.

"This place's nice." Toke brushes his fingers along a mosaic.

"I think it's supposed to look a little like Pompeii before it was torched or something," I say. "Part of its charm."

I unlock my apartment's door and a wall of hot air nearly knocks me over.

"Guess it's supposed to *feel* like Pompeii too?" He retrieves a fluorescent orange piece of paper that's been shoved under my door. *The air conditioning units are undergoing routine maintenance. We apologize for the inconvenience.* "Who the hell does routine maintenance in the middle of a heat wave?" He hurls his stuff on my rattan couch, plops down, and props his feet on my glass-topped coffee table.

I flush with embarrassment. "I guess the same people who choose to refurbish the swimming pool in the middle of summer?"

"Nice."

Silence as I rummage in my kitchen. There's an odd tension in my body, a pit in my stomach, and my fingers shake as I open a cabinet, stare, and forget what I'm looking for.

He's watching me. He's unbuttoned his tropical shirt and for the first time I notice the small tattoo of a fox on his left pectoral muscle. *Offer him a drink, you idiot.* Nothing comes out. I clear my throat. "Um, can I get you something?"

He sits forward. "In a minute. I'll get changed."

He vanishes into my bedroom, but leaves the door ajar; when I glance over, I can see him in the mirror. He drops his shorts. I flush and try to think of a drink I can make—what booze do I have in the house? I should look, but I can't stop peering at his—

—he turns so he can see me, and I pivot and crouch to check out my liquor stash, which I keep in the lazy Susan. Rum, amaretto, butterscotch schnapps, Southern Comfort . . . okay, I know . . .

"What's this?"

"What's what?" I pull out each bottle and set it on the counter above my head.

"Trophy."

I'd forgotten that was there—hadn't even thought to put it away. It's not something I like people to know about.

"Oh, it's nothing." I stand and close the cabinet door. "I won first place in a contest when I was in high school."

I glance over my shoulder; he's vanished from the mirror.

"Pineapple Princess, huh." He emerges from the bedroom and leans against the doorjamb. He's wearing a tank top that says GREAT BALLS OF FIRE and an orange pair of swim trunks.

God, he's hot.

"For hula?" He crosses his arms. "Think you'd be proud of that."

"It was a long time ago." I reach into the refrigerator and grab a can of pineapple juice—I'd opened it last week, so it might be a little sour, but with all that booze I don't think we'll notice.

"How come you didn't try out to be a performer?"

"It's not my thing, really." I lie and concentrate on measuring shots, dumping them in the blender.

"Sure. But being a waitress is."

"It's fine." I screw the cap back on the rum and reach for the amaretto.

"There's an opening. Right now. Turned down a girl just yesterday, in fact. I'd get you an audition."

I finish with the amaretto, add the SoCo.

"You'd get more respect around there."

He walks toward me.

"And." He leans over the breakfast bar. "You'd make more money. *Real* money. Three times what you make now. At least."

This stops me. Three times what I make now . . . *at least* . . . it'd be possible to save more than just on occasion, and that implant wouldn't be a *someday* dream anymore.

I look up at him. I imagine his hand running through my hair . . . my implanted hair. My *real* hair.

. . . No, Hailey. There's a reason you don't hula anymore.

How warm his hand would feel, in my real hair . . .

No.

. . . if we do hook up, because just maybe we will, I'll never have to worry about him finding out, about him leaving me.

Don't you remember the promise you made?

Only until I have enough to get my implants.

I hear myself say yes.

"Great. I'll talk to 'em. Set you up." He winks.

I just stand there. I'm not sure if what I've just done is a good thing, but . . . maybe, maybe I wouldn't get the job.

Come on, Hailey. You know you will. And then you'll get to be with him on stage every night, twice a night. I'll get to stand at a safe distance, but close enough to see the muscles in his body move as he works the fire knife—

"Now. What're we drinkin'?"

"Uh . . . " I get myself back on track. I add the last shot: schnapps. "It's this new thing. Pineapple Dream." I turn on the blender and shout over it. "One of the bartenders down at the Kahiki pool invented it and they were serving it for, like, six months, but the four kinds of alcohol were killing the taps so they were replacing like one every two weeks. I conned the guy into giving me his recipe so I could make it at home."

The machine whizzes to a stop, and I pour the drink into a highball—one in a set I'd also bought at the resort gift shop. There's a hula girl on each side of the glass.

When I pour the liquid in, I see the girl move. Her hip was shifted to the left; now it's shifted to the right.

Toke winks at me and takes his first sip. "Ahh. Kickin'."

I don't respond, because the hula girl on his glass, she cocks her foot again—from the right to the left.

He sets down the glass and comes around the bar to stand next to me. Close. Suddenly he touches my cheek; his fingers are cold from grasping the glass.

I almost pull away.

"What?" He blinks. "I said I liked it. More, please."

"Oh, I . . ." I take his glass and pick up the blender again, and this time my hands shake as I'm pouring the stuff in his glass, and it dribbles over the sides. When I pick it up to hand it to him, it's so cold and sticky it slides out of my hand, crashes to the coffee-colored tile floor, and shatters.

"Oh, shit." I scramble to pick up the shards, and he crouches with me and grabs my hand.

"Don't!" he says. "Don't. You'll cut yourself."

His hand is warm and firm; I feel a wave down my body, and something like coconut oil between my legs. He smells like hops and beach sand. I sense that something's about to happen, like maybe he'll charm me into the queen-sized bed my father bought me as a you're-a-big-girl-now-you're-moving-away gift.

I'm suddenly aware that my Batik wrap is open to expose my bathing suit.

"You look great." His hand settles on my cheek. "Seriously. You're so beautiful."

I close my eyes, feel his breath as he comes closer, his lips brush mine, and I start to respond and then—

—I suddenly feel hands, I'm sure of it, *hands*, yank on my wig. *Oh God Oh God who's pulling on my wig please don't let it come off!*

I shriek. Toke is so startled he yells too.

I touch my wig, touch it all over to be certain it's still there. Is he screaming because somehow my wig came off?

No. He looks at me. He's white.

My wig is fine.

"I'm . . . I'm sorry, I . . ." *Shit. Shit. Shit. Shit.* "No, no, I wanted you to kiss me, I did, really . . ."

But I can tell he doesn't believe me.

"Um," he swallows. "No. Sorry." Like he told me not to, he picks up a few shards of glass. "Let's go swimming."

Dammit.

He stands, dumps the glass in his hand in my trash. He goes into the bedroom to retrieve his towel, then grabs mine, the one that says DISNEY'S TYPHOON LAGOON and is in the shape of a surfboard. He stands by my door, holding it out to me. "Coming?"

I touch my wig again. It's fine.

"In a minute." I stand up, and my legs are stiff. I go into the bedroom, close the door, take off my wig, and put on my swim cap, the one that has synthetic tufts sewn into it to make it appear there's hair tucked up inside.

On my way out the door, where still he stands, frozen, I pass a glance at my kitchen—it's marble and full of hula girls; I have a hula girl clock, a hula girl statue, even a hula girl picture frame that says KAHIKI MOON RESORT. In it is my favorite picture—the only one I have of me and Toke together, backstage at the show when I brought him a cup of coffee and he wanted his friend to take the photo to prove that it wasn't beer he was drinking before a performance. I look at that picture, and wonder sometimes if I can ever legitimately show it to people and say, "That's my boyfriend."

When I look at Toke, he doesn't make eye contact. He's looking at his shoes.

I close the door and lock it, and down we go to the pool.

✦

My father didn't like to hug me, but he was still a good dad.

He was always encouraging me to be the best at everything. I'd bring home a story I wrote, and he'd say, "This is a good first attempt, but you need to fix this and that to make it perfect." He'd take me to Reed's to buy new clothes, and he'd say, "That's a nice color, but I think it makes you look a little heavy." Every time he pointed out something I needed to change, I'd work hard, dreaming of the day when I'd do something to the T and he'd say, "Wow, that's flawless! You really *are* unequaled!"

Sometimes it was hard on me, but I know it was because he wanted me to understand my hairlessness wouldn't make or break me, like it did my mom. She was a dancer. Then she got alopecia after she had me, and was so ashamed of it, she'd killed herself when I was too little to remember. He explained to me it was because she felt she wasn't perfect anymore, and he didn't want me to be like that. So, under his watchful eye, I had to excel at everything, and I always had to come out on top.

Somehow, in those moments when I had conquered something, I felt like I had a brand new perm, the thickest, most gorgeous head of hair known to man—just like the Breck Girl on TV.

There was only one other way I could make myself feel pretty like that, and that was imagining I was in the tropics.

I was always freezing. During the bitter winters, when the other kids were outside throwing snowballs in the yard, I was holed up in my room with the electric heat cranked to ninety degrees. I'd lie on my bed and long to be in my wall mural: a palm-tree-shaded beach with Tahitian blue water. Sometimes I could close my eyes and smell coconuts and taste pineapple. Oh, to be in the sun, away from this dreary place. If I were in the mural, I wouldn't have to wear so many clothes, and guys would go so ga-ga over my nice figure they'd forget all about my wig. I even envisioned myself, sometimes, in a grass skirt, doing the hula, and every man on the beach would stop and watch me. I'd never be cold again, and I'd have men.

I was fifteen—a sophomore—and it was Spirit Week at our high school, and a new girl had moved to town a month before. She was always alone, carrying her books like one might carry logs to the fire. She barely smiled, had sunken cheeks, and her skin had a strange yellowish tinge, like the color of lemonade. She always wore the same grubby knit cap, and some of the boys joked around that she wore it because she never washed her hair. No one talked to her.

Friday was Outrageous Day, and we were supposed to come to school in costume. At lunch, the other students laughed and giggled and played around; the class clown, Fred, had covered his body in green paint and wore a shredded T-shirt: he was the Incredible Hulk. He jumped up in the middle of the table and growled at his friends, who pelted him with french fries. The new girl sat by herself in the corner; she wore a grass skirt, coconut shells, a leotard, leis around her neck, and a bird of paradise flower in her hair.

Her hair. It was long—down to her waist—and it was thick, black, and shiny. I had *never* seen anything like it. I made my way over to her. She seemed oblivious to everything except her fries.

"I'm not trying to be weird," I said. "But your hair's really pretty. You shouldn't cover it up in that cap all the time."

She didn't look up.

I waited a minute, but I knew that was that. I turned to go.

"Why don't you sit here?" she said.

I stopped.

She smiled. "I'm Izzy."

"Really?"

"It's short for Izmerelda."

"No, I mean . . . you want me to sit with you?"

She nodded. "I don't see anybody fighting for the seat, do you?"

I stepped forward, lifted my leg over the bench seat and settled across from her. "My name's Hailey."

The spout on my milk didn't pull apart cleanly. I ripped it open and chocolate spurted in a fountain; some of it landed in her hair. "Oh, shit! I'm sorry!" I fumbled for the napkins on my hot lunch tray and stood up, leaning over the table to help her wipe it.

"It's okay. It's hair. It'll wash out."

I only half-registered her taking the napkins from my hand and using them to blot her tresses. For the first time, I wondered what that felt like. To touch your own hair, let alone shampoo it—and it probably didn't hurt, either. Washing my bald head felt like scrubbing a smooth potato—and sometimes it was painful, like someone was pricking my scalp.

I was jealous.

She finished. "See? All better."

I cleared my throat and sat down, feeling awkward—this had

gotten off to a bad start. "That's a cool costume. I totally love it."

"It's what I wear in my dance classes. I take Polynesian dance lessons."

I couldn't believe what I was hearing. "You take hula? There's a place around here that teaches that? Where?"

"Downtown Danbury."

My hopes plunged. She meant Main Street, where they filmed Hitchcock's *Strangers on a Train*. It was overrun with graffiti and populated by criminals and half-vacant buildings that either needed to be razed or repaired, like the old Palace Theatre. "I don't think my dad'll let me go down there."

"My mom waits with me. It's pretty safe. Maybe if your dad'll let you take lessons, you can come with us."

That night, I sprung the request on him over meatloaf and boxed mashed potatoes. "And if I spend money on these lessons, are you *finally* going to live up to your full potential?"

"Yes. Totally."

He chewed, then lifted his glass to his lips and took a couple of gulps of milk. "It's not going to be a repeat of the spelling bee?"

I could guarantee that—the spelling bee had been his idea, not mine, so it'd been very difficult for me to get into it and focus. The last round had been between me and one other kid who was so fat his bare flesh bulged from beneath his gray sweater. The final word was *mahogany*.

I'd lost.

"Mahugany, you spelled," Dad had said. "You almost had it. How could you not have known there's an 'o' and not a 'u' in that word?"

I'd wanted to defend myself and say the stupid woman had mispronounced the word—she had, in fact—but I'd known there really wasn't any excuse for not knowing how to spell it.

Now, I said, "No. I really want to do this."

He took another bite of meatloaf. "Where is it?"

I told him, thwarting his disapproving expression with "My new friend Izzy says her mom will drive us, and she waits there during the lessons."

And that is how I learned to hula.

❧❀❧

At the pool, Toke takes a step down into the shallow end; I dive in at the deep end. I feel a need to move, to untie every knot in my body. I take the water in long, easy back strokes and feel the sun frying my face; I've never been one for any kind of sun block, waterproof or not—we pasty white northern girls need all the sun we can get. I get back to the shallow end, stop, and clear the water from my eyes.

He's sitting on the top stair, looking at me. "You're a fish, aren't you."

"Yes," I sheepishly admit. "I love the water."

"That's why you wear the cap."

"The cap?"

"On your head—the swim cap."

I'd forgotten. I'd actually *forgotten!* Fear curdles my stomach acid. I stop breathing.

"Don't see many wearing those unless they're real balls-on serious swimmers."

"Oh!" I take a deep breath. "Right. That's me."

He stands up, comes down another two steps into the water. "You hula. You swim. What else don't I know?" He takes another step and is now into the water up to his waist. He wades over to me.

I'm embarrassed, thinking only about what he doesn't know and how his finding out would ruin everything. "I know. It looks dumb."

He pulls his hand from the water, sets it on my head.

God what if he figures out that's not real hair underneath . . .

Stop it, I tell myself. *No repeats of the kitchen.*

"No. I like it. It's different." He runs his hand down the right side of my head, over my ear, down my neck. "I'd wear one too, if I was serious. I'm not really a water person."

I just blink at him.

He shrugs. "I play with fire for a living."

I nod. "Right."

His hand travels down my arm. "Didn't even swim much in the ocean when I was in Hawaii."

I'm barely registering what he's saying, because his hand is touching mine, beneath the water line. "You went to Hawaii?" I envision myself standing next to him on a beach, a real beach. I've never been to a real beach.

"Lived there for a while," he says. "Back when I was mastering the fire stuff. More that I really wanted to embrace the culture. The gods, all of that."

His face draws closer.

"They have a legend, you know, about fire and water. They need each other. I could tell you about it."

"Um . . . " I can't say a damn thing.

"Relax." He cradles my hand and lifts it out of the water.

We stand there, my palm against his. His hand is large— really large—compared to mine. It's like setting a macadamia nut in front of a pineapple.

"It's true what they say, you know. About a guy's hands."

The palm touching his feels hot, but it's not from the temperature, and I don't want to admit I have no idea what the hell he's talking about, nor do I care.

And then I feel something brushing my left breast.

For a second I think it's his other hand, but when I try to (subtly) glance at my chest, it's not there.

There isn't anything there except my tankini's hula dancer pattern.

And the girl directly over my left nipple winks at me.

Stop, I think. *Stop.*

I feel something brush the outside of my left thigh. It's his hand. And it moves toward me, settles on my suit bottom.

I part my legs. My breath catches in my throat.

"You like that?"

"Yes," I whisper.

But there's another feeling. Something crawling. On my right breast, now.

It's his hand, I think, but then I realize no, one hand is beneath my suit bottom, teasing me, and the other . . . the other is on the small of my back.

Something slithers on my right breast. He's pressed against me, now, his mouth against my ear—

I try to pull away but he's strong.

"Relax," he says again.

Slithering. It's under both cups now, and it's . . . *oh God. It's starting between my legs.*

I can't stand it. I wrench away from him and there is the face of one of the hula girls on my breast, her mouth full of daggers, her eyes running with blood—

I scream and stumble away from him, swatting at my chest.

"What is *with* you?"

Gnashing. The girl on my left breast growls and her face distorts, melts—

"Forget it." He turns his back to me, making for the stairs.

The slithering stops.

"Wait—"

But he's already exiting. "You change your mind, come see me."

He trudges up and out, accompanied by the *spit-swish* sound of the water drops from his body pelting the cement. He goes to a patio chair and grabs his towel, slings it over his shoulder.

Then I remember. "Um, what about a ride?"

He doesn't even look back. "I'll call a cab."

Fortunately the basic, intermediate, and advanced hula classes all met at the same time, so carpooling with Izzy was no problem. Miss Alana, who taught basic, was very impressed with how quickly I learned the steps—she noted that, in her opinion, the ami poe poe, which isn't exactly hard (it's that counterclockwise turn on the left foot and stepping with the right)—is where an instructor can really tell if someone has the natural gift of sway. "You're exquisitely graceful," she said, and I was soon moved up to the intermediate, and then advanced level—which was the class Izzy was in, taught by Mrs. Palakiko.

That's when the trouble started.

It wasn't long before I'd mastered the advanced steps and routines, and by May, it was announced that the school was going to hold heats to select that year's Pineapple Princess—the advanced dancer who'd represent Danbury Diamond Head Hula Studio in the state (and hopefully the regional) spring competitions.

The Friday night of the competition, the studio's auditorium was full of parents—including my dad. He hadn't seen me dance at all, save for the couple of times he'd stuck his head into my room while I was practicing my kaholo and lele uwehe and whatever else.

As the twenty of us paraded out to the floor for the first heat, I thought I was going to throw up. My father was in the front row. We met each other's gaze, and he held up a palm and waved.

I closed my eyes and took a deep breath, and the heat began. Four girls were cut at the end of heat one.

I wasn't one of them.

Four girls were cut at the end of the second heat.

I wasn't one of them.

Four girls, gone, at the end of heats three and four. Two of them ran to their parents' arms, sobbing.

It occurred to me that this was really a pretty cruel way of doing things, but my pity for those girls dissolved when I realized there were only four of us left—*I'd* made it to the final heat! I could see Dad, clutching his Styrofoam coffee cup. He was beaming.

We finished, and the last ukulele note reverberated through the room. We held our final pose for several seconds, and then we were told to sit down and wait for the judges' final decision.

It was so quiet I could hear the big clock ticking on the wall.

At last Mrs. Palakiko stepped to the microphone.

"Our judges have come to a decision. Unfortunately, for the first time in Diamond Head's history, we have a tie."

I'd swear there was an audible gasp from the crowd.

"Since we all know there can only be one representative—and there is only one trophy, after all—"

Polite chuckles through the crowd.

"—the judges have decided there needs to be one more heat, as a tiebreaker. That final heat will take place here at ten a.m. on Sunday, after which we will have the awards ceremony and a traditional luau to celebrate."

My legs felt weak. This was it. Would I be named one of the final two?

I saw Dad shift in his chair, cross one leg over the other.

"The two dancers who will compete on Sunday morning—"

Someone's baby squealed.

"—are Izmerelda Palana and Hailey Bell."

Hailey Bell.

Hailey Bell! That's me!

The entire crowd of parents sprang to their feet in wild applause and cheers, and Dad—I'd never seen him run before—raced to me and actually lifted me off the ground, just like he used to do when I was little. He laughed and gave me a big kiss on the cheek. "When you're Pineapple Princess we'll celebrate. I can't wait to see my little girl with her trophy!"

At first, I basked in the glow of his love—I felt it coming off him, like the rays of the sun. And then a cloud shadowed over it, and I almost felt physically cold: I knew I wouldn't beat Izzy. True, I was a natural, but Izzy—there was something about her; she exuded a radiance and charm that I knew I didn't have. When she was doing the hula, she was a goddess in a grass skirt. Our execution could be identical, but that certain something she had would guarantee her the title.

I glanced over at her and smiled. She was talking with her sister, playing with her hair.

Her long, gorgeous, thick, oh-so-Polynesian hair *that moved with her when she danced*, as natural as the lapping of the ocean on the sand.

There was only one thing I could do to ensure I took the trophy.

"Dad?"

He put me down. "Yeah?"

"Do you think Izzy could sleep over tomorrow night?"

He frowned, settled a hand on my shoulder. "You should be practicing for Sunday, preparing to crush your competition, not having your competition over for playtime."

I blinked at him. "Please?"

He sighed, glanced over at Izzy, then looked back at me. "If I allow it, do you promise me you'll win?"

At that moment, it was a promise I knew I could keep. "Yes. Yes, Dad. I'll win."

He nodded. "Okay."

I smiled and clapped my hands in glee.

❧❦❧

That night, I'd set Izzy up on the floor in my room. We did girl stuff, painted our nails, giggled about the boy she liked and Izzy told me all about sex, since she'd actually fooled around before. She was too excited to sleep, she said, and then she held up her hand and offered me a pinky.

"No matter who wins," she said, "we'll be friends. Pinky swear."

I took her pinky, and realized it was the only finger on my hand that wouldn't fit in the handle of the scissors I had carefully stowed beneath my pillow.

Finally, two hours later, she was asleep.

I crept from bed, knelt by her sleeping form, and reached out to touch her hair.

It was like nothing I'd ever felt. Unlike my own wig, the hair was warm, alive, almost . . . pulsing. The feel of it sent small pins of excitement from my fingertips up through my arm. Wow. What would it be like to have this hair on my head? What would it feel like to brush it? And there was something else about it—scent. A faint whiff of something. I shifted my body and leaned closer, pressed my nose into the ribbon of it that snaked over my green shag rug.

It smelled delicious. Like coconut and warm chocolate.

I sat up. What was I thinking? I couldn't destroy such a lovely, exquisite thing.

Then I touched my own head.

It was slick and almost cold, like one of those plastic balls you buy for ninety-nine cents at Kreske's.

Yes, I could cut it. *I should have been born with hair like that. That hair is the only reason she's made it this far in the competition, Hailey, the competition that you deserve to win, because no one deserves unconditional love more than you.*

And Dad will give you that when you win.

Anger roiled inside me. I slipped my three fingers and thumb into the scissor handle. I cut. I cut and cut and cut and felt the hair die and grow cold as it stuck to my fingers.

Izzy snored through the whole thing.

When I woke the next morning, Izzy was gone—and the only evidence she'd been there were hair clippings strewn across the peach pillowcase.

"Where'd Izzy go?" Dad asked, sliding pineapple pancakes onto my plate.

"Oh," I said. "Her sister came to get her really early this morning. She wanted to go home and practice for a little while before the competition."

Dad stared at me for a minute, then smiled. "Hurry up and eat your pancakes. You should probably get back in your room and do the same thing. Early bird catches the worm and all that."

I nodded, and dove into my pancakes like I hadn't eaten in a week.

Izzy didn't show up for the final heat, so after a dance so the judges could watch me one last time, I was declared Pineapple Princess by default.

It deflated me a little bit—winning due to forfeiture—and for a second I wondered if Dad would say this wasn't going to count.

But he didn't. He simply said, "You would've won anyway."

That afternoon passed in a blur. I remember sitting at the head of one of the tables, next to my dad, who shook hands with every parent who came up to congratulate me. "Hailey," he said, "you are *finally* perfect. You're going to do something amazing with your life, now. I know you will."

When I got home, the scissors I'd used were lying on my pillow. I picked them up and started to make my way out to the kitchen to put them back in the drawer, and then decided that I'd rather never see them again. I threw them in the trash instead.

I never saw Izzy again after that—she wasn't at school the following week, and finally I heard she and her sister had moved away.

To this day, I don't know what happened to her. When I went to my ten-year high school reunion, I was told she never made much of herself; that she was living in some pitsy apartment up in Waterbury in the decaying brass district, another place, like Danbury, that looks like a bomb hit it.

✻✻✻

Growing up, I saw a lot of kids get picked on because they were considered freaks—they were too fat, they had too many pimples, one was albino. Technically, I should have been in that crowd. But I wasn't. Because I could cover up my hairlessness, it wasn't obvious I was a freak.

Being hairless made me vulnerable in a different way. I felt unprotected, like a baby chick, always waiting for that fox to show up and inevitably eat me. I made friends, I played, and I held my breath through every minute of each day, waiting for that moment when someone was going to discover I had no hair and my entire world was going to blow apart. I remember waking up every morning and thinking, *will today be the day someone finds out?* Sometimes it was such a sword of Damocles I wouldn't be able to concentrate on simple things like taking notes in class.

What was worse was that I was lonely—no one knew what I really was, and I couldn't show them. I spent a lot of time leaning up against a coat tree in the basement; it was layered with all my mother's coats and dresses that my dad had refused to donate. I'd wrap my arms around it and imagine it was someone who loved me unconditionally. A man who *knew* I was hairless and didn't care. Someone I could talk to about anything and everything and all I would get was support. All this imaginary person would say was "I understand," and "It's okay," or even, "I think your hairlessness is beautiful."

Then the eighth grade dance happened.

In reality, it had been a relief: the other shoe had dropped. The painful waiting was over.

But the heartbreak was just beginning. It wasn't even so much that I'd been exposed and that Peter didn't want me. It was that it fractured my fantasy: that someone who could accept me was out there. I'd lost all hope.

Until this afternoon.

I've drained the pitcher of Pineapple Dream, I've finished the bottle of rum, and now, fuck it, I'm on to the Southern Comfort, even though I can't feel my lips. That's right—I'm totally drunk. A slow kind of drunk, a haze on the brain, a my-limbs-don't-want-to-work-that-fast-and-I'm-content-to-sit-and-stare-and-think-about-thinking kind of drunk, a there's-a-tinnitus-in-my-ears kind of drunk, an it's-hard-to-get-around-the-apartment-without-grabbing-something kind of drunk. And I've just figured out the crazy hula girls—the ones on the glasses, the ones on my bathing suit—they're from inside me.

They're a warning: *You know better than to have hope. Don't go near Toke again. He will break you into so many pieces there's no way you'll be able to put yourself back together.*

Right now I'm the loneliest I've been in five years.

I don't do e-mail or Facebook when I'm drunk—especially not when I'm drunk and upset. More than a few times I've awakened the next morning to find I'd promised to loan someone money, admitted something shocking on somebody's wall, or posted something snarky in a thread in which I was the only dissenter.

Tonight's an exception. I do have one hundred and seventy-five friends on Facebook. Someone will talk to me.

I sit down at my laptop and boot it up.

The first thing I notice is on my timeline: several people have posted things asking me if I'd like to talk, or GIFs with little hearts. A couple say "I'm so sorry for your loss."

Odd. But at least I know there are people willing to talk, right?

The most recent notification: *Fred Rueck has sent you a message.*

Ah, the Incredible Hulk the day I'd met Izzy. He sent me a friend request maybe a year ago, but I haven't paid any attention to Fred since—last Christmas, I think, and even then it was just a stupid thing in my game requests, something like *Fred Rueck has sent you a Christmas Ornament using Santa's Sleigh!*

Curious, I click on his message.

I'm really sorry to hear about your friend Izmerelda... Kristen Hansen posted that she drowned in the pool where you work. I'm really sorry to hear it I knew u were friends w/her and did the hula 2gether. If u want 2 talk PM me & I'll send you my cell # or PM me your # and I'll call u.

This is what sticks with me: *she drowned in the pool where you work.*

The pool where you work.

I recall what Toke said this afternoon: *Turned down a girl just yesterday, in fact.*

Oh my God. Had that been Izzy? Was there a chance the girl Toke mentioned this morning had been *Izzy?* Had she really found her way down to Florida to revive an old hula dream?

No, that was impossible. No way.

I read it again, aware that I'm drunk. It explains the weird condolence messages cluttering my page, but that can't be right. I'd say Fred was pulling my leg, but for as big a joker as he is, he'd never do anything as cruel as this. I read it a third time. Izmerelda. How many other Izmereldas could there be in the world? And what the hell was she doing down here?

Suddenly, I feel like I'm being watched.

I hear a noise in my kitchen, as though someone's dragging something across the tile.

There's movement near the pantry. A shadow. Subtle, but there; no trick of the light.

I'm going to throw up.

The pantry door creaks.

Four fingers. Curled around the edge of the door.

Run, I think, but I can't move. I can't do anything but stand there.

The door opens. Slowly.

I can't breathe. There's no air.

A flash of a sickly whitish-blue forearm. The swish of something, like crinoline.

Or like a grass skirt . . .

The tap of a footstep on the tile.

The click of . . . of shell bracelets—I'd know that sound anywhere . . .

Go. Now.

Galvanized, I race to my foyer, grab my tote bag, and hurry out, slamming the door behind me.

My body seems to take the stairs faster than I can process going down them. Before I know it, I'm in the parking lot, near space 14-C, still not breathing, looking up at the second floor where my apartment is.

I lean over and empty my guts onto the pavement.

Strangely, I feel better—lighter. I take a deep breath. The air smells like chlorine, palm and vanilla; there's no moon, but the sodium lights bathe everything in a pale-pink glow. Down at the basketball court, a couple of kids are shooting hoops. The lights in the Community Center are blazing, and I see shadows inside, dancing. There is the sound of swing music—"In the Mood"— and in the distance I hear the cars on the highway.

There's nothing here to be afraid of, I think. This is your home. There are people around. Just go back upstairs, turn on every light and the TV, and you'll be fine. You're drunk and this whole thing has you completely spooked and now you're seeing even worse things.

But when I look up at my apartment slider, the sheer curtain shimmies.

I can't go back up there. No way.

I remember what Toke said: "You change your mind, come see me."

I know what he wants. I want it, too.

The girls on your glasses, the girls on your bathing suit. Remember your warnings.

Stupid girl! Toke probably doesn't have anything that even *resembles* a hula girl in his apartment.

Don't you want it? What's the worst that could happen?

You leave. You sleep in your car.

Wouldn't you rather sleep on a couch or in a bed?

I'll feel that sword of Damocles hanging over my head. I'll be waiting for that shoe to drop.

Wouldn't you rather not be alone?

I fumble in my bag for my keys, and my numb fingers and klutzy grip on items like my wallet and cell phone remind me that there's another reason I shouldn't go—I've been drinking.

I sigh and look up at the apartment again.

Fingers. There are fingers clutching the edge of one of the sheer curtains.

She's waiting.

His complex is only three miles up the road.

I can make it that far.

⁂

His apartment building is older, garden-style and only two floors—he lives on the first one, and I am fortunately clear-headed enough to remember which door he'd come out of when I picked him up this morning.

I knock, and suddenly feel like I'm going to pass out. *This is your last chance, Hailey; this is the last chance you have to call this whole thing off.* He doesn't come to the door for what seems like forever, and then, I think, *what if he doesn't answer—*

—it opens with a *click-swish* and I'm hit with the smell of beer and cigarette smoke. He's in a gray T-shirt and navy shorts and seems so much taller than he did this afternoon; then I realize there's a step up to enter his apartment. "Hailey."

I nod and force a smile, but I know it's a nervous one. "Yeah. I just . . . changed my mind, is all."

"Jesus, woman. You're practically white. You good?" He motions me inside, and the second I cross the threshold I feel comfortable and . . . safe; not what I'd expected to feel. I set my bag on the floor in the corner and glance around his apartment. It's not bright and typically Floridian—it's got walnut paneling. There are two mission-style futons. Gray-and-blue flecked rug. Cheap, badly put-together furniture, like the kind you buy in boxes at Walmart and assemble with flimsy included tools. No colors match: green cushions, maroon cushions, rust curtains, gold raised-velvet wallpaper.

I was right. There are no hula girls here.

I realize I'm not really drunk anymore, probably a combination of fear, adrenaline, and the fact that I'd puked up most of the remainder of the bottle of rum and the last couple of shots of SoCo before they'd had time to seriously take effect. "Fine. Like I said, I changed my mind."

Terrified I'll see the hula girl standing in the parking lot, I peer outside before closing the front door.

He motions to the futon. "Come. Sit."

I do. The cushion is much more comfortable than it looks; I sink into it.

He goes into the kitchenette and opens the refrigerator; I'm close enough that I can see all that's in it is alcohol, a couple of Chinese food containers, and what looks to be a pile of onion peels or something on the very bottom. "Want a beer?"

I'm not big on beer, but recall with horror that, yes, I had gotten sick, and yes, I hadn't brushed my teeth. I was going to need something to cover that up. "Sure."

"Miller Lite, Killian's Red, or Bud?"

We don't serve any of that at the Kahiki, so I don't really know what the difference is. I decide on the most interesting name. "Killian's sounds good."

"Woman after my own heart." He bends over and I hear him slide out a drawer.

For the first time, I notice a long mark on the back of his left thigh. It's like the amoebas I used to see in my science textbooks way back when, a big white blob fringed in a brown fuzzy ring.

I'm afraid to say anything, so I don't.

He struts into the living room and hands me the beer, then settles down on the floor across from me. "It's a burn scar, by the way. Really old. It was back when I first started training."

I flush with embarrassment. "I—I didn't mean to stare."

"Didn't know you were. Just everybody asks when I wear something short enough to see it, so I figured I'd get it out of the way."

I bring the bottle to my lips and can barely get past the smell of it—like rug shampoo and cat piss. I don't sip and say instead, "Weren't you afraid after that?"

"Sure. Was I supposed to give up? I'd already told myself the fire thing wasn't something I was going to fail at." He sips his beer and reaches for his cigarettes. "Every fear you have you can pretty much trace back to the fear of failure. All fear is rooted there."

I'm skeptical. "Fear of spiders?"

He shrugs matter-of-factly. "Fear of the failure to protect yourself."

"Okay. Fear of . . . sleep."

He lights his cigarette. "Fear of the failure to be impervious. When you sleep, you're vulnerable."

I think about the hula girls, how they're a defense mechanism and nothing more. But a defense mechanism—that's a manifestation of fear. The hula girl who chased me out of my apartment—her, too. But fear of what?

"And you're sitting way up there. I don't bite." He pats the floor. "Come down here."

I feel a flush. I join him, kneeling sideways.

I can see the bulge in his shorts.

Oh my God.

This moment is *here*.

I try in vain to suppress a nervous smile.

He shifts closer. "Don't be afraid of me."

"I'm just—"

He sets his burning cigarette in the ashtray. "Remember before, when I was talking about fire and water? How they need each other?"

"Yes," I say. Not that I care at the moment.

"Comes from Hawaiian legend. There's many variations. But there's one that says Pele, goddess of fire, was actually married to Kamapua'a, the god of water." He inches forward.

Our knees are touching.

Small shocks travel up my legs.

"Story says Pele got mad at him, chased him out of their home with lava all the way to the sea." He reaches out and takes my hands. "But it's the lava, its collision with the sea, that creates more land. Makes the island grow."

His hands. I could write novels about his hands, forceful with a fire knife but tender now, rough but gentle as he manipulates his large fingers between mine.

"Chase me to the sea," he whispers, and then his mouth smashes on mine.

His tongue butterflies between my lips. I'm overwhelmed by the taste of hops, the smell of beach sand and the white gas they use in his knife. Hot fireworks of want explode inside me in places I never knew existed as he bulldozes me to the floor.

Our beers spill. The ashtray goes flying. Something plummets from the coffee table.

Oh, God my wig. My wig is going to come off.

His weight bears on me and forces the air from my lungs, but I suck hard and sounds I don't recognize escape the back of my throat because this feels *right* and *wonderful* and *amazing* and all sorts of other words I couldn't really fathom until this moment.

"I want to be inside you right. Now."

Nothing excites me more than this. I watch him as he hefts off me and straightens up, wrestles with his shirt, throws it over by the glass sliding door that leads out to a small patio.

In the window stands a familiar figure.

Only it's not a hula girl this time.

It's Izzy, her eyes glowing like hot coals.

I scream.

He leaps off me. "Oh God. Did I hurt you? Shit!"

"No, no—it's not that it's not that it's not that, there's just . . ." There's what? What the fuck do I say?

She's gone.

He grins. "Oh . . . you're a screamer. When you get worked up."

"Yes," I lie. Eager to distract him, I sit up and work out of my tank top. I'm not wearing a bra.

He crawls back to me, runs his hands up my legs, using words like *smooth* and *soft* and that it's like I have no hair.

I try to quell the rising tide of fear, but he keeps going, furiously fingering the button and zipper on my jeans. He lifts me off the floor and works them down to my knees, then does the same with my thong and gasps. "You shaved!"

My breath catches in my throat. *Oh, shit.* "Is that bad?"

"No." His eyes meet mine, and he looks amazed. "I've never been with a woman who shaved and that's . . . something I always wanted. That's—" he stops.

He's looking at me—well, not *me*.

At the top of my head.

Panic grips my soul. The warm flush throbbing in every corner of me abruptly halts.

"Your hair is crooked."

"Um . . ." Tears well up in my eyes. I can't stop them. "It's—it's a wig."

Under my tense fingers I feel his arm muscles have gone taut and still.

There's a long moment. The only sound is the whoosh of the central air kicking on and the quiet hiccup of the tears I'm trying to control.

"It's okay." He shifts slightly off of me, puts his head down on my shoulder and wraps his big arms around me. "It's okay. Cry it out. When you're done, you can tell me."

When I open my eyes between jags I see Izzy in the corner, but I know she can't get to me because *he's* between us. I want to tell him the whole thing, everything, but I can't, not now when I know that the best I can hope for is these last few moments before it's a sure thing that this won't finish, that I'll have to leave and go back to my apartment, forced to hold on to only a few tactile memories and the fear that he'll tell everyone. That I'll become some backstage failed sex story shared with the other performers over a few beers while Izzy tortures me in every waking moment, in every hula dancer glass, clock, picture frame and bathing suit in my house.

I'm finally cried out. "I'm sorry."

"No need to be."

"I have—it's alopecia. It means I have no hair. Anywhere."

Stillness again.

"This is a bad thing because why?" His hand pets my shoulder. "Don't women spend fortunes on Brazilians? Razors? Nair?"

"But I'm *bald*."

"I don't care," he says. "Personally? Can't stand a hairy woman. This guy right here? Left women 'cause they were too hairy. I know. I'm a bastard. Just a thing I have."

I let this sink in. "What?"

"Can I see it?"

"Can you see what?"

"You. Bald."

I bite my lip. This is the one step I'm not sure I can take.

He lifts himself, rolls off me, and sits up. "Take it off."

Something comes over me, a peace I've never felt before.

He holds out his meaty hand. "Come on. Take it off."

I do.

He gasps and for one second I think it's in horror. He reaches up and touches my head. His fingers tickle and it's sensitive—no one's ever touched it before. I don't know whether to scream or wince.

"You're perfect."

I blink in surprise. I'm not sure I've heard that correctly. He can't mean that, can he? What the hell is going on here? Is he real? Is this actually happening? "Really?"

"God yes." His breath is hot in my ear. "Bed."

He stands up and yanks me to my feet and into the adjoining room, eagerly splays me naked on the bed, mounts me. I wait for the pain—like the stabbing of knives—that Izzy told me girls have when they have sex for the first time. Strangely, it doesn't come. All I feel is an odd sense of fulfillment, completeness.

I see Izzy in the doorway. Glaring.

But the whole world is different now. He's inside me, pounding, using words like *tight* and I feel beautiful and bold. I peer over his shoulder at her and feel remorse; that trophy, now, seems like a meaningless trinket, its value squat. It should've been hers. I never should've taken it from her. Never should've done what I did. "I'm sorry," I whisper.

Toke hesitates for only a second. "What?"

"Nothing." I shift so I can look into his eyes, wide open and boring straight into mine, unwilling for even a softening of her malignant stare to miss the thrill ride that is Toke.

There is fire and water, and no more fear.

※

When I wake up I'm not sure where I am at first, and then it all comes back: this is real, it's not a dream. I lift my head slightly and take in the room, but mostly what catches my eye is the trail of clothes that seems to wind from the living room into his bedroom. There's a pile just beyond the doorjamb—my green tank top, his navy shorts. Just south of that are my panties, and south of that is—

My wig. My wig that's never spent an unkempt night and always right next to me so I can put it on before I even get out of bed. There it is, on the floor, a tangled mess. In this context, it seems like any other piece of clothing—something I can wear or not, something I could live without while it sits in the hamper for a couple of weeks until laundry night rolls around. I look at Toke, who's on his back, mouth slightly open. There's something almost innocent about his expression. He fell asleep with my hand in his, or maybe he grabbed it in the middle of the night. It's warm, solid.

I feel something I've never felt before.

Safe.

I hear Toke move next to me. "What time is it?"

"I don't know."

"Crap." He rolls on his side, snatches something off the nightstand—his watch. "We gotta go to work."

Work. That whole life full of all-you-can-eat pineapple and rib platters and making sure the chocolate volcano desserts are smoking properly seems like it isn't mine. I sigh.

"We gotta." He shifts so he's over me. "No choice." He leans down, kisses my neck.

Inside me, things wake up, and this surprises me, since I'm also feeling a dull, raw ache to the point where I'll probably have to hit up the ibuprofen I keep in my bag for emergencies.

"Of course, I'm willing to stay here all day. If we don't want our jobs anymore."

I laugh, because at that moment I could easily say, *Yes, let's quit.* "Remember when you said you'd get me an audition to be a hula girl? Did you set that up yet?"

He stops and his eyes bore into mine. "Not yet." He touches my cheek, strokes it with his thumb. "Why—change your mind?"

I nod. I know what I have to do now.

"There's something I have to confess," I say, but I'm suddenly overwhelmed by the need to pee. "I just need to use the bathroom first."

There's a long silence. Then he says, "Okay."

I go into the bathroom and lock the door. You can tell a lot about a guy from his health and beauty aids. The shelf across from the toilet is crammed with cans of shaving cream, aftershave, and contorted tubes of hair gel. There are pumps of styling mousse and extra hold spray, nose hair scissors, tweezers, and a grubby electric clipper. A Kahiki Moon plastic souvenir cup explodes with several different kinds of razors.

I sit on the toilet and feel the urge to pee, stronger now, but nothing comes out. I don't remember Izzy talking about this. What if he broke me?

A trickle comes out. I scuttle back a little on the seat and look in the toilet, half-expecting and terrified to see that it's red, but it's normal, just very yellow, almost brownish. But there's definitely something just below my bikini line that isn't normal.

A hair. A curly, black hair.

It must be one of his, I think, but when I go to brush it off, it doesn't move.

It's a hair. It's *mine*.

I stand up, wipe myself, and grab the tweezers off his shelf. I pluck the hair and look at it, astonished. Where did this come from?

I fold it into a piece of toilet paper and chuck it into the overflowing garbage can. An irrational thought strikes me that he might find it, so I tuck it underneath some tissues and an empty shampoo bottle sprinkled with discarded Q-tips.

I wash my hands and think about how I'm going to confess. I look in the mirror and slowly mouth what it is I'm going to say . . . where am I even going to start? *Do you remember when you told me you turned down a girl for that job? Well, I think she might be the one who drowned herself in the pool and now she's haunting me?* No, holy crap. That sounds insane. *Do you remember that trophy? Well, when I was little, my dad wanted me to be perfect, and there was this girl and she had the most lovely hair and she should've been the Pineapple Princess but I was young, you know,* young, *and I just—I just wanted acceptance and so I cut off her hair, and that's how I won . . .* yes. It's a start, anyway, a start that is the truth. A terrible truth, but one that, somehow I know, I don't have to be afraid to share with Toke.

I notice a long, black hair in the center of my head. Then another.

I look more closely. There's a third.

There's a fourth. A fifth.

I seize the tweezers again and pluck them.

There's another. And another. And another.

Suddenly, the hair is everywhere. It's sprouting out of my nose and my ears, from the top of my head. I look down at my arms and legs and it's there, too, and above my bikini line. I'm filled with sheer terror. I scream.

Toke starts banging on the door. "Hailey? Hailey!" *Bang bang bang.* "Unlock the door!"

But I can't. I know I can't.

"Hailey!"

Izzy, burning-eyed and ferocious, appears in the mirror behind me. Her hair is wet and grimy, she's covered in mud and soot, and when she throws her head back and laughs, her open mouth is a filthy, black pit.

Apology not accepted.

ONCE, THE WORLD WAS DARK ENOUGH FOR SLEEP

I DO NOT LIKE the dark, but Mama makes me wear eye patches to bed.

She says it's because God made our thin eyelids in a time when the night was not an indigo gloaming sliced by the downtown sodium lights, and it is better to sleep in the true dark.

"It's deep and restful." She shoves the blankets beneath my mattress so tightly I can barely move. "Noise won't wake you up."

I do not tell her that sometimes it isn't the noises that wake me but the sense that someone is there. Or the memory of the movie with the reanimated baby chomping on a rat, which was on the television the night Mama and her boyfriend, Dillon, brought home my new little sister.

I do not tell her that I prefer that to the dark.

Until the night I slip off the eye patches and see what Dillon is doing to my sister in the pale salmon light.

Now I wish I lived in that time when God made people with thin eyelids, when the world was dark enough for sleep.

UNDER THE KUDZU

WILSON HAD HEARD that his hometown had been consumed by kudzu, but he hadn't expected it to be this bad.

The invasive, ivy-like vine and its large-lobed leaves had transformed the landscape. A burnt chimney kept watch over a kudzu-choked field; it reminded him of a strange land's guardian tower in some fantasy novel. Telephone poles loomed like wooly creatures with outstretched arms, and partially devoured signs announced SPE LIM and an obscured number. When he drove past the old mine where he and his friend Jimmy had often played, he saw the entrance was shrouded to nonexistence. He'd never gone into the mine—he'd never had the guts—but Jimmy had; Will mused that, in fact, Jimmy had probably been the last intrepid teen to explore it. Today's area kids probably didn't even know it was there.

The center of town was, oddly, deserted—it was July and it was hot, but in his opinion, not hot enough that people wouldn't be out and about. Still, it looked as though things had been closed for a while: he spied a half-consumed car in the Safeway parking lot, and the kudzu had engulfed the side of Pickins's Movie House, the marquee of which sported some broken letters and holes. The sidewalk at Cornflower's Drugs was green, and kudzu had even tentacled around the two coin-op kiddie rides out front that had been there forever: the fire truck, which probably hadn't been painted since he was a kid (he could see gray instead of red patches between the leaves), and the sun-faded alien spaceship.

It did look as though the drugstore was still operating—there were uncovered cars in the parking lot—but the interior's fluorescents weren't on.

It's Sunday, he thought. *They were never open on Sundays anyway; maybe that hasn't changed.*

Where *was* everybody?

Will licked his lips: his mouth was dry. He'd drained the two cans of ginger ale he'd brought two hours into the long-haul drive from Maryland, and he hadn't stopped to replenish. He remembered how, on hot days, he and Jimmy would skip buying soda at the movies so they'd have enough money to hit Planket's Creamery for Icees—

Of course. Everyone was probably at the creamery.

But Planket's didn't seem to be where he'd thought it was. The sign was there, and it looked polished, as though it'd been recently replaced; the parking lot had also been repaved—the burnt-nuts-and-plastic smell of fresh asphalt permeated his car. But when he pulled in, all that was in Planket's place was a large green—

Wait. That *was* Planket's.

It was covered in kudzu.

There were three other cars in the lot. He pulled up next to one and stared at the massive carpeted hulk in front of him.

He could see the door, and a couple of kudzu leaves partially covered an old MasterCard logo—that 1970s tan and orange circle thing. His parents had had one of those cards, and whenever they'd whipped it out it meant something magical was about to happen; a long-desired dream was about to come true.

Pinpoints of white fluorescent bled through slivers between the leaves: Planket's was open.

Go in, he thought—but he hesitated.

Because he remembered what had happened to him the last time he'd gone into a kudzu-covered building—admittedly, it had been fake kudzu, but it didn't matter. The terror was still real.

It was 1977, before the kudzu had completely invaded, and the most exciting event all year had arrived: the church carnival. It was usually crappy—the same three tired, dilapidated kiddie rides: a helicopter contraption, a bug roller coaster, and a mini-train that chugged past grotesque dioramas of fairy tale characters (Little Miss Muffet's spider scared the daylights out of him, mostly because of its red eyes and foaming mouth). But the year Will turned six was different: the buzz had been that the children's corner was getting a new ride.

A haunted house.

His older sister, Cyn—who'd just turned thirteen and was cusping on all things forbidden—salivated for months. "Get all fired up, Will, 'cuz that spook house is gonna be the first thing we go on!"

But on that morning, Will stood, hesitating, in front of the towering, fake-kudzu-covered house that was Creepmore Manor. Owls, their yellow eyes bearing down on him, popped from the plants. A mummy strapped on a big spinning wheel wailed and moaned, and a moving mannequin dressed as a gypsy—a pretty woman that reminded him of his mom with her bundle of dark hair, ruby-red lips and glittering purple gown— shrieked and pointed at him. The owls hooted, the mummy spun faster and faster, the gypsy taunted him, and then, suddenly—

—a door above the Creepmore Manor sign flapped open and out thrust a pair of long, green, gnarled hands. "Come on in, kiddies! Hee hee hee hee hee!"

Will jumped. "I can't, Cyn!"

"Can't what, you big ol' chicken?" She set her hands on her hips. She was wearing a Wonder Woman costume, because all the kids liked to dress up for the carnival. Will never participated; he didn't see the need to pretend to be something he wasn't. "Go in there? Come on, it's the hottest thing!"

Will took a step back, feeling the candy apple edge up his throat. "No."

"There's nothing scary in it. It's for kids, you know, and aren't you bored of the same old stuff like me? I know you are. So, so bored. And if it doesn't do good, this might be the only year they have it, you know."

Two of the boys from his first-grade class—T.K. and Jimmy—skipped ahead. Actually, he hadn't known Jimmy too well just then. He wouldn't become Jimmy's best friend until weeks later, when they collided in the movie theater, spilled both of their popcorn tubs—and pooled their money to get a replacement to share.

Well, the other boys were going. Will supposed he could, too.

Cyn grabbed his hand, tugged him to the ride entrance, and presented the man with six red paper tickets. They bounded up the platform, which felt like it was about to give way, and the carnie ushered them into a two-seated bright pink car. The front was the purple-striped, yellow-eyed face of the Cheshire Cat. Will didn't like the teeth—they were fangs. He was sure, from the Lewis Carroll picture book he'd read, the Cheshire Cat didn't have such big fangs. But they climbed in, and the car rolled forward and hooked a sharp right into the darkness.

A sneering, clown-faced bunny leapt from a panel in the side wall and startled the hell out of Will. He screamed and shut his eyes, and throughout the rest of the ride, he didn't open them— not once—but the noises and the threats and the coarse laughter were enough to do the damage, and Will was sure his heart had stopped when, just before their car burst forth back into the light, a deep, throaty voice snarled, "I'll never let you out of here!"

That voice echoed in his head for so many nights afterward. He'd wake up in his room, expecting to see whatever it was that had said it—he hadn't seen it, but what had it been? A raccoon with a bloody face? An evil witch with a salivating grin? A troll with rotten teeth? Each time he woke screaming, he envisioned something different.

He vowed to never go anywhere under kudzu again.

Now, as he sat in front of Planket's, he was in the grip of that fear. *You've been in there hundreds of times*, he thought.

But those occasions had been different: *you remember, it was starting to get covered with the kudzu when you were in high school, but Mr. Planket was always out there whacking at it with a machete, cursing, to the point where if Mom was going to pull in there and she saw him, she'd change her mind and drive right by. "Such foul language," she'd say. "It's the kudzu, that's what it does, cursin' at it doesn't make it better. Plants don't respond to that kind of thing."*

Will knew that wasn't true. He'd read a study on plants in one of his many science magazines. Some botanists filled two soundproof rooms with plants. In one room, they pumped classical music, and the plants grew toward it and flourished. In the other, they played acid rock, and the plants shied away from the speakers, some of them even shriveling and dying.

By the time Will was eighteen—two years before he roared out of town for good—the kudzu was harder to control. Some of the houses had succumbed, the abandoned ones in particular, like Mrs. O'Dell's, which everybody joked was haunted anyway. He'd always felt that in those houses a certain evil lurked, like the place's very walls would know what was in his soul, all of his wrongs, all of his mistakes—

Stop it, Will. Planket's isn't one of those houses. What's wrong with you? Just go in, buy an Icee—and maybe somebody can shed more light on your sister's accident. As was typical of everyone in town,

Officer Marcus, who had called him about Cyn's death, hadn't been that forthcoming:

"Wilson. Wilson Hale."

"That's me."

"Good."

There had been a long silence.

"Who's this?"

"This is Sheriff Daniel Marcus."

Another long silence, and Will remembered feeling he hadn't been sure how to react. Baltimore didn't have a sheriff. It had cops, but not anyone who referred to himself as sheriff. "Uh . . . listen, if it's about that parking ticket I got last week . . ."

"I'm in your hometown, Wilson."

A pit of acid had opened up in his stomach then, because he had known something was wrong. He'd crossed his office, outside of which his secretary sat, typing away on her computer, and closed the door. "Yeah?"

"Sorry to have to tell you this, but your sister, Cyn . . . she's been in an accident. She . . . passed away."

Will had sunk into his chair and stared at the ashtray Cyn had sent him for Christmas—an unusual gift, considering he didn't smoke. Suddenly it had hit him that he wasn't that surprised by her death . . . a couple of years before Will had moved away, there had been something . . . not quite *right* about her. She'd started doing all sorts of strange things—burying her childhood teddy bear, painting the bathroom mirror black, making herself vomit—and her eyes had had a haunted look, like something else was in control. And then she'd just let herself, her looks, her body, everything . . . go.

At the tender age of twenty-four, she'd given up.

And she'd never left Wodeston.

"What kind of accident?"

"Car."

Long silence.

"Did she hit someone, or did she just run off the road, or what?"

"Nope, no other vehicles involved."

"Did someone check out the car?"

"Yup."

"Did they find anything?"

Another long silence.

"Nope."

That had been the extent of the conversation, but Will had known a chunk of his vacation time was about to disappear. There was no one to bury his sister but him—he'd have to go down and make the arrangements. And that house of his mother's that Cyn had lived in needed to be cleaned out, fixed up, and sold—that was, if the kudzu hadn't completely eaten it alive.

Now, he heard a door bang and saw someone emerge from around the back corner of Planket's. A man in a ratty T-shirt and mud-spattered jeans stopped and shielded a hand over his eyes, looking at Will. Then the man jerked—as though he'd been hit with several thousand volts of electricity—and bolted straight for Will's car, wailing and waving his arms in the air.

Will panicked, rammed the stick into reverse and backed out. *What the hell was that*, he thought, heading out of town toward the direction of his sister's. The farther he went, the houses and structures were more and more smothered by kudzu, to the point that he wasn't even sure he'd be able to *find* his sister's house, and if he did—

—if he did, would he want to go inside?

He shuddered.

He rounded a corner, startled by the back end of an inert, bright red hatchback thrust across the lane directly in front of him. He slammed on the brakes—

The last thing he remembered was the shock that went through his body as the cars collided.

The thing that brought Will back to consciousness was the blaring of the other car's horn, which in the dream he'd been having was his sister, yelling. She'd opened her mouth, which was black as a pit with dark blue ink leaking from the corners, and out had come that horn sound.

He wasn't sure how much time had passed; in Baltimore, he could tell from the change of the light, the way it fell between the buildings. But here, the sun—or lack thereof—was falling into the kudzu and being promptly, it seemed, swallowed.

He tried to move, and surprisingly, found that he could. He was sore, but didn't think anything was broken. Then he realized if the car horn was going off, it meant someone had still been inside the car when he'd crashed—and the person's head was now probably slumped against the steering wheel. He didn't remember hearing the horn before the collision.

Suddenly panicked, he reached for the door handle and tugged.

It wouldn't budge.

He tried again. Nothing.

He tried to peer out the window, which miraculously hadn't broken, but couldn't see if the door was jammed. He unsnapped the seatbelt, smashed down the airbag—his face burned, but he was too panicked about thinking he'd just killed someone who might've possibly been alive to worry about it—grabbed the door handle and thrust his shoulder into the car's driver-side door—

It popped, *creeled*, and came open.

He felt dizzy, so he sat for a minute. The sky was a strange color, not quite blue, not quite gray, and a filmy haze hovered above the road.

He stepped from the car and made his way over to the other vehicle. It had apparently spun and drifted not sideways into the gutter, but head-on; the hood was wedged into a telephone pole so covered with kudzu it looked like a giant sloth Will had seen in one of his dinosaur books when he was a kid. He'd been terrified of that prehistoric sloth: what if he was in the woods and he ran across one? "They're vegetarians," his mom had said. "No reason for you to be afraid of a vegetarian—it's not going to eat you. You really shouldn't run your life based on fear. Especially of something that died years ago."

Someone was slumped against the steering wheel, all right.

He wondered if he should call someone. *Don't move the victim,* he thought, *call 911,* but as he circled around to the driver's side door he was certain he'd seen her someplace—

—she had dark hair.

Like his sister Cyn.

"Uh, hello?" He crept forward.

The horn stopped and the woman sat upright, screamed, then shouted, "Let me go, dammit!" She panted, looking at him.

He took two steps back.

"Your car—you were in the middle of the road, and I—I was coming around the corner, and I hit you."

A rivulet of blood ran from her nostril. "I . . ." she glanced around, confused, then out at the trees, and screamed again. Then she was still, resting her head against the seat.

"You . . . you feeling okay? I have a cell—"

"No!" The woman was suddenly animated again; Will noticed her eyes were a strange shade. They weren't quite brown; they weren't quite blue. "No, no, don't do that!" She reached for the door handle and began thrusting her shoulder against the door. "Get out. I have to get out—"

"Whoa, whoa, stop!" Will came up fast on the door. "Stop. You're going to hurt yourself. Now your whole front end's off its block, so the door's not going to open. See?" He pointed to the part where the driver's side door met the hood.

She was still panting.

"See?"

Cautiously, she reached for her seatbelt, unfastened it, and peered out her window at where he was pointing.

"I can get you out through your window."

Her expression softened, her breathing slowed, and he thought he saw her smile. "Really?"

"Really."

"You . . ." she glanced over her right shoulder. "You have a car."

"Well, I do but . . ." He shrugged. "I hit you, and my whole front end looks about as bad as yours. Doubt we'll be going anywhere in it. And anyway, we should both get checked out. I'll call 911—"

"No, don't. Please don't."

"I think—"

"Don't call anyone!" She burst into tears. "Don't call anyone."

"Okay!" Will held his hands up. "Okay, okay. I won't. But you're bleeding."

Her expression changed again. He watched her look down at her blouse, a white and pink-flowered baby doll, and she plucked at the smocking, touching the blood. She leaned into the rearview mirror and checked her reflection, lifting her hair, touching the cut on her right cheek. "It's not so bad. I don't live far from here. Can you walk me home?"

Will hesitated. Something didn't feel right.

"Please . . . I don't live far at all."

The low-lying mist on the road thickened; the kudzu around them seemed to move. Will was suddenly aware that another car could come around the corner at any moment and slam into both of them.

"Okay."

He saw her take a deep breath.

"Now, what you're going to want to do . . ."

But the girl grabbed the Jesus handle to her left side and pulled herself through the window with almost no effort, landing on her tan spike heels and nearly keeling over. He reached out to steady her.

She stood for a second, teetered a little, then straightened.

"You okay? I mean, to walk? Any pain anyplace?"

"I think," she said. "I think I'm . . . I'm all right. My head's sore."

They stood looking at each other, and Will felt strangely drawn to her. A light scent surrounded her, too, like . . . hot honey and . . . strawberries. "Stay here a minute." He went back to his car and forced the passenger door open, pulling out a first-aid kit. "I got some stuff in here, we can clean up that blood a little bit—"

She took a step back. "No, no. Just leave it. Really, it's fine. My parents' house isn't far from here."

Will was puzzled.

"Well, let's at least call . . . what's his name? Officer Marcus, or something."

"No! No, don't call him."

"Well, someone's going to find your car sooner or later. Mine, too."

"It's all right," she said. "Let's wait until we get to my parents' house. We can call from there and everything'll be fine." She stiffened again, looking nervously over her left shoulder.

"What is it?"

"Nothing, I just . . . thought I heard something."

He looked around at the road. "Yeah, well . . . I have to admit, this place sure is a lot creepier than I remember."

She eyed him. "You don't live here."

"Used to." He nodded at her shoes. "You really shouldn't walk in those things; you've been through enough."

She shook her head. "I'll be fine." She pointed back in the direction from which he'd come around the corner, back toward town. "My house is that way."

He looked up at the sky again. "You think we'll get there before dark?"

She nodded. "Yeah, it's only about a mile."

They started the trek, neither of them speaking. Will marveled at the quiet for a while, and then, as though his head had cleared, he remembered what he was doing there. And with dread: What would he have to do to get the car fixed, and what about Cyn? She was in the town morgue, and Wodeston didn't even have a funeral home, but it did have that tiny cemetery—the cemetery they'd all played in as kids.

It had seemed so far away back then, death, something that couldn't possibly happen to them. Funny—Cyn had been spooked about playing among the tombstones, whereas it hadn't bothered him at all. "It's all out in the daylight," he'd told her once. "It's not like they bury you in a cave."

Of course, that was before he was old enough to understand that the stones marked a body. For some reason, he'd never thought a cemetery was anything but a bunch of stones with names on them.

"I'm Helene."

He was startled, and stopped.

She wasn't next to him.

He turned. She was standing, apparently, where she'd announced it.

"Oh, I'm . . . Will."

She nodded, and came up to meet him again. "So, what are you doing here, Will?"

"I'm here for . . . well . . . my sister, actually. She died . . . uh . . . a few days ago."

He'd taken a few more steps before he realized she'd stopped again. When he turned to look at her, she had a worried look on her face, a pout on her lips.

"You're Cyn's brother?"

He was surprised—and *more* surprised that he *was* surprised.

It was a small town. His sister had never left. There was probably a death here once a year, and everyone would know about it. It made sense.

"Yeah. Did you know—I mean, you know of her, but did you know her?"

She looked down at her feet. "I did, yes."

"I mean, were you friends, or—"

Helene started walking again, passing him. "Let's not talk about this right now."

"Wait!" Will ran to catch up with her; he gripped her arm, and she screamed when he grabbed it.

"Let me go!" she screeched. "What, you want all the neighbors to come running out thinking I'm being attacked?"

"Well, stop screaming and none of the neighbors *will* come out!" The ludicrousness of the statement hit him: there were no neighbors around here, only kudzu.

She was panting, glancing about furtively.

"I just . . ." he said. "All I did was ask you a question. Marcus, he told me nothing. I'm here to bury her. I just want to know how she died. That's all."

"A car accident," she said, rubbing her arms and shivering. "That's all I know."

"You don't know anything either?"

She shook her head, but was still looking at her feet. "No, I don't."

"And what about you. You remember your accident?"

Their eyes met, but then she looked away. "I don't remember. I probably swerved to miss one of those damn squirrels."

He could sense it all over her, that she was lying, and it irritated him. He was just done with it, done with the caginess, done with being stuck in the middle of this creepy kudzu. He wondered why he was even walking this girl home. Why should he? "Fine." He started walking back in the direction of his car.

"Where are you going?"

"Back to my car and doing what I should've done: call the police."

"No, no, you can't!"

He felt her touch on him, and it sent waves of . . . shock, pleasure? He wasn't sure . . . up his arm.

"Please don't, I—I need you to come with me." Her eyes were pleading. "My parents—they'll kill me—"

"You're a little old to be worried about what your parents think, aren't you?"

"You don't understand; if they find out—"

"Find out what. What? What are you hiding?"

She was silent for a moment. The kudzu rustled in a sudden breeze. Then she said, "You don't understand."

"Then talk to me," he said. "All I want to know is what really happened to Cyn, and I'll walk you home, and our quality time'll be through."

"She . . . I talked to her a few hours before the accident."

Will took a step toward her. "And?"

"And she was . . . she was very agitated. She said she was going for a drive. There was no one in the car with her, I know that. She just went for a drive and took that corner a little too fast. She hit the pole just a few yards from where I hit, actually."

Will eyed her suspiciously.

"That's it. That's all there is. Please, will you come with me now?"

He nodded despite himself. It wasn't an answer for him, not enough of one, but he knew what he had to do: walk her to the edge of her drive—that was it, he wasn't going to get involved in a let's-have-dinner-with-the-parents-affair—hike on back to his car, call Officer Marcus, stay in the next town's hotel overnight, and deal with everything in the morning. He'd dig for more answers from some of the other townsfolk.

"And yes," she said. "I will miss Cyn. Many times, she was the only person I had to talk to." She'd stopped at the edge of the road. "We're here."

Will was confused; all he saw was another thick jungle of kudzu in the threatening shapes of giant, hairy walking men. A tunnel of the stuff ended at a large lump.

A large lump with a chimney.

She pointed. "That's my house."

Will felt like a rock had lodged in his throat. It was a house, like the one that Cyn had begged him to go into that day. An unknown. Someplace dark, someplace scary, someplace where things were lurking. He took a deep breath. "Well," he said. "If you're sure you're fine now, I'll be heading on my way."

"You really should come down. My parents will be so grateful."

"I got you home," he said. "I have to go back, and call Officer Marcus, and deal with the cars—"

"No, really, you have to!"

Her eyes were like his sister's then, and for a moment he thought it was her, Cyn, and he flashed back to a long-forgotten day, a day when he'd left her there, alone, at the doorstep of the first completely kudzu-covered house in town: Mrs. O'Dell's. He was eighteen and trying to figure out what he was going to do with himself after high school; she was twenty-four, and the kudzu fascinated her to the point where she'd enrolled in the county community college's summer botany program.

She was at first enthralled with the kudzu's magenta flowers, the ones with yellow tubes thrusting out of them like wicked tongues, the ones that smelled a little bit like hot honey and strawberries. Cyn began venturing from the road into the deep woods to pull them out and weave them into the braids of her long, chocolate hair.

Soon, she grew bored. She wanted variety.

"Someone told me about a place where there's white flowers!" she said. "We learned in class that white flowers are really, really rare. So I'm going."

"Only if your brother goes with you," Mom had said. "They may be just plants, but I don't see the point in wandering off into them by yourself. You could get hurt."

Even at eighteen, the prospect struck fear into him—but he'd never say no to Cyn or his mother. In the end, he failed them both anyway, because the memory of Creepmore Manor had never been exorcised, and he'd stood there in front of Mrs. O'Dell's abandoned kudzu-covered house, sweating in panic, temples throbbing—and then legs pumping as he ran, as fast as he could, stumbling over the kudzu that seemed to rise up and hook itself around his boots.

He had left Cyn behind.

She'd come home hours later, not quite right. It was like she was always someplace else after that, there but not. What if his abandonment had changed her life? What if she wouldn't be dead now if he'd made a different decision?

"Please," Helene said now. "Please."

He swallowed. "I'll walk you as far as the door."

They made their way through the dense stuff, all the while Will growing colder, though he didn't know why. And there was something else, too: he almost felt as though the kudzu whispered around him, goading him, urging him to go farther—

Helene stopped walking. "We're at the steps," she said, though to him nothing looked much different from the forest floor. She put one foot on a stair and then another, and slowly, Will made out the pattern of three steps leading to a porch. "Come on," she said. "My parents really would like to meet you. They knew your sister pretty well, you know."

He followed her up the first step. He took a deep breath. Second step. Deep breath. Third step. The porch. The door. He thought he heard movement from inside the dwelling—the creaking of a chair, the soft thump of heavy footsteps.

He wanted to run.

Then he remembered his sister again.

He squeezed his eyes shut and slipped his hand through the kudzu, and it pricked and tickled, sending a shudder up his spine.

He found the handle. It was cold and clammy. He gripped it and began to turn, using his full weight to get the door open.

The smell of stale beer, rotting baloney and cow dung wafted from inside, and another smell, like hot honey and strawberries—

He turned, and he ran. All the while, he felt the kudzu, closing in, breathing in his ear, reaching out, scratching his face.

The car. He knew it wasn't going to start, and it was a mile from here, but he had this amazing urge to get to it, to *force* it to start, he didn't know how, to get out of this town, get out and never come back. Screw the house, he was sure it was like all the others, covered in kudzu, people huddled up inside, living their darkened, tomblike lives as day in, day out, the vines spread . . .

He reached the road, stood in the lane. Which way was out of town? To the left. Yes, his car was to the left. He'd been heading out of town before the accident, and Helene's house had been back toward town. They'd come a mile *toward* town—

—he thought about the position of her car.

She'd been heading out of town.

He recalled what Helene had screamed when she'd first come to: *Let me go.* Their conversation: *She was very agitated . . . She hit the pole just a few yards from where I hit, actually.* His conversation with Officer Marcus: *Did they check out the car? Yup. Did they find anything? Nope.* Helene: *I probably swerved to miss one of those damn squirrels.* Creepmore Manor: *I'll never let you out of here!*

He felt sick.

Cyn had been trying to leave town.

Helene had been trying to leave town.

Something had stopped them.

Wind rousted the kudzu animals around him and he thought again of the giant sloths. It was a mile, he knew, to his car, another four miles, he knew, to the town line. He stood in the middle of the road, dreading every step he had to take, trying to ignore the smell of hot honey and strawberries as daylight faded.

MUJINA

I FIND THE painting at a tag sale, and know I have to have it. It's a lush watercolor of a deadly curve on the Hana Highway on the other side of the island, a curve I navigated twice a day on my commute to Kihei, a curve just beyond the home we had to leave because of the injuries I sustained in the accident.

The waist-high canvas rests against a dilapidated bamboo chair. An ozone-laden breeze tells me if I'm going to buy this painting, I'd better do it soon—gray clouds bloom above the big mountain; lightning strikes pound the summit, and there are distant rumbles of thunder.

Across the Manilagrass under the palms, a plump, aging woman in a yellow blouse and turquoise earrings sits on a low stool. She shakes her head as she dickers over a jeweled box with a woman in a white pantsuit.

A raindrop.

I rest my weight on my cane, and with my free hand lean the painting toward me. Despite its resting against the damp cushion stuffing cauliflowering through a rip, the canvas's brown paper backing is pristine, marred only by a fluorescent orange sticker which indicates she's asking a hundred dollars.

147

"Gala?" asks Lani. She works at our art gallery and insisted on being my driver once I was released from the hospital. She appears beside me and tucks a strand of her long coffee hair behind her ear. "You really like this?"

I'm not sure whether *like* is the right word, so I'm slow to answer. "I do."

"Well the strokes are exquisite, but . . . are you sure? I mean, wouldn't this . . . bring back bad memories?"

I can't remember anything from the night of the accident; my last memory is of drinking a glass of wine by our pool. "Maybe that's what I need."

Lani protests, but I'm already hobbling across the grass to Yellow Blouse, the blades pricking my bare ankles. She is Japanese. Her face is round and wrinkled; I can see that those wrinkles aren't necessarily from age or even from the Hawaiian sun.

Another raindrop.

"The painting over there." I motion with my head.

The woman rises on wobbly knees. "What painting?"

"The one against the chair."

She hobbles too. I wonder what, because of my damaged leg, my gait will be like when I get to be that age. I've already put on twenty pounds due to lack of mobility.

"Mama, where are you going?" A young woman in a red shift and a carved wooden hair ornament rushes to Yellow Blouse's side. "I told you I would handle anything like this."

"Paintings." Yellow Blouse's brow is creased and her mouth is smashed into a grimace. "I told you not to put out any of her paintings!"

"I know you did, but we . . . we have more than we can fit on the walls, Mama."

Despite the uneven ground I beat Yellow Blouse to the painting and wedge myself between them. "I'll give you one fifty."

"It's not for sale," the woman spits.

"Mama," Red Shift says.

"It. Is. Not." Yellow Blouse scrutinizes me with hard eyes.

"I'll give you double."

Red Shift's eyes grow wide. "Nariko would be so excited. She'd want to see her art sell."

Now it's clearer than ever that I *must* convince them—they know the artist.

Yellow Blouse turns to her daughter, and the two argue in one of the forms of pidgin spoken all over the islands. A whisper in my ear whisks my attention to the painting, and I swear I see a frond of foliage move as though it were real. I reach to touch the canvas.

"Don't." Red Shift seizes my arm. "Mama says she's changed her mind; you can have the painting."

Relief washes over me.

She holds out her hand. "I'll take the money."

I rummage in my straw handbag and pull out a wallet fat with cash intended for a long day, but I'm sure now this is our final stop. "Who's the artist?"

"My sister." She looks down at her feet. "She passed away."

Yellow Blouse shouts something angry at her daughter, throws up her hands, and waddles away.

"Mama wants me to tell you Nariko was killed by a *mujina*," she says. "A woman without a face."

I'm about to ask for more detail, but there's another raindrop, then two. I signal Lani, who is paging through a rack of dresses, that we're leaving.

"That's why she's changed her mind," Red Shift says. "She thinks you are a very kind person. You seem gentle and responsible, like you would never do something like hide from the consequences of your actions."

I'm confused. "What does that mean?"

"Did you buy it?" Lani interrupts.

I nod.

"Have a nice day." Red Shift makes a stiff exit.

Lani carries the painting to her Nissan and pops open the hatchback. "What was all that about?"

"Nothing." I make my way around to the passenger side door. "Listen, I . . . I'm tired. How about we grab lunch and head home?"

❦

I have my husband Michael hang the painting over the teak buffet in our Kihei apartment. It's a far cry from the sprawling, multileveled Polynesian-inspired home off the Hana Highway we sold for the sake of medical expenses and my health. We still have a distant view of the Pacific, but it just isn't the same; the new canvas, therefore, becomes more of a comfort than I thought.

"Why would you want that?"

I'm surprised he isn't as thrilled about the purchase; it's something that as curator at our gallery he probably would have snagged for one of his annual exhibits on local artists. "It reminds me of home."

He kisses my neck. "You *are* home."

"You know what I mean."

He pulls away from me. "Yes, well."

I shouldn't give him such a hard time. He's stuck by me, even when I woke up from the accident and couldn't remember—at least at first—who he was. Even as I'm facing a future devoid of everything that made me who *I* was: his right hand, the do-it-all wife, my job as the gallery's first lady who handled all the volunteer coordination and fundraising activities.

"How about some lunch?"

He rummages in the cabinets as I sit on our orchid-patterned couch and admire the canvas; my thoughts turn to Nariko. Did this particular stretch of the Hana have meaning to her? Like me, did she travel it every day, know it as well as her own skin? I can almost feel the breeze on my face, smell the coconut palm and kahili ginger; the road is a place of wonder, a place where the thought *this is what heaven must be like* is not uncommon—but so is *watch your driving*. On occasion, someone never arrives at his destination, and inevitably the car is found crumpled at the base of a cliff.

I hear the pounding of footsteps and a shadow flits past.

It scares the hell out of me.

Michael appears at the threshold of the kitchen. "You okay?"

I limp as fast as I'm able to the sliding doors to the balcony, but I know there's no way anyone could've run by because it's simply not that wide. "I saw something black just—rush by me."

"Maybe it's your eyes getting worse. When's your next appointment?"

"Next week." While part of my peripheral field of vision is damaged—and sometimes I'd swear I'm seeing something dark move in the corner of my eye—I know that I saw this. "But this is different."

"You sure?"

"Yes. It was really there."

There's a long silence. Then he says, "How about grilled cheese and onion on pineapple bread?"

Maybe, I think, *it was just a large bird.*

❦

Michael is at work. I'm sunk into the living room sofa, my back resting against one of a dozen orchid-spattered throw pillows. The sliding door is open, and the breeze fills the room with the scents of salt water and palm. It's not as strong as it was at the Door of Faith Road house, but it brings me back to my last memory—my glass of wine by the pool the night of the accident. It always ends there.

I hear the footsteps again, that frantic running I heard yesterday. I put my book down and sit forward, cocking an ear, thinking *it's just people tromping about in one of the surrounding condos,* but then I see it down the end of the hall.

A short, human-shaped shadow.

My breath catches, because I know what I'm looking at—I've seen those shows about haunted objects. *Mama wants me to tell you Nariko was killed by a mujina. A woman without a face.*

I'm fascinated and terrified.

"Who are you?"

It doesn't move or make a sound.

What feels like a cold fist clutches my heart. *"Who are you?"* Fear twists my gut. "Are you Nariko?"

There is no response.

Without taking my eyes off the figure, I fumble for my cane. "I'm not going to hurt you, I—"

The footsteps pound as the black thing streams toward me, sails through the air, and hurls itself into the painting.

I scream.

Silence, save for the heaving of my own breath and the tittering of the canvas against the wall. The painting's image roils like the surface of a pond, then stills.

Shaking, I clamber for the cell phone and dial Lani's number.

It rings a few times before answering *Aloha! You've found Lani, but if you get this message I'm probably . . .*

She *always* picks up when it's me.

An audible, feminine sigh draws my gaze to the painting. In the middle of the highway's serpentine curve, something sparkles, something I'm sure wasn't there before. I maneuver around the couch to get a closer look.

That is *definitely* new.

The glittering pile in the middle of the road has, curiously, almost a three-dimensional quality, as though something has been added to the paint. I stretch to touch it, but can't quite reach.

Get the step stool.

Balancing on a stool is a dangerous prospect; if I fall, I could endure another injury, or worse, unknowingly jar something loose. I've heard horrendous tales of bone chips breaking off, getting into the blood stream, and causing aneurisms years later.

Is Nariko trying to tell me something?

I set the teak stool in front of the buffet. After several seconds of debate on how to mount the thing, I step up.

The stool wobbles, and I land on my back on the hardwood floor.

Shit.

The wind knocked out of me, I close my eyes and focus on my breathing, thinking *just forget it*; when I look at the painting again, though, the glittering pile is now accompanied by a trail of reddish footprints.

I try again. This time I press my full weight on the cane, stand one-legged, and use my bad leg as a third point even though I can't put much pressure on it.

The footprints are sticky, and the glitter pile is sharp; a painful sting makes me withdraw my hand, and there's a smear of red on the heel and a wine-colored bead of blood on the pad of my index finger.

I recall my wine glass breaking.

Oh my God. The night of the accident I dropped a wine glass on the pool deck, it shattered, and a piece of glass pierced my foot! Yes! I left bloody footprints on the kitchen tiles!

I remember!

My cell phone chimes "Music Box Dancer" and I lose my balance, plunging once again to the floor. By the time I get to it, it's on its last phrase before voicemail.

"Gala? Oh my gosh, are you okay? Do you need me to come over?" Lani says. "I'm just . . . I'm so sorry I couldn't get to the phone . . . hold on for one minute."

I hear the mouthpiece jostle, and she says, muffled: "*Stop!*

Stop." Now she's clear again. "Sorry about that. It's pretty crazy here today. How's the painting?"

"Oh my god the painting—there's this woman, Nariko, she has no face, she's a mujina—the woman in the painting—I mean it showed me something—"

"What? What the hell are you talking about?"

"I remember, Lani! I remember something!"

There's a long silence. "You do?"

"I remember breaking—I broke a wine glass by the pool!"

"Are you serious?"

"Yes. And I cut my foot on the glass. There was blood on the floor."

"Are you sure it's just not wishful—"

"Oh no, I remember. There's hope! Eventually everything will come back to me!"

"Gala."

Her forceful tone stops me. "What?"

"I'm . . . glad you remembered something."

"I did."

"I want you to sit down for a second."

"I don't want to sit down. This is the best thing that's happened in months—"

"Gala, what did you mean by 'The woman in the painting showed you something'?"

I'm suddenly back on Earth, and aware of how insane what I've just told her sounds. "I mean . . . I meant. It wasn't a woman, actually, I mean, she was—like a shadow."

"Like a shadow you might be seeing as part of your peripheral damage?"

Outside, the distant cries of gulls; a gust of salt-smelling wind rustles the celery drapes.

"Listen . . . I don't doubt that you remembered something. And I think it's wonderful, I do. But the doctors said some—odd things could be happening to you for years after. Remember that? I'm just asking you to keep that in mind."

I look at the painting and discover the glass shards are no longer sparkling in the midday sun; in fact, it's like the glass was never there at all.

"Do you want me to come over?"

"No."

I know what I saw.

I know Nariko will give me another clue.

When Lani hangs up, I sit on the couch and wait.

⁂

If Michael was a painting, then I was the brush, and we were a masterwork.

We were dirt poor Cranbook Academy art students, subsisting on boxed macaroni and cheese and dollar menu burgers until his parents passed and he inherited their estate. We graduated, married, and pursued his dream of moving to Hawaii and our dream of owning a gallery—Galerie Island.

We spent every day together: he handled day-to-day operations, acquisitions, exhibitions; I planned all the opening events, coordinated staff and did everything else. We were always busy, we won Best in State awards three years in a row, and we were profiled in *ARTnews*. We'd finally gotten everything in order for a new wing, which would take us down a historic rather than contemporary road, housing pieces related to the folklore of not only the native Hawaiians but others who'd settled here.

In the few weeks before the accident it wasn't uncommon for him to be working extraordinarily late, and for me to assume the duties of getting dinner on the table. Still, our life together was a

Starry Night of beloved art, spectacular fundraisers, and stunning evenings under the Hawaiian moon.

Then came the accident, and it all ground to a halt.

⁂

I sit and watch the painting for more signs, for my mujina, Nariko, to speak to me. The dinner hour looms, and I consider ordering out. As it encroaches, however, I realize I shouldn't do anything of the sort. While dinner isn't an easy task—doddering around the kitchen with sharp objects in hand is more than slightly precarious—making it is an important step back toward normal.

My legs sore from standing, my arms sore from chopping onions, coring pineapples and sautéing prawns, I put the rice on to boil and sink into a cypress kitchen chair. I notice that on the counter, a bottle of Volcano Red sits next to the last hand-painted damask wine glass I own.

Michael won't be home for another hour, and I contemplate a drink, but then decide against it; the details Nariko has shown me are still too tenuous, not yet fully ingrained, and I don't want to do anything to erase them. I review them again: the night was cool, and our pool's green lights had turned it an inviting shade of lagoon. I was on one of our rattan chaises, looking up at the stars. The Cat's Cradle—what the West called Orion—caught my eye. *Cat's Cradle, where there are no actual cats and no actual cradles, but it fills the time.* That was from a Vonnegut story or something, wasn't it? I drained the wine glass—wait, it didn't slip from my hand.

I threw it.

I threw the wine glass.

Why?

Now I stare at the painting. *Nariko, what have you to tell me? Give me another clue—*

When my cell phone peals "Carol of the Bells," I jump. It's Michael, and at first he's talking to someone else.

"Sorry about that, honey," he says. "Listen, I'm . . . I know you're probably already making dinner, but I didn't think they needed me here, and it turns out they do—I've just—with the opening right around the corner of the new wing there's just so much, and . . ."

My heart hurts. "I understand."

I hear him lean away and shout, "I'll be right there!" He's back with me. "I have to go."

"I know," I say. "Go do it. This is a big deal."

In the background, I hear a woman laugh.

I rise to turn off the rice, and a wisp of a cool breeze kisses my neck.

I turn toward the living room.

The painting.

Nariko has left something for me.

In the middle of the painting's highway, a note—a lined yellow Post-It, the kind Michael always uses because without the lines his words are a too-close-together jumble.

I drag the step stool over to the bar and climb up.

The Post-It's bottom edge is curled so I can't read it, but I'm scared to pull it off—what if it damages the paint? Just like that, as though Nariko has been reading my thoughts, it slowly unfurls.

It's Michael's handwriting.

It reads: *Been called to check out some new work. Want them before someone else gets them. Probably out all night. Sorry.*

Yes! That night, he left me this note, but it was . . . I had dinner ready, and he was overdue. I called him. He didn't pick up the phone. He called me back an hour later, citing this note. And then I filled my wine glass, went out to the pool, and looked at the stars.

I dial Lani, who again doesn't answer, but this time I leave her a message.

❧❦❧

"So I'm not understanding this," Lani downshifts. We are on our way to Safeway; Michael was out all night and is still sleeping, and I want to pick up some coconut pudding. "This ghost—"

"Mujina."

"Okay, mujina, whatever her name is—"

"Nariko."

"Right, she put a Post-It on the painting?"

"Yes! I know it sounds insane. But it was right there, the yellow-lined one Michael always uses, plain as day." We're passing through a neighborhood of pastel-colored ranch houses. Beach morning glory creeps over white clapboard fences and plumeria trees shade the manicured lawns.

It's all so deceptively peaceful.

She's quiet for a moment. "Do you have the Post-It now?"

"Well, no, I . . . it . . . I never actually had it in my hands. It vanished."

She nods.

"You don't believe me."

"It's not that, it's—"

"I remember things, Lani! What about these details? I mean, I can't be making those up!"

"No, of course not." She puts on her blinker and prepares to turn left onto the Piilani Highway; the landscape is now brown grasses and rocky outcroppings. "I'm just . . . can you *trust* what you're remembering? What if you're confusing what happened that night with a different one?"

"You think this isn't real. That it's all in my head."

She doesn't respond. We turn onto the highway. Ahead of us, there is the swell of the mountain, brown in the sun, pale blue in the shade of passing clouds.

"I'm not doubting you at all. I'm just saying we both know you had severe injuries, some to your head." She slows to a stoplight. "To be safe, maybe we have to entertain the possibility that what you're recalling isn't exactly what happened on that particular evening."

"This is the first bit of clarity I've had! How can you do this to me?"

She puts the car back in first gear as the light turns green. "I'm just looking out for you."

I want to scream. Scream at her, maybe even shake her. I press my lips together and we trundle past slopes punctuated by kou trees. "Pull over."

She glances at me. "What?"

"Pull over."

"Are you okay? Do you feel sick?"

"No. I'm getting out."

"What?"

"Pull the fuck over!"

She just glances at me again and keeps going.

I seize the wheel.

"What the hell are you—"

I manage to steer the car into the gravel shoulder, where it comes to rest against a rise.

There is nothing but the *whoosh* of blissfully ignorant passing cars.

"Are you trying to kill us?" she finally asks.

I don't answer; I open the door and struggle out.

"Where are you going?"

"Home."

"You can't walk that! It's almost two miles back to your place!"

I seize the cane, slam the door, and move as quickly as I can over the gravel shoulder. She's yelling out the window of her Nissan. Pain wrenches my hips and back, but I keep going.

Eventually, a taxi swings by and offers me a ride.

Michael stands in the living room with his arms folded across his chest; the glass coffee table is littered with empty Pipeline Porters. "Lani called me. That was incredibly stupid. You could have gotten killed. You could've gotten *her* killed!"

I hitch into the kitchen, because it's time for that glass of wine I should've had last night. "I have to start learning how to get around by myself sometime."

"This isn't the way to do it."

I prop my cane underneath the avocado kitchen counter and press my belly against it for balance. "We have to start somewhere." I grab the Volcano Red and my glass, then rummage in the drawer for the wine opener.

He comes up behind me, reaches over, and takes the bottle from me. "We need to start with getting rid of that painting."

The comment hits me full in the chest. "What?"

"Lani told me everything." He sets the bottle down with a *thunk*. "She says you insist the shadow that you see is some kind of—woman that's showing you things. Do you have any idea how that sounds?"

"But I'm starting to remember what happened—how do you explain that?"

He doesn't say anything; he pulls a church key from his jeans pocket and opens the bottle.

"Lani says she knows the tag sale where you got it. We'll take it back."

I grab his arm. "No! No, please."

He pours me a glass of wine. "How much did you pay for it?"

"I'm so close to remembering what happened—"

"How much?"

"I don't care what you guys say, I *am* remembering, and Nariko—"

He puts the wine in my hand and walks into the living room, heading straight for the buffet.

Oh God, he's going for the painting. I put down my wine and rush to the threshold of the kitchen.

"Wait! Listen, I—you're right. You're right, okay? I was thinking on the cab ride home how crazy this all sounds. All of this—it isn't real, and I've latched onto this because I'm so—I'm so fucking desperate to have my life back!"

He looks at me. There is pity in his eyes.

"Do you remember?" I don't have my cane, but I manage to limp toward him. "Do you remember our lives before all this? How happy we were?"

The quiet is filled with the hum of the ceiling fans. I watch his eyes, and find it strange that he can't look into mine; he's looking at the floor. He heaves a deep sigh, and then walks to the sliding door and looks out at the sea.

"Please, Michael. Can't you just let me have this?"

More quiet.

"I'm sorry." He turns. "I just—I wasn't thinking. We'll keep it. At least for now."

As he walks past me into the kitchen, I could swear he gives the painting a nervous glance.

✣✤✥

For days, I sit on my couch and stare at the canvas, certain that Nariko will give me more.

When Lani and Michael ask me how things are, I affirm their suspicions that what I was seeing was due to the peripheral damage, and *Oh, by the way, my doctor's appointment is soon, and I'll be sure to tell him about it.*

Sometimes I talk to the painting, ask her to come again. But I see nothing new, and I remember nothing more.

By day four, I feel like a fool.

Maybe this *is* all in my head, and the only pieces of memory I got back were ones my brain was going to recall anyway.

Angry, I stumble to the buffet and grab the step stool. Fuck this, I *will* give it back to Yellow Blouse. I can't lift the painting and balance, so eventually I knock it down with my cane. It crashes against the buffet, knocking a crystal vase to the hardwood, and lands facedown on the floor.

I'm stunned by my own actions. What if I damaged it? What if I've ruined the ability for her to communicate?

Then, on the canvas's brown paper backing, writing appears.

Writing I recognize as Lani's.

I toss my cane aside and drop to my knees, crawl toward the painting to read it.

It's a love letter.

To Michael.

I'm shocked and hurt, but not surprised, because I knew this before, didn't I? Or at least, I suspected. Of course I did. All his late nights—far too many than would be justified for the new wing, I wasn't stupid—Michael's guilt gifts, the pair of hand-painted damask wine glasses among them, and strangest of all, Lani ingratiating herself to me, going that extra step even then in that almost forced way . . .

I had no proof of any of it.

Now the night returns.

I made his favorite meal, pineapple rice and prawns. After it sat for about an hour, I decided to open a bottle of Volcano Red and wait. Two more hours went by. I called him. He answered and asked, "Didn't you get the Post-It I left you?"

I hadn't seen it because it'd fallen off and slipped beneath the stainless steel refrigerator, probably when I was ducking in and out to get dinner ingredients. A dirty yellow corner stuck out, and when I reached down to pull it free—*Been called to check out some new work. Want them before someone else gets them. Probably out all night. Sorry*—something else came with it: a gray linen envelope.

Inside was a love letter.

From Lani to Michael.

Making plans for a future without me in it.

I read it three times as I felt my insides turn to stone. Then I opened a second bottle of wine, went out to the lanai, and looked at the Cat's Cradle: *there are no actual cats and no actual cradles, but it fills the time.*

My marriage was a fake.

I hurled the empty wine glass, it shattered on the pool tile, and I cut my foot without caring, because I was seething, and I was about to—

"*Mujina.*"

I'm jarred back to the present. That was a distinctly female whisper, like the hiss of a cobra.

"*Mujina.*"

The Hana painting vibrates, and a dark head of stringy black hair rises up out of the paper backing; bloody hands emerge and seize the sides of the canvas, and a white-gowned, blood-spattered girl crawls toward me. She lifts an unnaturally twisted arm in my direction, her broken fingers clawing for me. *Mujina.*

I scream.

She disappears.

Her black hair. Her white nightgown.

That night. I went to the bamboo basket by the door and dumped its contents to get my car keys. I was going to find Michael and Lani and catch them in the act.

Only I didn't make it that far, did I? Drunk and angry, I was trying to navigate that deadly section of the Hana Highway when a dark-haired girl in a white nightgown darted from a stand of rainbow eucalyptus trees into the road. I slammed on the brakes, but the girl's body punted into the air like a rag doll. My car skidded toward the cliff, and everything went black.

The dark-haired girl was Nariko.

I never saw her face.

I never saw yours, Nariko hisses.

Red Shift: *Mama wants me to tell you Nariko was killed by a mujina. A woman without a face. She thinks you are a very kind person. You seem gentle and responsible, like you would never do something like hide from the consequences of your actions.*

Oh my God.

I am mujina, the woman without a face. *I* killed Nariko. *I* killed her because I was drunk and angry.

She didn't deserve to be a victim.

But now I know who does.

When Lani answers her phone, I say, "Let's go for a ride."

DOORS

OR THE FIRST TIME in the two decades of making this same, frequent, six-hour drive to Provincetown, Elise's knees were stiff when she got out of the car. A second sign that she was getting old; two weeks ago on her fortieth birthday, she'd suddenly noticed age spots—faint but unmistakable—on the backs of her hands. She checked them again now, and even in the fading January daylight she could see them. They seemed to be getting darker, in fact.

She sighed and opened the trunk. She hoped she would age gracefully. This would be her last trip. Her mother, who had still lived in the Bradford Street house Elise had grown up in, had died this past fall. Elise was going to spend the next month cleaning out the place and making arrangements to put it up for sale.

The process loomed. Mom had always been a hoarder of junk. Not good junk, like antique dolls or rare China. Not useful junk, like Christmas gift bags that could be reused or jars that could be cleaned out. Mom's junk was from the beach. Boxes of smooth stones, baskets of shells. And the worst: bowls of seagull bones. The only saving grace was the junk had, at least, been stacked in the corners so a person could walk.

After Elise's father had died and Elise had moved away, however, Mom had started gathering driftwood, dirty bottles and cans, and dried-out seaweed. The collection had outgrown the corners. It had swallowed every available surface and was a layer deep on the floor. It had become so bad that when Elise visited she stayed in a hotel.

Until five years ago. Her mother had become so frail it was necessary for Elise to visit once a month. It was hard to find a place to stay: in the summer, everything was overbooked; in the winter, the bed and breakfasts and beachside motels closed down. It was feast or famine. The feast was a hassle, because she had to make plans months in advance. The famine had a creepy air. She imagined the darkened windows of the inns eyeing her as their NO VACANCY signs creaked in the winter wind. Even when she was younger, she'd wondered why they hadn't just put up signs that said CLOSED FOR SEASON. To her way of thinking, No Vacancy implied that the empty buildings were indeed not empty at all; that in fact, they were full to capacity. The people moved out at the end of the summer. And that was when the ghosts, or God knew what else, moved in.

So she'd rented a small apartment in a converted shingle-style house on Commercial Street. And here she was, getting ready to stay in it for the last time.

A door banged. Her neighbor, Pete, emerged from his apartment, lit a cigarette, and walked toward her.

"Hey." His voice was deep and heavy. Pete was single and a loner—like herself—who'd confessed that Elise was pretty much the only person he hung out with. They'd been known to tie one on together in each other's apartments during her stays, catch movies at the Cape Inn or hit the bars more than a few times.

She smelled the sea, and the reason for her visit pressed on her again. "Thanks for ordering those dumpsters for me."

"No problem. They'll be at your mom's first thing tomorrow." He stuck the cigarette in his mouth, went to the back of her car, and hefted her suitcase like it was his own. Then he slung one of her grocery-crammed recyclable shopping bags over his shoulder. "How was your drive?"

"It was great. No traffic, nice and sunny." She reached into the trunk and grabbed her toiletry kit. "Has it been this warm here all week?"

"Yeah, we've been in a thaw. But bad rains, too. You missed those. Like monsoons." His boots made sucking noises in the muddied path to their doors. "Which reminds me, be careful in front of your place. It was wicked muddy so I put some cardboard down. And in the big storm two days ago your door kept blowing open, so I went ahead and changed the latch, and now it's pretty tightly closed so you can't just push it open anymore."

"You didn't have to do that." She knew he was one of the luckier year-rounders who had a steady job with a construction company in town, but that he enjoyed doing handyman work on the side, so much he'd earned the nickname Rent-a-Pete. Still, even though they both considered each other friends, she'd always felt a barrier between them, and she couldn't decide if it was *don't take advantage* or *don't get too close*. He'd offered to order the dumpsters and she'd let him, since he'd insisted a friend owed him a favor anyway. But now he'd been careful to lay down some cardboard and fix her broken door. "How much did the hardware cost?"

"Nothin', don't worry about it. I had extra stuff in the shed." He took a key from his pocket and unlocked her door, motioning her inside while he flicked his cigarette into a galvanized metal bucket on the concrete stoop. "See? Now you got a real lock that actually works."

They stepped inside. Pete set the suitcase near the front door and the grocery bag on the kitchen counter. "I'll get the rest of your stuff."

"Really," she said. "Just leave it. I can get the rest." She admired the apartment's uncluttered openness: the cathedral-ceilinged lower floor's streak-free windows embraced the view of her small yard and hibernating rose bushes; the eight windows in the upstairs loft washed the white walls in the gold cast of the sinking sun. But it was little comfort when she remembered the task ahead of her at her mother's.

She noticed that while she'd been having these thoughts, he'd been unpacking her groceries.

"I can do that, Pete. Really."

He stopped and looked at her. "You're not coming back after this—I know that. With your mom gone, there's no reason to keep it. You're going to put your place back up for rent and I'll get stuck with a neighbor I can't stand."

She laughed; he'd referred to the person who'd rented the place before her as Pretentious Polly. "Lightning doesn't strike twice."

"Exactly." He opened the door. "I'll be back."

She watched him through the glass. He rummaged in the back of her car, pulled out two more boxes, closed the trunk, and headed toward her. She quickly tried to look busy. When he returned, she was stacking Lean Cuisines in her fridge.

"This is all you had back there," he said. "After you're unpacked, wanna go down and get a beer or something?"

"No." She shut the freezer door. "I'm pretty tired." The truth was, as glad as she was to see him, she wanted to be alone. Open a bottle of wine, maybe finish the whole thing.

He nodded. "So what time do you want to go tomorrow?"

Elise blinked. "Go where?"

"To your mom's. You didn't think I was going to let you fill two dumpsters by *yourself*, did you?"

Her cheeks flushed. She had never let anyone she knew in her mother's house. When she was growing up, she'd been so ashamed of the clutter the two friends she *did* have weren't ever allowed over. She was afraid if they saw the freaky things her mother collected they'd leave her. "Pete, I appreciate the offer, but—"

"Come on, El. I took the week off and put myself on call to get you started, and I can pitch in on the weekends," he said. "You've got nobody to help you with this. I don't mind."

"It's not that. It's that . . ." What? What was she going to give for an excuse? "I—I really *want* to do this alone."

She felt tension between them, though she didn't know why. He didn't say anything. He just stood, looking at her, seemingly puzzled. Then, after a long moment, he heaved a sigh, held up his hands, and said, "Okay." He went to the door, set his hand on the knob, and looked back at her. "If you change your mind, you know where to find me."

He left, and a second later, she heard his footsteps on the other side of her kitchen wall.

❧❦❧

Just as Pete had promised, the two dumpsters were camped on the lawn: brown behemoths plastered with bright red *TRASHMASTERS! Truro, Mass.* decals. They were the largest available, but she suddenly wished they were big enough to just pick up the entire house and cart it away. She knew the place had been falling into disrepair since her father had passed, but she hadn't realized just how bad it had become.

The house was a Cotswold cottage style, the only one of its kind in town. She sadly realized she'd have been proud to grow up in it had the place not been such an embarrassing mess—it was perched on prime land overlooking Commercial Street and the bay. Its brown shingles were weather-beaten and fading, ivy choked the front sitting room windows, the roof sagged, the white gutters angled unnaturally, and the garden was a tangled mat of dead plants. A dirty, chipped wrought iron bench sat next to a cracked birdbath full of greenish ice.

She shivered in the wind, and reached into her pocket for the keys.

The front door was stuck, and she shouldered it; it popped open with a *thwuck*. The wind chimes Mom had hung on a nail on the back of it banged, tinkled twice, then crashed to the floor.

The first thing to hit her was the smell—faint sulfur, perfumed soap, and dust. She stepped farther in and something cracked beneath her foot. *I'm going to get killed in here if I don't put some lights on*, she thought. She palmed for the wall switch and flipped it, but the overhead light didn't come on. It must have blown out—she'd kept the electricity going so the pipes wouldn't freeze. She felt her way toward the half-moon hall table, and reached for the lamp. The toggle was stuck, but she persisted. When the light came on, she grimaced in disgust.

Bowls of bones lined both sides of the hallway. There was just a tiny path for her to sidle through to the kitchen. *Again.* Because the last time she'd seen her mother, about a week before she'd died, Elise had cleared it out.

❧❀❧

It was late September, and Elise had received a call at work from the guy who delivered her mom's groceries. Her mother had hurt herself, though the guy didn't know how. "She's okay now," he said. "Just some cuts and bruises. I called the ambulance and she's in the hospital."

She'd had to throw some clothes in a bag and make the rushed trip home. It turned out her mother was all right—no broken bones, nothing serious—but it was then that she'd realized she had to do something more than just visit once a month. The conversation she'd known would someday be necessary was going to have to happen *that day*. The thought of having to deal with it made her angry, afraid, and full of dread.

She'd picked up her mom at the hospital and had barely spoken to her the whole ride back to the house. Instead, she tried to decide how she was going to broach the terrible subject. The house would have to be cleaned out. It would have to be repaired, put up for sale. And her mother would have to be moved—but where? She didn't want her mother living with her. There was no room, anyway. She had a tiny little apartment that was neat and orderly and only had a few pieces of furniture. Perhaps specifically spartan in reaction to her youth's forced immersion in her mother's clutter. Should she place her mother in an assisted care facility? A nursing home of some sort? Where the hell did a person even start with a project like this?

By the time they'd gotten to the house, she was frustrated and enraged. After a long, difficult navigation through the bowls of bones and baskets of shells in the hallway, Elise cleared off a kitchen chair, deposited her mother in it, and put on water for tea. After, that is, she'd found and washed the kettle, which was covered with sticky grime.

"We have to talk, Mom." She opened the cabinet where she remembered the tea cups were kept.

"I know you're worried about me, but I've been doing very well lately."

Elise grabbed a cup. It was chipped and a crack ran down its interior. "I wouldn't call this accident *doing well*. What happened?" She reached for another. It had a broken handle.

"I . . . I just fell, that's all," her mother said. "I've been so busy working on things."

"You fell." Elise wasn't sure she believed her. She reached for a third cup. Broken. "I think we have to talk about your future." A fourth cup. This one had a chunk out of the bottom and had been badly glued back together. "What the hell? Do you have any cups in here that *aren't* broken?"

"I haven't used those cups in ages," her mother said. "I don't have time for tea anymore."

Elise stopped what she was doing and closed her eyes, trying to center herself. Then she turned and faced her mother. "Look.

I'm just going to come out and say it. I think it's time we work on cleaning this place out and putting it on the market. I can look into getting you a place near me."

Her mother fiddled with a paper towel on the table; Elise watched her fold it, crease it, unfold it, press out the crease. "I think this has been working out fine with your visiting me."

"No, Mom."

"It has."

Elise sighed and rubbed her temple; a painful throbbing had come out of nowhere. "It worked for a while, yes. But I'm trying to be realistic. It's time for things to change. It's not safe for you here anymore."

Her mother was still worrying the towel. "I don't know what you're talking about. I'm doing important work here."

"Yes, I know." She tried to keep from groaning; she had been listening to her mother say that for the past five years, and knew that what the older woman defined as *work* was wandering the beach. "I know, but maybe it's . . . maybe it's work that you could do at the new place."

Her mother smiled faintly. "There are no beaches in New York City, dear. I have to be *here* to do my work."

Elise pressed her lips together, then returned to her search for cups; she found two acceptable ones, finally. Filthy with a layer of dirt, but intact. Her stomach lurched. "Mom, look at these." She held them out. "You don't clean; you don't keep yourself up. I realize that this is hard." She went to the sink and turned on the water. "But you won't have to worry about it anymore. Someone else can do it for you."

"This is my house, and I intend to die in it."

The cup Elise was washing was so caked she had to scrape the film off with her fingernails. The process nauseated her. "Mom. Really."

"I can only do my work here."

Elise shut off the water. "Dammit! Your only work is *hoarding*. Period. That's what you do, that's what you've always done, and that's what you'll continue to do. You can't take care of yourself anymore. I'm going to come up here every weekend and start getting rid of stuff whether you like it or not, and I'm going to start looking for another place for you to stay near me. That's the end of it."

"How *dare* you—"

"And until—" she rummaged in a drawer for a garbage bag. "Until I can get you out of here, I'm starting today so at least you can *walk*."

"What are you doing?"

She shook the bag open, moved into the hall, picked up a bowl, and shoved it into the bag. "I'm doing this because it's not safe. You can't have all this stuff blocking the hallways. You're going to end up really breaking something."

"I need those things! You leave those bones where they are! If they break—I want you to leave them there."

She picked up another basket. This one smelled of sulfur. "Not sea bones, Mom. I'm talking about *your* bones. In *your* body. You were lucky this time. You might not be next time."

Her mother was quiet for the moment. "You can put them in the bag and put them in the living room."

Elise picked up a bucket full of bottles and crammed it into the bag. "The living room is full. When was the last time you could even sit in there? I'm not going to trade one obstacle course for another."

"Put them on the stairs, then."

"They're going where they should've gone years ago."

The teapot screamed. Elise kept throwing stuff in the bag. Her mother got up from the chair and moved into the archway.

"Don't you throw out my things," her mother yelled. "I don't go to your apartment and throw out *your* things!"

"I don't have piles of worthless shit in my apartment!" Elise was shocked at how loud her own voice was, at how mean and damaging the phrase actually sounded. Her mother didn't respond, and Elise didn't bother to look at the woman's expression; she had work to do.

"Don't throw them out—*please* don't throw them out. *Stop it*!"

"I won't watch you live in piles of garbage anymore!"

"You get out, young lady. You get out of my house right *now*!"

Elise stopped and looked at her mother. It struck her that, old as Mom was, frail as she seemed, she was still formidable. She suddenly felt like she was ten, and her stomach roiled.

"*Get out*, young lady. Go back to your city. Go home."

"Mom—"

"Go."

She looked at the hallway, felt the weight of the bag full of baskets and bones in her hand. At least the hallway was clear now. "Fine."

"And you leave that bag here. Put that down right now."

The way her mother had scolded her snapped her out of the fear. She *wasn't* ten. She was an adult. An adult who *functioned*. And in one shrill, angry burst, she fired: "The next time I come back here, I'm throwing *everything* out!"

Silence. Elise knew she'd really done it now, and in a childlike reflex, she almost burst into tears and cried out, *I didn't mean it.*

But she kept her mouth shut.

"You." Her mother said, low and threatening. She hobbled toward Elise. "You will never be able to get rid of my things."

But knowing her mother couldn't catch up, Elise turned her back and dragged the heavy bag out behind her.

The teapot was still screaming when she reached her car.

Elise closed her eyes and tried to shut out the memory of that day. It had been their last exchange.

Hopeless and overwhelmed, she took a deep breath and decided the best thing to do was to go from room to room, scout things out, and turn on all the lights. Pull back the heavy drapes, open a few windows, and let in some air. Check out what was in every closet. Get a sense of what she was dealing with. Make a plan.

She brushed her hands on her jeans and went back to see what she'd stepped on in the hall. She stooped to study it.

It was a dried sea star. Sugar stars, they were called. She'd broken one of its arms. She remembered when she was little she'd been fascinated by them. When they were alive, she picked them up and their suction feet tickled her palm; when they were dried, they looked almost edible. She remembered wishing they were sugar-coated cookies. Now she was amused at the childish thoughts.

Gingerly, she picked up the pieces and set them on the hall table. She decided to start upstairs.

Upstairs, where she hadn't been in . . . *years*, now that she thought about it.

She turned on lights as she went. All the rooms on the second floor branched from a narrow hall that ran the length of the house, and each room had sloped ceilings and a single window—though all the doors, including the ones to her mother's bedroom and bathroom, were closed. In fact, it looked as though not even her mother had been up here in ages. The hall was littered with paper, cloth, and other detritus; lining the walls were more baskets and stacks of what looked to be driftwood.

She crept down the hall, stepping carefully, occasionally crunching something underfoot.

There was an unsettling rustling at the end of the hall, and a piece of newspaper moved. She thought she saw something skitter past her.

Great. Mice.

She made it to the end of the hall, to her old bedroom. She had left so much behind when she'd gone. Her bedroom was as good a place to start as any—whatever was in there was probably hers. She could toss it all and feel accomplished. She reached for the knob.

It didn't budge.

She tried it again. Was it stuck?

No. Her mother had installed a locking knob on the door. It was locked.

"Mom!" She called out, even though she knew her mother wasn't there. Fine. She turned to the room across from hers—it had been her father's study.

There was a locking knob on that door, too.

She tried to calm herself. *Fine, go to Mom's room.*

Her mother's room. The bathroom. And even the linen closet. All locked.

Her breath caught in her throat and panic seized her. *Wait a minute, Elise,* she thought. *There have to be keys to all these rooms. Probably in the kitchen somewhere.*

The kitchen: that disorganized hole full of dirty dishes, broken cups and overstuffed drawers.

She made her way back downstairs and started her search. Drawer by drawer. Cupboard by cupboard. Grubby spoons, knives, forks. Napkins, potholders. Nails. Nails, tarpaper, hammers . . . and these looked *new*. She went into a few more drawers and cabinets. New tools were everywhere. Keys. *What I need to find are keys.* Bowls of screws, tacks. Piles of newspapers.

No keys.

In her desperation, she stopped rummaging and started rooting, stopped rooting and started removing. Soon she was pulling the drawers out, dumping their contents on the floor.

She could've sworn she heard a voice. Her mother: *You will never be able to get rid of my things.*

"Oh, yes I am!" she screamed. In response, something clunked upstairs. "Oh, yes I am! I don't care if I have to break down these doors, I will get rid. Of your. Junk!"

She sank to her knees and burst into tears. She wasn't strong enough to break down any of these doors, or even know how to go about doing it short of using an axe, and then it was going to cost her a fortune to replace everything.

Pete. She could call him. She could ask him how to get the doors open without damaging them.

She collected herself and reached into her pocket for her cell phone.

It wasn't there. Had she left it in the car? No. She'd wanted it with her, in case . . . in case she fell over all the junk. In case she had to call someone because she was hurt. It had to be somewhere in the house.

She got to her feet and painstakingly retraced her steps, checking every inch of where she'd walked, kicking aside papers, wrappers, sticks. After a good forty minutes and she still hadn't found it, she decided to check the car. *Just check it*, she thought. *Maybe it fell out and it's on the seat.*

She opened the front door, dismayed when she saw that the skies had opened up. It was pouring, and the violent wind bent the trees and shrubs nearly horizontal.

Shit. She pulled up her hood and made a mad dash for the car, her booted feet landing in massive pools and runoff in the crumbling driveway.

And then she saw her cell phone. In a puddle, just outside her driver's side door. It must've fallen from her pocket when she'd gotten out of the car. Knowing it was futile, she picked it up to see if it still worked.

Nope, dead.

She had no choice. She got in the car and started the ignition.

As she drove the two and a half miles back to the apartment house, she focused on calming down, formulating what she'd say to Pete, rehearsing how she'd say it. She parked the car and splashed her way up to his door. She noticed the cardboard pieces he'd put down in front of both of their stoops were little more than soggy, ineffective sponges.

She knocked on the glass of his outer door. Nothing.

She knocked again.

Footsteps, and then the inner wooden door pulled open and there he was, beer in hand, in his usual paint-spattered jeans and sweatshirt.

And before she could stop herself, she burst into tears. "All the doors are locked and I can't find the keys and I don't know how to get them open and my mother's house is a mess!"

There was no response. She just stood there, crying and hating it, wiping her runny nose on her sleeve.

Finally, he just blinked, pushed the outer door open wider, and took a step back. "Jesus. Come in out of the rain. You're going to catch pneumonia."

She stepped inside, and he pulled out a chair at the kitchen table. "Sit."

She did.

He brought her a box of tissues, went to the refrigerator, opened a beer, and set it in front of her. "You've changed your mind about me helping, I guess."

She pulled a tissue from the black box and blew her nose, then said, "No, I just want . . . I don't know what I want." She shivered.

"What's going on?"

She took a deep breath, blew her nose one more time, and then said, "Sorry."

"That's okay. It's fine." He set his hand on her arm.

She looked up at him, startled.

He withdrew his hand.

"No, that's all right," she said. "It's actually kind of warm. I'm freezing."

He went to a hook near the door and brought her one of his zip-front sweatshirts. "You can take off that and put this on. If you want."

She hesitated. It *did* look warm, and her sweater coat was soaked. She stood up and did as he'd suggested. She zipped the jacket, suddenly noticing it smelled . . . good, *like nutmeg*, she thought. She sat back down, blew her nose again, and sipped the beer.

He didn't say anything; he just watched. Then: "So the doors are locked?"

"To all the rooms. And I have to get in there to clean them out. Do you have a special tool I could borrow or something?"

He was amused. "Not really. You'd have to pick the locks. I got a lock-pick kit in the truck, but it's kinda something you don't just do; it requires practice. But I'm pretty good at it. I could do it for you."

"No!"

"Fine." He took a step back, leaned against his kitchen counter, and folded his arms in front of his chest. "You know, I don't *get* you."

"I mean, I'm sorry. I . . . " she took a deep breath. "The reason . . . the reason I didn't want you to help is because . . . she has a lot of . . . had a lot of . . . stuff."

There was a long silence again. Then he shrugged. "So what? Most older people have lots of stuff they've accumulated over the years."

"You don't understand. It's a mess. She was a hoarder. Of weird shit."

He frowned. "Weird shit?"

She nodded. And then, slowly, she told him the whole story, the words feeling sharp and foreign. She realized it was the first time she'd ever discussed it. But no expression on his face showed shock, or disapproval, or anything. When she was finished, the only sound in the room for a few moments was the soft murmur of the weather girl talking about gale warnings. Pete drained his beer.

He turned to the sink and rinsed out his can; he wiped his hands on a towel and leaned against the counter. "So what do you want to do? I mean, really? What would you like *me* to do?"

"I want all the doors unlocked. Or opened. Without them being damaged." She sniffed. "And I want every item in every single room thrown out. Furniture, everything."

"Okay. I think that's a relatively easy problem to solve." He tossed the towel in the dish rack. "You want to go now, or you want to wait until later or tomorrow?"

She thought about this. Again, her mother's voice came back to her. She realized that she was a little scared of what might be behind the locked doors. And that if she waited, she might lose her nerve.

But she was glad, in a strange way, that Pete was going to be with her.

"Now," she said.

⁂

The house's dark green front door was banging in the wind. Pete shut off the truck engine, and both of them sat there, staring, the sound of the rain drumming on the roof.

She shifted to look at him. He was eyeing the house like he would an adversary, and she was suddenly aware that his doing this made him more than just her drinking buddy. She caught a faint whiff of nutmeg, and then her embarrassment took over again. "Look, maybe . . . you're absolutely sure there's no way you could just *tell* me how to use the kit."

He was still staring at the door, but then he turned to look at her—and his expression was one she'd never seen on him before. It was almost as though he were annoyed. "Come on. Make up your mind."

She nodded, and then simultaneously, they opened the doors, stepped out, and made their way to the house.

She could have sworn she heard him make a noise of disgust when he entered, but when she glanced at him, he wasn't even surveying the scene; he was fiddling, instead, with some tools on his keychain. "Why don't you show me the first door you want opened."

"Um . . . it's upstairs." She cleared her throat. "It's my old room."

The stairs creaked beneath their feet. She wondered what he was thinking; she contented herself instead with trying to listen to every sound he made, whether or not he sighed or grunted. But she didn't hear anything from him at all, save his boots behind hers. When they reached the top step, she heard that skittering from down the hall again, and the air felt closer than it had before—closer, and more rank. Like rotted lettuce and urine.

"I . . . I think there might be mice," she said.

"Or something else. We might want to be careful when we're going through all this stuff."

They arrived at her door, and she took a step back to let him through. "This one." She rubbed her arms, suddenly chilly. "This is it."

He examined the door knob, and then worked with the tools on his keychain. "This lock's pretty standard. Easy enough."

She felt safer with him standing near her—an odd feeling she'd never had before—so she took a moment to look more closely at the condition of her surroundings. The coffee-colored paint was chipping, and in the corner above the window she saw what was clearly water damage, a black-and-green blotch haloed by yellow. All of this was going to be expensive to fix, and Mom hadn't left much in the way of money. It occurred to her the easiest and fastest way out of this mess, once the place was cleaned up, was to fire-sale it. Dump it for as little expense as she could get away with—there were only a few small bills to pay off, and everything after that would be hers—and be done with it. It wasn't easy to get nice old homes in Provincetown, and even this one, in the shape it was in, would make someone very happy.

"Voilà." Pete pushed the door open and jammed the tool ring into the pocket of his jacket.

A smell like turpentine and asphalt drifted from the inside. She stepped across the threshold and gasped.

Everything of hers was gone. Her bed, her dresser, her lamps. Even the two framed pieces of art—both Cubist and possibly the only things she'd considered keeping—were gone. Instead, there was a single chair, piled high with junk, just to the right of the door, and the room was stacked, nearly floor to ceiling, with pieces of metal, cardboard, and wood. "This isn't my stuff," she said, more to herself than to him.

"You said this was your room."

"Did she throw out my things?"

She felt his hand on her shoulder, and she suddenly felt so dizzy she leaned into it. Her mother had thrown out her things. Yes, it had been stuff she didn't want, but it had been *hers* to throw away.

Her knees gave out.

Pete caught her.

She heard a crash behind her, and she realized he'd managed to clear off the chair with his free hand. It shifted and creaked when she settled into it, but it held.

He crouched, facing her. "This isn't your stuff. You're sure."

"No." She leaned forward and ran a hand through her hair. "I have no idea *what* all this is." Her head throbbed, and her mouth filled with saliva; she thought she was going to throw up, but managed to quell it. She felt as though she'd been robbed.

That same feeling she'd had when she'd come home to her apartment a few years ago: the door had been hacked open, and her TV, DVD player, and jewelry box were gone. She hadn't been able to sleep for weeks—and it wasn't because of the missing items, or out of the fear the person might come back, or even because she was running scenarios in her head of what might have happened had she been home. It was because *someone* had touched her things. *Someone* had been in her private space. Everything in her place had felt dirty.

She recalled the day she'd tossed her mother's things in a bag right in front of the woman. Is that what her mother had felt?

Stop it, she thought. *What you threw out then was junk, and it was for her own safety. You weren't tossing out her photos or her bath products or her dishes or her furniture. You were throwing out junk. What Mom got rid of, in this room, that was your bed. Your dresser. Your lamps. She threw out perfectly good, usable stuff in favor of this . . . crap.*

"We might still find your things," Pete said, as if he'd been listening to what was in her head. "She could have just moved them someplace else."

She nodded and took a deep breath.

He patted her leg, then went to one of the piles near her and pulled something out of it. "This looks like tar paper." He held it up for her to see—it was a square and a triangle pushed together. Shaped like the side of a simple house. "And this—" he pulled something from a different pile. "This is aluminum."

She was aware he was rummaging, and she was suddenly comfortable with him doing it.

"These materials had to be cut this way. If she cut it she'd have to have tools, like a jigsaw, or else she found it or bought it this way. But . . . there are thousands of pieces here."

She looked around, and he was right. The same odd shape was cut out of several different materials, all of varying sizes. "Where did she get all this?"

"More importantly, what was she planning on doing with it?" He tossed the piece he'd been holding back on its pile, which toppled and landed on a coffee can. The can tipped over, spewing galvanized nails on the one clear patch of hardwood floor.

"I know what *I'm* going to do with it."

He looked at her. "You okay? You look a little pale."

"I'm fine."

He seemed to accept this answer.

Elise stood up, feeling almost vengeful. "I'm going to get some boxes and start getting rid of it all."

"You want me to open up the other rooms?" He shoved his hands in his pockets. "I mean, I can open up the other rooms and go, if you'd rather."

She realized he was offering her privacy. And at that moment, the thought of being alone in the house, of going through all of this—no, she corrected herself. The thought of being without *him* in the house—was terrifying. "No, I . . . would you help me throw all of this stuff out?"

He nodded. "If you want. I mean, if you're sure everything's going to the dumpsters and there's no sorting, we can probably get this room all done in just a couple of hours."

"I want that."

He heaved a deep sigh. "Okay, then. I'm gonna step out for a cigarette and then we'll get started." He left the room and turned the corner.

She suddenly felt like she was being watched, watched by all the odd pieces of metal and tar paper and wood and whatever else. The pile he'd tossed the metal piece on shifted again.

She hurried out into the hall. "Wait—"

He turned. "Yeah?"

"I'll—I'll go with you. I mean, not to smoke, I just—"

He smiled. "Come on. I think we could both use some air."

✻❦✿❦✻

Elise was surprised at how touching all the items and putting them in boxes, then hearing that tinny *thunk* as they hit the bottom of the dumpster, made her feel. She'd expected it would be liberating, but it was exactly the opposite. She thought back to the person who had stolen her belongings from her apartment, and she somehow thought that when he took them he'd gotten some kind of satisfaction from it, as in *if I sell this TV I can eat this week,* or even, *if I sell this TV I can buy my drugs.* Taking her things had been, probably, some sort of means to an end for whoever it was. This had no such quality. She was tossing out this—junk—and when it was done, all she would have was an empty room, and a dumpster full of worthless things. And there was a sadness underneath it all, too. She actually wished her mother were here to tell her what all this *was.*

And why it was so important she had to toss out Elise's things to make room. It wasn't like the house was small.

They were halfway through clearing the room when Pete said, "So, you're really going to go, huh? You wouldn't consider just fixing this place up and moving back into it?"

"It's falling down, as you can see. It's kind of a train wreck."

He shrugged and tossed some balls of twine into the box he was filling. "This is the kind of work I do every day, you know. I could fix it up for you over time. A side project. It's nice. Around here, if this were fixed up, it'd cost a pretty penny to buy."

"I know."

"So you've considered keeping it, then?"

"No." She bent over to retrieve another pile of house shapes. "I just want everything in this place thrown out right now."

"And then you'll think about keeping it? Or you've decided?"

She was suddenly annoyed. "I've decided. What's here for me, really? Except the past, I guess. That's a dead-end street."

"I thought *I* was."

She had finished setting another stack of house-shapes, this pile fashioned of cardboard, into a box before what he'd said registered. She looked at him. He was watching her.

"What?"

He turned away, toward one of the last three piles in the corner. "Never mind."

"No." She took a step forward. "What did you say? I honestly didn't hear you."

He blinked. "I said, 'I thought I was.' Meaning, *I'm* here."

She felt her face flush, and she smiled nervously. "Well, of course you're here. You *live* here."

His expression changed. "That's kinda not what I meant."

It occurred to her then that she *did* know what he meant. She had known all along what he meant. She opened her mouth to respond—

—but he'd already taken offense.

"There's beer in the truck. Why don't you go get it and I'll . . . start opening up these other doors."

The way he'd said it was snappish, clipped.

"I didn't mean to—"

"It's okay," he said. "I get it. I'll open up these other doors, and you can do what you want and go where you want and do whatever."

"But it's not that—"

"We've been dancing around this for five years. You haven't noticed?"

She looked at the floor. "No. Really."

"Right."

"I'm not lying. I swear I'm not."

"Go get the beer."

She hesitated for a moment, but knew she couldn't convince him. She hurried through the hall, down the stairs, out to his truck, and set her hand on the six-pack. Then she considered not going back inside. She glared at the decrepit place, recognizing that right now finishing this project was too much for her. She could walk away. Walk away from the house. Walk away from him. Turn off the electricity; let the damn thing rot.

But she heard him calling her: "Elise! I think you'd better see this!"

She swallowed. For the first time since she'd been at Pete's asking for help, she felt terrified about what she might find.

She slammed the door to the truck and walked as quickly as she could over the uneven, muddy ground. At the base of the stairs, she set her hand on the newel post; it was sticky. "Are you okay?"

"Wow," he said.

She ascended the stairs. "Is it . . . is it really bad? Worse than my room?"

"No, I mean . . . wow. You never told me your mother was an artist."

"What are you talking about?" Her voice was so loud she must have startled another mouse; she heard something scurry behind her, but she kept moving down the hall.

"I'm in here." His hand stuck out from the doorway to the room that had once been her father's study.

She approached and peered inside.

Her mouth fell open.

The room was crammed with houses. Six inches high, two feet high, three feet high, five feet high. Houses made from driftwood. Houses covered with tar paper, tacked together with nails, covered in beautiful shells. Gleaming, silver chimneys made from old cans. And each house . . . each house had windows and doors. And each window or door revealed the houses' interiors.

They were full.

Full of seagull bones. Full of nails. Full of broken glass. Full of shells, full of crosses, full of sugar stars.

"Oh my God," was all she could say.

Pete nodded at their surroundings. "Every room on this floor—even the old bathroom—they're all full of these things. They're really intricate . . . must've taken years."

"Many years. I . . ." she recalled what her mother had said—she was doing work, or she was doing good work, or something like that. "I had no idea she was doing any of this."

Pete bent over and moved the three-foot-tall structure blocking her entrance slightly to the side, then stepped over another two or three small houses, turned, and reached for her hand. "Come on in—watch your step."

She marveled at his bare hand for a moment, struck by the deep lines in his palm.

"I don't want you to fall."

Their eyes met. She bit her lip and took his hand, and he helped her over. And then she let go and rubbed her arms, feeling the enormity and the chill of all of it. The sad little houses. The lovely, sad little houses made of broken junk.

But the houses were full. They were all *full* of something. Just like her mother's house had been full of something. Full of the sounds, maybe, of her mother *working*. And what was Elise's life full of? Her little apartments were empty. Her life was empty.

She and Pete stood there in the quiet.

Pete was the first one to speak. "Look, I don't . . . I don't mean to be telling you what to do. But I don't think you're going to be able to throw *this* stuff away."

"I know," she said, remembering the sugar star she'd crushed under her foot, wondering if maybe it could be glued. She reached for his hand, and he took it. "I know."

There was the sound of dripping water coming from the corner of the room. It made her think of tears.

Outside, it rained harder.

ROOTS

THE ONLY PLACE I see my daughter Anna's face now is on a milk carton.

She was just five years old when she wandered out the back door into the woods behind the house and disappeared, but in that moment, less traumatic but still painful, I lost more than the Anna I loved. The other women on Merrow Street— neighbors, friends, confidantes—withdrew; they didn't understand because they still had *their* children. Oh, certainly, in those first days they were all aflutter, alighting on my doorstep with their lasagnas, cookies, and wine. Two weeks in, their voluntary visits tapered off, and despite my well-in-advance invitations, they had their excuses: Bethany was in the weeds picking up after the girls; Diane had to take Derek and Tyler to soccer practice; Sabrina had to give Miranda her piano lesson. I knew, of course, that they weren't really that consumed; they hadn't been too busy for me when I had my Anna. They regarded me as though I had an infectious condition; as though the loss of a child were viral; as though being near me were to guarantee that one day their children would disappear, too.

Nick has become distant, but I don't blame him; instead of the minutiae you discuss with your husband—*how was work, don't forget we're heading to the Sheltons' for cocktails on Friday night, I took the van in for the oil change today*—that which *isn't* minutiae casts a pall over everything. Work and cocktail parties and oil changes are too trivial, but we can't really talk about that *the little girl we made is missing* thing either, because that is too overwhelming. So yet again we eat another meal of broiled salmon and saffron rice, our last meal before he goes on yet another overseas business trip, in silence.

I used to miss him when he went on business trips. Now the only thing I miss is his laundry.

I've taken to gardening, the only activity that seems not to remind me of Anna. Before she vanished, there wasn't a garden of any sort behind my house. In autumn, the flowerbeds were buried beneath dead leaves; in spring, dandelions sprouted through the rotting wood chips; in summer, some withered stalks thrust up around the grubby, cracked birdbath. But after Anna went missing and my friends went away, I grew roses, geraniums, and forsythia. When that was done, I moved over to the area near the woods and put in hemlocks, careful, *always* careful to never plant in the area where I thought my Anna would have trodden in case she returned and couldn't find her way back into the yard.

In our neighborhood, the houses are abreast with nary a hedge between them, and sometimes I sense my former friends watching me. Busy with their children, indeed; they seem to have plenty of time to stare at a grief-stricken soul on her haunches, clawing rocks from the ground.

There is the one in the pink house next door who isn't busy with her children because she has none—Onja, who grew up in Madagascar but moved here when she married Grant. She was from the capital city there. I imagined it a lush, rainbowed place full of parties, because Onja is always dressed in the bright colors of a plumed bird and her speech is melodic, even though sometimes it's difficult to comprehend. This works both ways, though, because when she first moved in—two years before Anna went missing—I invited her for ladies' night. She asked what she could bring and I told her, *salad*, since I knew my other friends liked to grandstand with their oysters Rockefeller and mango martinis; no one would deign to bring simple greens. Onja showed up at the door with rice and a carved coconut full of sauce that reeked of chili and ginger, an appetizer no one touched.

She also regaled us with odd stories. She told us she was born because her relatives perform a ritual in which they unearth their ancestors' bodies and replace their burial clothes—women who cannot conceive, like her mother, jam a piece of the old shroud beneath their mattresses as a cure. And she told us that she knows there is such a thing as a man-eating tree, which flourishes deep in the Madagascar jungles and has claimed its share of wayward explorers since the island's discovery.

Diane, tall, broad, and pear-shaped, was still busy poking fun at a putrid death shroud as a fertility treatment when Bethany, who lives in the green house next door, bulldozed the conversation. "Every culture has its—antiquated cures, but—a man-eating tree? Really, now." She has four small girls, and I could never imagine how she could've given birth to them just about one right after the other when she's shaped like a string; I was tubby after Anna and still can't get rid of my pouch. "That's absurd!"

"Not so much." Onja sipped her martini. "You hear of the Venus flytrap? The corpse flower? They eat meat."

Bethany, who always reminds me of a chicken when she's gossiping, pulled her head back and looked like she was about to cluck. Instead, she daintily wiped the corner of her mouth with a napkin and said, "But a *tree*, as big as you're saying, that just reaches out and grabs people? That just doesn't make any sense."

"The Mkodo tribe, they sacrificed young women to the trees. To ensure that they would have good harvest."

Bethany squawked in laughter.

"Be amused." Onja set her empty glass on the counter and met Bethany's stare. "These trees, they have *fanahy*—intelligence, character, part of a man that is forever a *soul*. They know flesh from flesh and they can pick-choose their victims."

That quieted everyone down; Bethany looked at me in the ensuing silence, then gathered up the dirty appetizer plates. Diane, Sabrina, and the other women demurred to the sitting room and helped themselves to the Linzer tarts I'd served on my bone china.

While the others had been unsettled by the story, I was charmed by it; Onja was quite an entertainer. Although I never invited her over again. She wasn't one of us; clearly, she never would be.

Today I'm weeding the garden, pulling up stubborn pachysandra that have been threatening to choke my roses, and I hear Onja say to me, "Christelle, you have such a good garden. I brought you this."

I stand and brush the dirt off my knees, even though I'm certain I have a smudged face and root-threaded hair. Onja, stunning in a yellow and pink blouse, carries a chartreuse and orange ceramic pot adorned with purple crosses. In it sits something akin to and twice the size of a pineapple, but where this common fruit's angular leaves should be are hairy, purplish-green, sinuous strands, their tips curling, pulsing . . . moving like the tentacles of a squid.

My stomach knots.

"Something for your garden." She holds it forward.

I take a step back. "What is it?"

She smiles. Her teeth are faultless. "It is a *tepe*. A sacred tree. A man-eating tree."

It doesn't look big enough to be a tree, and I'm sure she is sowing more stories. "Oh, come now. You were just making conversation."

She furrows her brow. "It was no story. I gave you the truth. Here it is. For you."

In her green house next door, Bethany stands at the picture window in her dining room, looking into my yard. She's sipping a mug of something, and next to her is the youngest of her four blonde girls: Kathy, who is the same age my Anna was when she disappeared. The child rushes to her side and pulls on her pant leg.

Bethany notices I see her staring, and shuttles her daughter away from the window.

"You need someone who will not run away on you," Onja says. "Someone you can love and care for, someone who will always be there."

I just stare at it.

"Take it." She thrusts it into my hands.

I have no choice. I wrap my hands around the cool ceramic.

"Plant it." She turns to go back to her pink house.

I watch her retreat across the lawn. I see Bethany has returned to the window and is eyeing me again. I remember my husband will be in China for another three weeks.

Someone who will not run away on you. Someone you can love and care for. Someone who will always be there.

The serpentine appendages quiver and reach.

"Onja!"

She turns.

"It won't—it won't eat me, will it?"

Onja throws back her head and laughs, a loud guffaw. "You are its mother now. It does not bite the hand which feeds it."

I like the sound of *mother.*

"How do I—take care of it?"

"It will eat bugs and perhaps a small animal which crosses its path when it gets big enough. If you really want it to grow, give it love—talk to it; it will listen and know your soul . . . and give it meat. Raw steak. Four times a day and it will grow like the size of your house in a fast way." She nods, turns, and continues back to her house.

Something touches my breast. It is one of the tree's tentacles. It stirs something inside me, something I've not felt in a long time. "Come now, baby," I say, letting the tentacle curl around my finger; it is cool and muscular. "Let's get you planted."

The tree needs someplace safe, so I choose the spot in the woods at the point where I've often imagined Anna entered; it is far enough in that it is away from Bethany's prying eyes. The tree is not hard to plant at all; even its roots seem to have their own mind, and it practically buries itself when I set it into the hole I've dug. I'm wrapped in a scent like melon and peanut butter.

I go to the market and fill a reusable shopping bag with raw steak, chopped meat, chicken, and pork.

When I return, I haul my bag down to the tree's base; its hairy appendages creep toward my bare ankles. At first my breath leaves me in fear, but then I remember *you are its mother now*, and I hold my ground.

They caress my leg, and warmth penetrates my bones.

They move to the bag of meat. There is hesitation; the tree seems to be aware it cannot eat the plastic and Styrofoam packaging. I tear the sustenance free, and watch as the worm-like things grope to lift it from the ground without much success.

"Here." I gather it in my hands and hold it up. "It's for you. Food."

There is a blast of that melon and peanut butter smell again, something I will eventually translate to mean pleasure. It slides the steak from my palms and places it inside its crown, where it eats.

At first, the tree is only waist high and doesn't consume as much as I'd expected; it is at several pounds per day. But Onja was right; the tree grows so fast that it isn't long before I'm making a daily trip to the market and filling a cart to the brim. Sometimes I clean out one whole section of the meat counter and have to drive to the superstore across town.

The women certainly pay a bit more attention to me now, but it's only in the stores. They rush about with their clingy children at their waists and try to sneak by without talking to me; they don't ask me what I'm doing with all this meat, but occasionally I hear *she's lost her mind, tut-tut, poor dear* and the like drift from the end of the seafood line or the soup aisle. But this doesn't upset me as much as it used to; now, I have the tree, my baby, to take care of, to talk to.

"I don't miss those women anymore," I tell the tree, whom I have given a name—Anah—as I sit at his base and slash open tightly-wrapped packages of raw lamb chops. He is eager today; his tentacles tremble like the tails of excited cats, and the sounds he makes are like the ecstatic whispers of children. Today Anah seems to say, *They aren't like you, Mother. They aren't special. They're just plebian women with plebian children pursuing plebian interests who won't leave anything behind except something else that will die.*

I take a deep breath and pet the spikes of his dark brown mottled trunk. His tentacles coil down and press my cheek. *How could you talk with people who do not understand your loss, your grief? They go smugly about their worthless lives.*

"But I have you now." I pat his jagged bark a bit too hard and slice open my palm; I cry out, and blood drips to the ground.

Anah emits another smell, like plantains and rotten meat. Tenderly a tentacle turns my hand and creeps inchworm-like across the wound. He rolls the tentacle's tip in my blood and places it in the orifice that is his mouth, the inside of which I cannot see, for it is far above my head now. Someday I want to see the inside of his mouth, for I want to understand him as he understands me in this world where no one else does.

⁂

I feel sometimes in the stores that the checkout boys are looking at me, and am terrified that one day I will be out in the parking lot, loading up the van, and that the police will come and ask me what the hell it is I am doing with such a huge quantity of meat. It gets worse when he is up to two and three carts of meat per day, so I buy memberships at wholesale clubs and cruise the circuit within a sixty-mile radius.

I'm so hungry, Mother, he says on the day I have noticed he is as high as the roof of the house.

I offer him a skunk I'd hit with my car.

I need more food than what you give me, Mother, he says. *The animals that wander and the meat you give are not enough to sustain me, and if I don't get enough nutrients, I will die.*

He lowers a trunk-thick tentacle; its tip is brown and withered, its pulsing tonguishness dry, brittle like scorched bark in a wildfired wood. I tell him not to worry; I will devastate the meat counters in every market, superstore, and wholesale club, capture every stray and swipe every roadkill from here to California if I have to, because he is not going to leave me the way my Anna did.

Still, on the quietest of nights, I swear it's the sound of his weeping which drifts through my open bedroom window.

⁂

Bethany's youngest, Kathy, has vanished.

There is the process with which this neighborhood is so familiar: panicked *Have-you-seen?* phone calls. Hysterics. Police. Human chains combing the woods. Search dogs and high-intensity lights fading the night sky to blue. There is yelling and chaos; there are lasagnas and cookies and bottles of wine, and then when it all dies down, I am the only one left Bethany has to talk to, to weep to, and the other women stay away from us, even though Bethany has three other girls. She pays them little mind, now, and is only focused on Kathy, the one that is gone.

Welcome to my world.

The night Kathy disappears, I lie in my bed and swear I hear my Anna talking, perhaps playing with her dolls, inviting them for tea or dressing them up in tiny clothes. I get up to check to see if it's her, but it isn't. This condition lasts for five days. Each day the sounds diminish; each day the noises get weaker, almost as though my Anna is physically dying, or that her ghost is fading from this plane. And each day I go into her room, exactly the same as it was the day she left, to find that it is never her. I tell Bethany that this is what she can expect; she will begin to think she hears Kathy, calling her name.

Anah's illness has abated. I am relieved.

Bethany tries to drop in on me at the worst times, as when I am in the middle of preparing Anah's next meal or bleaching up after it. I don't let her in, making the excuse that the house is simply not in any condition for visitors, and spend a lot of time at her house instead.

"I understand." She motions to her sink. "I can barely do the dishes every day."

Three days before my husband's scheduled return, Anah falls ill again, and this time it is worse. It seems as though by each new feeding another tentacle has begun to brown, wither, split.

I continue to feed Anah. I consider reaching out to Onja. One day, the phone rings. It is Sabrina from down the street.

"Miranda was playing in the yard, and when I went to check on her she was gone! Have you seen her?"

I tell her no, I have not seen Miranda, and I know that by evening the whole missing-child-search process will start all over again, and so I need to hurry and feed Anah before the men with the dogs and the hats are crawling all over the neighborhood, and then it will be me and Bethany spending lots of time at Sabrina's house. We will have our own club.

I go down into the basement where five-year-old Miranda is bound by heavy-gauge rope to a chair; she squirms and tries to jump it a distance from the pile of Kathy's things—her shoes, her dress, her hair bows—in the corner. Miranda is gagged, but I know I will have to knock her out completely so the neighbors won't hear her; I will do what I have to do. Her plump little body plus the meat cuts and roadkill should be enough, at least for now. Bethany has three more girls. Diane has two boys. Sabrina has a son—Miranda's brother—who is almost twelve.

I think of all the other women in the neighborhood, and how soon it will be that we'll see *all* our children's faces on the milk cartons.

Then, at last, we will all understand each other.

THE THING INSIDE

SHE AND REESE had never talked about it, what their dead baby had looked like. They'd both seen it, something Kristina would forever regret, even though she couldn't quite recall the image; it lurked, fuzzy and blurred, at the edge of memory. She remembered blood, lots of it. She remembered a dripping shape. She remembered the feel of Reese's large, hot hand around hers and his screaming, as well as a foreign sound that had left her wondering why the doctors had let a tortured cat into the room.

Then she'd realized the sound had been coming from her own mouth.

They'd tried to discuss it, a couple of times, but the words had remained unspoken. Then, when she'd gotten pregnant again, that'd been the burial of any further attempt.

Now, as she sat in the passenger seat of their Grand Cherokee and watched the fleeting Texas landscape as they trundled toward Austin, she wondered what was truly ahead. During the earliest weeks of this second pregnancy she'd fallen into catastrophic depression, spending hours in what would have been their son's bedroom, all painted robin's egg and graced with spruce furniture and stuffed bunnies. It was then Reese had decided they needed a new environment, someplace in which they could both pack that horrifying undefined visual in a cardboard box and forget about it.

"You comfortable? You're quiet," he said.

"I'm fine." She rested her hand on her protruding stomach. "*We're* fine. This is just . . . very different."

"Far cry from New York." He reached over, set his hand on her knee. "No more dark skies. Well, once these fires clear."

Despite the promise of sun, they hadn't chosen Austin; it had chosen them. Reese had agreed to stop firefighting. His brother's position in the state Fire Protection Office had secured him a desk job processing certifications, and as several thousand acres had been burning for months due to the drought, he was guaranteed overtime. Their new brick house wasn't too far outside the city, in Bastrop, close enough to conveniences but isolated enough so Kristina would have peace. Everything had fallen into place so quickly, so cleanly, it'd felt perfect. But the dense gray smoke chunneling in the distance, the thick smell of hot tar, soot, and mesquite coming through the A/C vents, and the taste in her mouth—left from when they'd passed the carcass of a charred cow and she'd made him stop the car so that she could get sick under the relentless August sun—was changing her opinion.

She shifted in her seat. "Can we stop? I just feel like I could use . . . a cold drink."

He eyed her.

"Like juice! Just juice."

His gaze lingered before returning to the road. "Sure. Soon as we see someplace."

A Mobil station sign glowed against the smoke from the distant fires, and she laughed at her own surprise—she'd expected some decrepit shack plastered with antelope skulls. *See,* she thought, *this is gonna be fine.*

Reese pulled into a slot next to the handicapped space.

She reached for her door handle.

"I'll get it." He whipped the keys from the ignition, climbed out and went around.

"I'm not crippled, you know."

"Every little bit helps." He held out his hand. She took it and stepped onto the pavement, noticing it felt soft.

The place was just like every other chain—fluorescent lighting, immaculate tiles, aisles rainbowed with Nutter Butters, Pringles, Oreos; the faint smell of burnt coffee and cherry cleaner.

Reese squeezed and released her hand. "I'm going to get the bathroom key. Do you need it?"

"No, but give me a minute." She'd had no problems with incontinence during her last pregnancy; this time, it had started almost immediately.

He kissed her on the cheek. "Get me a root beer."

She heard him talking to the cashier while she, not knowing what she wanted, headed toward the back of the store. She neared a long waist-high bin and stopped; inside, the Lone Star and Dos Equis beer cans on ice gleamed like rubies, emeralds, and topaz. She had never been a beer drinker, but on a day like today, one would've been a godsend.

She moved on, reaching the coolers and grabbing his root beer. She settled on a cranberry juice, made her way to the counter and rummaged through her satchel for some cash. When she looked up to hand her bills to a gangly, flannel-shirted kid behind the counter, what caught her eye was the giant, furry, mounted head of what looked to be a rabbit with antlers growing out of its skull.

Its malicious stare startled her.

"What *is* that?"

He looked surprised and stroked his immature excuse for a beard. "You never seen one?"

She smiled politely. "No, we're new to the area. Moving to Bastrop."

"Well, that's a jackalope." He tapped in a few numbers on the register, which emitted high-pitched beeps. "Cross between a jackrabbit and an antelope."

She laughed but realized it was more out of nervousness than anything else. "Interesting. Nice sense of humor you've got down here."

He frowned. "No, they're real. My brother, he's a big dude at UT at Austin, he studies 'em."

The register drawer sprang open and she heard the *schwick-schwick* of her change scraping against the molded plastic.

He put the change in her hand. "See, they're actually just these rabbits all infected with this virus, it's like a papa-whatever, sorta the same shit that causes cervical cancer, and they all end up like that, all rabid and with horns growin' outta their heads. They're mean, they imitate people's voices, and they get pretty big, too."

She dropped the change in her wallet, anxious to get away from him and the thing. She was sure it was watching her.

He leaned over the counter and lowered his voice: "You know, some stupid town in Wyoming claims it's the capital for jackalopes, but they've got nothing on us. The state park in Bastrop, plenty of places for jacks to live there. Wyoming only says that because what the fuck else they got? That skeleton volcano or something?"

Apparently, she thought, *he's never seen* Close Encounters. "Devil's Tower, you mean."

"Yeah, right," he said. "Devil's Tower."

She looked at the beast again and shuddered. Something was tugging at her, but she didn't know what. Had she seen something like this on one of those shows, like the *In Search Of*s she used to watch when she was a kid?

"Thanks." She grabbed both drinks and started to the door. "I'll be sure to steer clear of them."

"They *are* real, you know," Gangly Kid called after her. "They even got a Latin name. Things that aren't real don't get Latin names." He twisted his body under the overhang where the cigarettes were stowed and pointed to a gold plaque on the mount. "Le-pus tem-pera-men-talis."

"Thanks," she repeated, because she didn't know what else to say. Then she sat in the Jeep. She watched Reese come out of the bathroom, go inside, come back out again. When he climbed into the driver's seat, she was grateful.

"Did that kid say anything to you in there?" she asked.

"No. Why? He say something to you?"

She cracked open his root beer, passed it to him, and filled him in on her encounter. "Did you see it?"

Reese shook his head and backed the Jeep out of the lot. "No."

"It was gross. It was all . . . deformed."

He stopped the car and looked at her, and she felt that familiar tension that signaled she'd gotten too close to the flame. There'd been a lot of those moments lately.

"Don't," he said at last. "Just don't. Just a weird kid, that's all."

Then he jammed into first gear and they were moving again, but no matter how many more disturbing sights they passed— clouds of smoke, the occasional burnt animal—she couldn't get the leer of that jackalope out of her mind.

✦✦✦

Their new house was much as she'd recalled, brick-faced and large-windowed, but the grass was dead, and the once-lush mesquites loosed brittle leaves. The tangled branches reminded her of that . . . *thing*'s antlers, and it didn't look as though the trees in the woods surrounding 2nd Avenue's houseless cul-de-sac had fared much better.

"Home sweet home." Reese busied himself with his keys. "Wait here. I'm going to open us up."

She watched him approach their stained-glass front door and noticed something else: the potted bushes on the stoop were also dead.

She heard rustling and turned toward it: the cul-de-sac. There, at the edge of the woods, a cat-sized, brown *something* moved.

Her breath caught in her throat.

It turned to look at her. It was a jackrabbit. Just a normal jackrabbit, chewing thoughtfully. She chided herself. Of course there were going to be rabbits. The realtor had said there was lots of wildlife, and beyond the woods was a lake, and there was a nice state park—

The state park in Bastrop, plenty of places for jacks to live there.

She heard the *thwuck* of the front door. "We're in!" Reese yelled.

Startled, the rabbit leapt into the woods.

Reese emerged, opening the back of the Jeep.

"How far are we from the state park, exactly?" She reached for a box marked KITCHEN.

"Oh, no. You're not carrying a damn thing." He waved her away, hefted the box into his arms. "The park's a few miles north. Why?"

"No reason."

He eyed her with what she took to be mistrust.

She followed him into the house, but when the smell of varnish and fresh paint nearly overwhelmed her, she stopped.

Reese put the box on the counter. "You okay?"

"Yeah, I just—strong smell." She took a deep breath. "It didn't bother me when we saw the house."

"'Cause you're further along now. Come here." He settled his arms around her. "It's going to be different this time. You'll see."

She kissed him on the mouth, grateful for the taste of him, like root beer and pine. It'd seemed to her like months since they'd really enjoyed each other; after she'd gotten pregnant again the whole focus had been on being careful, taking it easy, keeping her calm, and, finally, moving. They leaned against each other in the quiet and then she heard, from somewhere, *thump.*

She pulled away from him. "What was that?"

He shrugged. "Acorn or something on the roof. House is only one floor, remember?"

They'd purposely chosen a one story; Reese hadn't wanted her climbing stairs this time around.

Still, something didn't seem right, and even though she was grateful she'd never have to worry again about getting the call that he'd been killed on the job, she wished he didn't have to start work for at least a week so she could settle in before being alone all day . . .

It's going to be different this time, like he said. Don't you trust him?

"Now." He rubbed her arms. "I'm starving. Don't suppose anyone delivers subs out here."

She laughed. "I don't suppose anyone delivers *decent* subs out here. Maybe we should settle for barbecue."

"Too spicy for you."

"No," she said. "I think I'm craving it, actually."

She heard it again: *thump.*

She trusted him. She just wasn't sure if she trusted herself.

❧❦❧

It wasn't as if there was nothing to do, but during the day Kristina still wished she weren't alone. She emptied boxes, stowed towels, organized pots and pans, and decorated their bathroom with the Caribbean-themed ensemble populated by festive (*frankly, creepy*) stick figures that Reese had bought with cheer-up intentions.

The house was almost too open; there were so many windows that from any room she could see the lawn and surrounding woods. The Texas light was different from the light in New York, however. There, afternoons were soft gray, chick, or lavender; here, they were golden-olive-rust: if heat had a color, this was it. There was something stark about it, stark and unforgiving. Even the shadows were too bright.

They hadn't brought much furniture, because Reese wanted new things, and she hoped they would buy them soon, because despite her unpacking, her footsteps still echoed. In a vain attempt to absorb sound, she left emptied boxes in the rooms instead of shuffling them to the garage. She'd just finished the few in their bedroom when she found one Reese had top-shelfed in their master walk-in. When she reached for it, she couldn't quite grab it, and it crashed to the floor and broke open.

Out spilled the baby clothes she'd gotten at her shower.

She remembered that morning, being caught off guard not because her few friends had surprised her, but because, in her superstitious family, no one *ever* threw a shower before the birth—it was considered bad luck. At first, she'd faked her glee; eventually, though, the tiny booties, burp cloths, and elephant-and-bunny patterned jumpers had assuaged her discomfort, and by the end of the day she'd been *excited*.

Now, however, she reacted to the pile of still-tagged clothes as she would a litter of dead kittens. She sank to her knees, her sobs bouncing off the pristine walls, shiny floors, polished countertops.

She'd calmed down and had just resolved to get a trash bag when a movement caught her eye.

Out on the lawn.

She stood, wiped her eyes, peered out the window.

Blinking back at her was a rabbit the size of an adult golden retriever.

An adult golden retriever with antlers.

She froze, fearful that it could leap at her and break through the glass.

Its expression seemed to change. As though it had emotion, as though it could read her mind and was thrilled that she felt threatened. It opened its mouth and snarled at her, baring several dagger-like teeth.

She bolted for the bathroom, yanked down the blinds, locked the door, and perched on the edge of the tub. For a moment, the flamingo and chili stick figures on the shower curtain seemed to move, but she wasn't going back out there. She'd wait here until Reese came home—

She felt a gush between her legs.

She'd wet herself.

Well, I can't sit here soaked.

She ventured into the hall and through every room, cautiously creeping up on each window from the side, in case it was waiting.

It wasn't.

She recalled the jackrabbit outside the woods the day before. *Silly. Your eyes are blurry with tears; those probably really weren't antlers but sticks or something and you got confused.*

She pulled fresh clothes and while she was showering decided not to mention the creature to Reese.

This became increasingly difficult over the next few days. At night, she'd startle awake and out the window spot what she'd swear were two or three of the beasts back by the line of trees, watching her. When she took out the garbage, she'd catch a fleeting swatch of fur ducking around the house. The thumping on the roof became frequent. And sometimes, when she was in the bathroom, she'd hear scratching on the other side of the wall.

Finally, one night at dinner, she said something.

"Jackalopes, huh?"

"Yes." She focused on a piece of lettuce in her bowl. "I told you all about them at—"

"I know what you told me." He set down his fork, wiped his mouth with his napkin. "Last time it was trolls, Kristina."

"But—"

He reached across the table, set a hand on hers. "You want me to check around the house?"

She nodded.

He found nothing; he'd even waited up at night. The thumping continued, and each time they heard it, he'd gone to check and discovered only acorns. Yet during the day, she still saw jackalopes—more of them, even, and babies, too. Once, she pulled down every blind in the house, but all that yielded was the sight of their shadows, following her from room to room.

Reese became increasingly impatient.

"I checked everywhere. The garage. Back by the well. Even a few hundred feet into the woods. There's nothing. It's how pregnancy affects you, and I know you're spooked, but maybe you could leave the TV on during the day to keep you company. Or go out."

"It would help if I weren't here alone all the time," she argued. "They didn't say you were going to be in that office seven days a week."

He opened the fridge, grabbed a root beer, and cracked it open. "I have to be. The state's in crisis. Everything's burning. Hopefully it's just for a bit longer."

But she knew what she was seeing wasn't caused by her pregnancy, and the next day she Googled *Ways to Get Rid of Jackalopes*.

She learned that the female's milk was medicinal. That they only gave birth during lightning storms. That they were masters at mimicry, even of a person's voice. That they were shy (*my ass*) unless approached (*and then God help you*). But all she had to do to capture them so she could kill them was put out bowls of whiskey and wait until they were too drunk to move.

Whiskey.

Jack Daniels, her old, comforting . . . dangerous friend.

She hadn't drunk much during her last pregnancy—at least not that she remembered. At first, she'd only taken a couple of sips here and there because of that burning need she could neither ignore nor defeat. Then she'd down a glass at noon to get the edge off the loneliness, the fear of that call telling her Reese wasn't coming home. She'd exchanged that for a couple just after he left for work, so she could focus on the household chores; later, she'd added just one glass after he was asleep, to knock herself out. It hadn't added up to much. Not really.

And the women in her family had always spoken the truth, that there was a membrane that protected the baby, so she hadn't been drinking enough to cause . . .

You swore to him you wouldn't touch another drop.

She wouldn't. This wasn't for her.

This was for those damn jackalopes.

A round trip to the Rite Aid liquor aisle later, Mr. Jack Daniels was eyeing her.

She looked away. *No. No. No.*

She went to the cupboard, grabbed a Tupperware bowl for the bait, opened the bottle, and poured.

God, it smelled delicious. The cleansing sting of alcohol, charred wood . . . a hint of maple.

Have some. Just a sip, said a voice in her head.

No. She stopped pouring.

Come on, said the voice. *You'll feel so much better.*

I said no. She opened the microwave, set the bowl inside, and slammed the door shut.

"Walk away," she spoke aloud. "Walk away, pull yourself together, and then you can put the bait outside."

But she didn't walk away. She stood, staring at the open bottle.

And then she found herself rummaging in the cabinets for anything she could use as a rocks glass. Reese had tossed them long ago, so all she found was a Pyrex measuring cup. She looked back at Jack, then into the cup, which had markings: 2 OZ, 4 OZ, 6 OZ. She could have two ounces, just two.

Relief awaits you inside, a nice cold drink that understands you when no one else does . . .

She opened the freezer, seized the ice cubes, listened to their soothing music as they hit the glass.

Now, the voice had changed its opinion: *You promised.*

It's no big deal, she argued back.

"It was no big deal last time either, was it? And look what happened," Reese's voice echoed from the empty foyer.

Shit! The one day he'd come home early! "I was getting a glass of—"

No one.

"Reese?"

No response.

"Reese? Are you home?"

Not a sound.

She rushed to the garage door. It was open, but there was no Jeep. He wasn't around. No one else was in the house . . .

But the garage door had been open. Her eyes drifted to the pages she'd printed about the jackalope: *masters of mimicry, including the human voice.*

. . . except maybe one of them. In her house.

A flickering near the trash caught her eye, and she heard a low growl.

There.

A jackalope. A littler grayer than the one at the gas station, but one nonetheless. Staring, baring, snarling.

Another *thump* on the roof.

A second one appeared.

They upset the garbage cans, which shifted with hollow thuds—

—and then there were three. The one that appeared to lead the pack was the golden retriever-sized creature she'd seen around; a thread of mucus dangled from the corner of its mouth.

They advanced.

She dove through the door and slammed it, backing against the wood, her chest aching as she struggled against what felt like an inflated balloon inside her.

She beheld the J.D. on the counter. Still. Absolutely still, quiet, as what she imagined an ash-buried landscape might be like.

Clink!

She jumped.

An ice cube in the Pyrex had melted, shifting.

Don't drink any. You need every drop to get those fuckers drunk. There were three, they were big, and one fucking fifth of J.D. might not be enough.

But suppose it was. Once they were wasted, how would she slay them?

A knife.

There were knives in the house, somewhere. Reese had packed them away, hidden them in those dark weeks between the stillbirth and the new conception, forced them both to use plastic knives. But he wouldn't have thrown them away, she knew that. They were probably in one of the kitchen boxes.

She eyed the first box he'd brought in; he'd placed it near the back slider, stacked others on top of it.

That's the one.

Thump. Thump.

They were trying to get in.

The thumping became banging became shuddering, and she turned to the door, squeezed her eyes shut and pushed with everything—

"Are you kidding me?"

Reese's voice.

She slowed her breathing, opened her eyes.

"I said, are you kidding me, Kristina? Are you *fucking* kidding me?"

She turned.

It was him. He was standing next to the counter, holding up the open bottle of J.D.

She was still panting but managed, "Oh, no, I'm not drinking—"

"I can't believe you're pulling this shit again!" He brought the bottle down against the marble counter. Glass and brown liquid fountained to the tile, but he'd only broken the bottle's neck. He slammed it down, chest heaving.

Her face burned. "But I'm not! I'm not! I swear, it's—"

"It's what, Kristina? What?"

Still shaky, she swiped the printouts from the counter, thrust them at him. "Here!"

He rolled his eyes. "We've been through this, Kristina. Last time—"

She couldn't stand it anymore; her flesh crawled. "That's because I was *drinking* last time, okay? I admit it, I was a drunk, but this time I'm not! The kid at the gas station said these things are real and vicious and they imitate people's voices and I heard you talking when you weren't here and there's been *growling*, and *banging*, and I see them all the time in the yard and they stalk—"

"Stop!"

For a moment, there was only the sound of her breathing.

He said, "Okay, I'll bite. What's the whiskey for?"

She cleared her throat, read: "It is believed a jackalope can be caught by putting whiskey outside. It will drink and become intoxicated, and then you can capture it without it mauling you to death." She turned the text to face him. "Wikipedia, see?"

He crossed his arms. "A fifth."

"They're really big. But they're so big I don't think even a fifth's going to be enough."

He nodded, pressing his lips together. "And what are you going to do when you catch them?"

"Kill them." She felt a pain in her lower back, rubbed it. "They could kill the baby, Reese. We can't have this."

He just stood, and she was relieved: he believed her.

Then his expression darkened. He grabbed the broken bottle, marched to the sink, and poured the booze down the drain.

She panicked. "No! Don't! We need—"

He smashed the bottle against the porcelain basin and glowered at her. "Do you think I'm an asshole?"

The phrase felt like a slap. "No—"

"You. Promised."

"I—"

"I. Nothing. You think I *wanted* to stop fighting fires? You think I *wanted* to move all the way down here?"

"You—"

"Bullshit, Kristina! I gave up doing something I loved to get the pressure off you so you wouldn't drink and our baby might have a brain!"

The words hit her full in the stomach. "What?"

"Our baby had anencephaly. No brain, no spinal cord. Whatever was there looked like raw giblets. Thank God it was born dead!"

She fought the bile rising in the back of her throat, succeeded when she stopped trying to picture it. She took a deep breath, could barely eke: "But you said you didn't remember eith—"

"I fucking remember! Of *course* I fucking remember, I hadn't spent the previous nine months drunk off my ass! It was horrifying, Kristina! It's burned into my brain! Right here!" He pressed his thumb to his forehead. "I see it when I sleep! I see it all day long! And I see it when I look at you!"

He stormed from the room, slamming their bedroom door so hard the house shimmied.

She collapsed to her knees and threw up.

When her head cleared, she desperately wanted J.D., and lamented its loss.

Then she remembered the bowl in the microwave, and for the first time, something else: her baby's swollen, misshapen head (*aliens in* Close Encounters): one eye lidless, the other the size of a tangerine; a bulging, plum-colored cheek and the smell of rancid meat and alcohol.

She set her hand on her stomach. No. Not this time.

She toed into the bathroom and curled in the tub.

The creepy Caribbean stick figures felt like old friends.

⁂

She woke up in their bed, and from the light, she could tell it was afternoon; the glowing red letters on the clock confirmed nearly four. She called for Reese, but there was no answer; she padded into the kitchen, dimly recalling it was Sunday of Labor Day weekend but glad, for once, he was at work.

The broken J.D. bottle was gone, the spilled whiskey had been wiped away, the Pyrex was upside down in the dish drainer.

Thump.

Scratch, scratch.

Had Reese found the bowl?

She opened the microwave door, relieved for the sweet whiff of burnt maple. The bowl was there. Still half full.

She reached for it, set it down on the counter.

Her cell phone. Ringing.

Reese.

"Listen to me. There's a brand new fire, like an hour ago. Just north of the state park, not far from the house. This one's a storm, and it's moving fast. We're being evacuated."

She pulled up the blinds. A thin haze of gray smoke filtered the sun. *At least it's not so bright anymore.*

"Honey?"

"I'm here."

"Pack. Essentials, grab only essentials. I'm on my way, I'm coming to get you out of there, okay?"

At the edge of the woods, there were seven pairs of eyes. Their owners were hopping furiously toward the house.

You won't have time to get them drunk, now. You're going to have to do this the hard way.

She went to the kitchen.

The hard way.

With a little lube to help.

No.

"Honey?"

Yes. You have no choice. Just a little bit. It won't hurt anything. Not just this once.

"Kristina?"

"Yup." She balanced the phone between her shoulder and ear and lifted the bowl to her lips.

"I'm sorry about last night. What I said."

She took a long swallow. And another. God, it was like hot honey on a sore throat. "I know."

"Just pack."

"I will."

She hung up. The smell of fire was in the air, all right, but she felt calm.

She returned to the living room. The jackalopes had multiplied; a raft of them was gaining ground.

The knives. Find them.

From the kitchen pile she hurled one box after another aside until she got to the last one. She struggled with the tape, destroyed the box cover; inside, stacks of Bubble-Wrapped packages.

Thump, thump, thump

She glanced into the living room. Outside, clouds of smoke blacked the sun.

The fire was coming. And so were they.

She started to cough, grabbing bundle after bundle, tearing into the plastic with her untrimmed nails: soap dish, pitcher, cutting board—

At last. The expensive boning knife. She was getting somewhere. Where was the chef's knife—

She heard the shattering of glass in the living room. The jackalopes funneled through the window and swarmed her.

The big one poised on her stomach. She felt its asthmatic breathing and low growling, like the purr of a rabid cat, in her body. A bloody thread of mucus dripped from the corner of its mouth onto her shirt.

Her hands trembled. *Do it, thrust the knife into it right now and this will all be over . . .*

The thing snarled savagely. She felt its pressure on her belly, on her baby, smelled something like mold—

It was about to go for her throat.

She raised the knife as high as she could and came down on it.

Labor-like pain splintered her innards. She opened her eyes.

There was no jackalope.

There was only the knife thrust deep into her rounded belly, blood geysering to the shiny floors.

DECONSTRUCTING FIREFLIES

Co-written with Nathan D. Schoonover

MY SON LIKES to take things apart, and perhaps before The Shortage mothers would've written this off as the typical penchant of boys. But mothers before The Shortage did not live on farms populated by Barn Boys who camped out in the old cement milk house, doing dickens with the whiskey. Mothers before The Shortage did not have to listen to the Barn Boys howling at night as they rewire the chickens and make bets on how fast they can get them to lay eggs before the birds' hard ruby eyes roll back in their heads and their feather coverings catch fire in a rain of sparks. Mothers before The Shortage did not have to worry about husbands with byrotechnic degrees teaching their sons that harming the animals is okay—not only do we just breed more in the laboratory, but the metal they're made from prevents them from feeling pain.

Jigger, Hap, and Lair are not the worst my husband could've found for Barn Boys, despite the influence they've had on little Nate. They spend their days doing useful things: oiling the pigs' joints when the mud seeps through their skin; feeding the cows and fine-tuning the chickens' groins so there's enough eggs down the market shelves, which keeps us out of trouble with the government. They fix the tractors and keep the plumbing running smoothly. They till the fields every day without having to be told, and they know which chemicals enhance the growth rate of which plants. All of that's good: there's little time for policing. We're responsible for feeding all of Cleghern. Have been ever since the Collier farm over in Newton burned to the ground last year. Collier had such lazy Barn Boys, you see, that the man himself had to waste his afternoons baling hay and shearing the meat off the cow frames. He could only keep up with his lab production late in the p.m., and one November midnight he passed out from exhaustion and knocked into the AutoWeld. When it tipped over, the whole place went up.

Still, it's at night I really worry about what goes on by the single burning lamp behind the milk house's shoddy window. If I have to ensure my husband stored my grandmother's oak-frame bed or Spode china out of harm's way, I go down in daylight. I wouldn't want to be around the boys at dusk, because that's when the booze comes out. You see, gargantuan Jigger, hat-headed Hap and hairy Lair, since they don't have dental insurance or go to the doctor much, attribute their rock-solid teeth and robust health to the unique blend of ingredients brewing in the homemade still.

Despite what I do, little Nate is always down there at that hour. He is fascinated that Jigger doesn't use the message pad to summon the cows: he calls them in to pen by just cupping his hands on either side of his smeary mouth and making a noise through the neat hole above his upper lip—a hole, he claims, put there by his daddy's stubbing out a cigarette when he was my son's age. At least, that's what he told Nate, who believed it with all his heart and came running to tell me. Nate's very bright, but he's impressionable, and after that he'd asked Jayce, "Could you make a cigarette hole in my upper lip?" Of course, that was out of the question, so the only unsavory habit he's been allowed to pick up from Jigger is taking things apart.

Little Nate is obsessed with the workings of the farm—not how things are done, but how things are *un*done. How the milk gets drained from the cow's udder; how the big hay rolls get cubed down into bales; how the thin layers of skin over the cow frames are shorn free and become steaks next to his father's six-egg breakfast in the morning; how Hap dissects a distributor cap. He'll watch the boys clean their stunners, and then come inside and seize something—my mixer, my blender, or the kerosene lantern, for example—and take it apart. He doesn't hang around to watch anything go back together, which is why I spend my afternoons, when I'm not choring, reassembling. But Sunday morning, he took apart his bedroom lamp and shrieked while I scrambled like a short-circuited cockroach and barely pulled it together before the dark fell. Now that he's torn apart that lamp four mornings in a row, I'll have to curtail his time with the Barn Boys.

Saturday was Sporting Day, and Jigger, Hap and Lair went hunting. Jayce had created a couple of eighteen-point bucks, as I recall, and that's what they were after, but they've got an endless amount of time to hunt since there doesn't need to be a deer season anymore—people like my husband just keep filling the woods. I think, honestly, Jayce spends too much time breeding herds just so he can keep his good Barn Boys around and sharp. That day, though, they didn't get that eighteen-pointer. They brought home a dozen bucks, all between four and twelve points. We're supposed to refurbish the deer frames, heads and all, to use them for next year's herd. So when they carted them all in on the back of the flatbed truck, singing like young men who had just experienced sex for the first time, little Nate ran out to see.

The boys spread the carcasses out on the lawn and dragged them down to the butchering slab to disassemble them: shear off the skin and meat, tear out the wires, and chop off the heads. I looked out the kitchen window and saw Nate standing there, far enough away so he wouldn't be showered with guts, watching. And it was the *way* he was watching, unmoving, the early summer breeze twitching small pieces of his blond hair, that made me stop peeling the onions.

The boys hurled the heads into a pile on the side, and from a distance, it looked like caramel raisin pudding. I shuddered. There was something sad in those eyes—even if they were just diamonds underneath the coal-colored LiquiGel Jayce uses. I wondered what the last image their eyes registered could've been. A field of sunflowers? A white moth? Did it hurt when the bullet ripped through their flesh coverings?

Jayce swears it doesn't, but I know better because he makes them with nerves. They feel something, I'm sure.

Jigger crouched down, pointed to the pile and spread his hands wide, shaking his head, and I wondered if little Nate asked him if he was gonna take the heads apart. I expected the boys would soak them in solvent. That's what you do to clean the skulls before refurbishment: you just let them soak until the brains, eyes and sinews turn to mush and only the metal frames are left. But they didn't. They piled the heads onto a large tarp and dragged them over to the cold cellar, a stone structure built into the hill next to the house. Hap climbed up and Lair gripped the heads in his stubby-fingered hands as Jigger lit up a corn silk cigarette. They lined up the heads in a row on the roof. They were going to let those heads rot and fester and smell in the sun for three weeks and let nature and the maggots take care of most of it.

Little Nate came bounding inside and dashed up to his room. It overlooks the cold cellar, which meant he was going to see those heads in the morning when he woke up and at night before he went to sleep. At bedtime, I tried to settle down with Jayce, but instead of seeing his wiry gray hairs bend in my breath, I saw those vacant, soulless eyes staring at little Nate, clutching his toy screwdriver as he slept.

I decided I didn't want those things eyeing him, so I crept into his room, carefully avoiding the litter of rusty farm tools and pieces of old cars Hap lets him have, and flicked on the lamp. I squinted my eyes to try to see the deer on top of the cellar, and thankfully, the room's reflection on the glass had curtained them for the moment.

On Sunday, the dawning of God's day, the lamp incident happened. It has happened every morning since.

I figure it'll pass, but it doesn't. Every morning Nate awakens, takes the lamp apart, and forgets about it until before dusk. Then he cries that the lamp must be back together before nightfall: "They'll come in, Mommy! But they'll stay!" While he screams, I scramble to get the lamp reassembled before Jayce returns and starts yelling about how things that cost him good credits are being treated around this house. Usually, I haven't even put the lamp back together entirely correctly: the harp is bent, the shade's akilter, the socket's crooked on the base, and the wires are exposed so it might even spark in the night and set the peeling wallpaper ablaze. Then I tuck little Nate into bed, but he can't fall asleep with the light on. However, I suspect if he wakes in the middle of the night to a dark room, he'll start shrieking when he gets a look at those heads. So after he's asleep, I creep back into the room and switch on the lamp.

Supper is late tonight because I thwarted another lamp incident before finishing the venison. I set Jayce's plate down in front of him and rummage in the drawer of the old metal cabinet—one that's outlived its usefulness in the lab—for a knife and fork.

"That was quite a lot of nice venison we got on Saturday," I broach the subject.

"Yeah." Jayce lifts his utensils. "This looks good. New formula's an improvement over last year."

I hate the way he speaks of the meals that include meat. It makes them sound about as appetizing as motor oil.

"Might want to get used to lots of stew, loaf, and pie," he says. Outside, I hear the Barn Boys yowling, and I wonder if they've started their dickens early tonight. "After what the boys brought in on Saturday, we're going to be eating it into next summer."

He sets down his knife and considers me with a solid gray eye. "What's the matter, babe? You having problems with them killing things again? I can tell them to do any more slicing and dicing down at the slab past the corn field, so you don't have to see it."

I hate the way he brings that up all the time, too. While it's true that since the miscarriage I haven't exactly been keen on watching them slaughter animals, it has nothing to do with the fact that I understand this is what we do with our lives. We create or slaughter, we donate or eat.

"No, I don't have a problem with that," I say. "What I have a problem with is the heads on the roof of the cold cellar and the stink. Why can't they just soak the damn things in Postmort?" I sit in the rickety chair across from Jayce and pick up my fork. The handle is slowly twisting off it. I reach for the cloth napkin and unfold it across my lap.

"That's not the way Jigger likes to do things, Ilse." He shoves in a mouthful of creamed chipped venison. It'd looked delicious when I'd set it on the table, but the thought of the deer's brains and the white film of maggots in them has repulsed me. "They like to do things natural."

I get up from the table and take my plate to the porcelain sink, which is due up for its monthly bleach and rebugging. "There's very little that's natural anymore."

He shrugs. "Natural won't work. Cloning the whole animal takes too long." He sips his tea. "These were older models anyway. I'm not even going to refurbish them this time around. I'm coming up with a faster, sleeker design. Just let them have their fun."

"It's sick and unnecessary."

"Ilse, I told Jigger the boys could keep these as trophies."

The bugs in the sink stretch their elasticized arms and grip pieces of venison from my plate. It's always bothered me that although they're metal, they never seem to lose their appetite; when they hear the clank of the plates against the porcelain, they emerge like feisty snakes and snatch their meals. But that's why Jayce traded for them: they're expedient models that leave no trace, and the fines for wasting food these days are pretty high.

I'm sick of the metal beasts. "And where are they going to put those ghastly things?"

"Probably on top of the milk house," he says.

I shiver. "When people come in the driveway, that's the first thing they're gonna see."

"I know. But they're proud of 'em. These are trophies, honey. And good trophies means they'll stay around longer."

"I don't like little Nate staring at those things. Do they have to be across from his room? Could they set them elsewhere?"

"It's really the best place. The sun shines intense and hot there. There's no shade." He lifts his glass of orange juice; for the first time, I notice he's got a gut. A small one, but it's there. I should cut the sugar out of his diet, but it probably wouldn't do any good since I know he has a few nips of bourbon in the lab. I don't care that he drinks, as long as he keeps the production up and doesn't take the habit out on us.

"Well, Sunday while you were in town doing the goat thing, he took apart his lamp and couldn't get it back together. Which was fine, until the sun started to pull down and he was screaming and crying," I say.

Jayce sets down the glass and burps. "His light's been on every night. He's afraid of the dark, that's why he's throwin' a fit."

"No." I turn on the water to rinse off the now picked-clean dish. "*I've* been putting his light on. If it's on, he can't see the deer heads. He can only see his own reflection."

"Well, stop doing that. You're probably freaking him out. He's thinking there's ghosts in here, or God knows what." Jayce is gentle; although I imagine in his mind he's muttering, *Foolish woman, your silly ideas,* he won't say it. He just frowns, squeezes a piece of overdone toast in his fingers, slaloms it through the gravy, and pops it in his mouth. A dollop of juice dribbles over the gold band on his fourth finger. "Kid might not cut it as a byrotechnic. Not the way he's going." He takes another mouthful of his venison. A chunk drops from his chin to the plate. "Maybe I should start having him spend time with me in the lab."

That thought doesn't appeal to me, either. So he'll grow up like Jayce, putting things together with no sensitivity? I cast my eyes to the sink. The bugs have retreated to the drain now, but their pointed appendages have left gray scratches in the porcelain that'll have to be buffed away before next inspection. "I never should've let him watch them disassemble those deer."

"I told you, it's a good thing for him to get used to seeing. If he doesn't make byrotechnics, he'll be a great Barn Boy. He'll always have work."

I look out the window. The boys aren't in the milk house yet: Lair's sitting on a log, brushing his long hair with what looks like a couple of tines of old pitchfork, shortened and re-formed; Hap's knelt down on the old well cover, blocking his hat with a brick; Jigger spits. "That's what I'm afraid of."

He pushes his plate away and stands up, comes over to me, sets his hands on my hips and kisses the back of my neck. He smells like ammonia, burning hair and a faint something else, his characteristic musk that makes me think of the seven ferrets, his first projects, that we kept in the upstairs room before little

Nate was born. I feel him sigh against my back. "Do you have plans tomorrow?"

I think. Just the usual chores, maybe some shopping. "Not really."

"Why don't you take him to the zoo for the day?"

The zoo, where Jayce gets the DNA. The zoo is the last bastion of live animals. Well, live totally *organic* animals. The ones that aren't extinct. Each state has one zoo—there aren't enough natural creatures to fill more than that—well, except for Wyoming. Not as many things died there, I guess.

Jayce toys with a curl of my hair, which has sprouted a few grays. In the mirror, when I see them, they remind me of spring dandelions in the field. "It'll reinforce that the things we slaughter here aren't real beasts, not really, and that'll make him feel better. Maybe it'll even inspire him to come and watch me assemble things."

I don't see how this will make little Nate feel better, because he'll just go and see the deer and then come home and see those empty, haunted, soulless eyes staring at him in the night. But I concede.

✾❀✾

We're naturally up early around here, so I load little Nate in the truck, along with a couple of sandwiches, thirty credits and the Farmers' Card and start the long drive across the state.

The zoo is expansive, as open and wide as the photos I've seen of Africa. We stroll through the aviary. The rocks are spattered with bird waste, and I reach out to touch it. There are still germs, but I don't let that stop me. I haven't seen bird crap since I was a little girl, and looking at it makes my eyes hurt because it is good and real, the kind of good that oatmeal would be after not having tasted it in a dozen years. The Inca terns, their feet bright as poppy petals, move so differently. Warm, squirming, lighter than the ones Jayce makes, and their sounds are notes that make songs, not pre-programmed tunes with clicks at their conclusions.

The bellies of the Siberian tigers sway when they pad across the grass and plunge into their man-made pond, swatting at fish with their paws. To watch them eat, the twist of their heads in one, smooth motion, makes me long for a cat. Not the cat Jayce made me—pretty and white and puffy and perfect Katrina—but a cat. One that still knows when it's hungry because its stomach tells it, not because the timer in its brain has gone off.

In the reptile house there are matamata turtles, their flattened heads maneuvering like leaves at the bottom of the spring where we draw the water, and little Nate laughs, because, he says, "The leaves have eyes!" He presses his hands flat against the glass.

"Mommy, will their eye coverings come off? Do they have diamonds or cobalts or emeralds or rubies?"

"Those," I say, crouching down, "are real eyes. Like ours. When the animal dies, they will rot clean through and there'll be nothing left."

A keeper in khaki goes to the right of the diorama all decked out with fake giant fronds and dirt. He opens the door, and there's a musk-wet-mold smell like carpet in a flooded basement, and that, too, brings me back to that time when there were turtles. Real turtles you could keep in a terrarium. I had a little snapping turtle. Pappy. Pappy the snapping turtle. When The Shortage came, we had to eat him.

I buy little Nate an ice cream at the stand disguised as a giant butterfly. Within a few minutes, vanilla ice cream and strawberry sauce coat his chin. He points to the camouflage-netted dome rising like a giant egg behind a tangled gateway of branches. *Insect World*, the sign announces. "Can we see the bugs?"

"Haven't you ever seen the real ones on the farm?" The outside insects are the only creatures not manufactured; there are special farmers who just breed live bugs. Plant life has become so important, and there have been few successes in imitating pollination.

There are also not many decent parts to eat on most insects.

He shrugs and bites off the point of the cone, sets it on his mouth, and sucks. The ice cream drains like a lowering lake. "Yeah, but I can't catch up with 'em to touch 'em."

So we wander through the magical door, and there's a floral rush of scents, wild geraniums and blue flag irises, blueberries and black-eyed Susans, Mexican sunflowers and mint. Butterflies are in avid flutter, like small colorful confetti. "Welcome to the Butterfly Garden," says the lady in the turquoise uniform. "Don't pick the flowers and don't touch the butterflies."

Which is, of course, exactly what Nate does. He crouches by a patch of daisies and waits for a harmless comma or red admiral to come by; when one settles on a nearby nettle, it doesn't move when he pinches his fingers together and picks it up. I glance around to be certain no one's looking and then grab his sweaty hand. "We don't want to do that, Punkin. We can't afford the fines. But over here there's a pond. Would you like to see that?"

I know he wouldn't. He camps by a thistle to wait for a painted lady, and after that it's a long afternoon of watching him touch each unfortunate mourning cloak, checkered skipper, and white peacock as though he were tinkering with a clock; he pokes their thoraxes and brushes their wings with his pinky.

I sit on a bench to rest as Nate wanders over to look at a glass room where there are pupae hanging from branches, looking like tiny pieces of rice.

It reminds me of the maggots that must have been in those deer heads.

I see him slip on a pair of headphones, and he stands completely still, that same kind of completely still he was the day he'd watched them bring the deer home. His pale green shorts have a smear of dirt up the back, and I remind myself to instruct him not to wear his dress clothes when he's out watching the boys mess with filthy things.

He trudges back to me, his eyes bright with curiosity. "Does the sun carry the spirits like my lamp?"

"Like your lamp?"

"Yeah. The deers come into my lamp at night and light it up, and in the morning, I take it apart to let them all out so Daddy can use them again. Is that what the sun does? Like when I help Daddy? It sucks up the old spirits of the dead things and then puts them back into the butterflies when they're sleeping in the hanging bags?"

I chuckle, not only because it's cute, but because I hear Jayce's voice in my head: *Foolish woman! He thinks the souls are turning on the lamp!* My actions have created a regular quagmire in his child brain, and it was so obvious! Next to us, a father is hoisting his strawberry-haired tot with flushed cheeks up onto his shoulder, and I hear snatches of soft words, farmers and bugs and real, and I decide I will stop this lamp business, once and for all. "They don't go into your lamp, honey. That's me. Mommy turns on your light for you so you won't be afraid if you wake up."

He blinks at me, pooching his lower lip out and furrowing his brow so that I can see the miniscule lines that will one day become wrinkles, perhaps when I'm no longer around. Then he looks up through the dome netting, maybe at the veins of canvas that plunge his face into serpentine shadow patterns. "The sun doesn't take souls?"

"No. The sun is—it's gas. It's hot gases that warm the Earth and make the plants grow, and it nourishes the butterflies, but it doesn't carry their souls."

Silence again. He reaches up to slip his sticky hand into mine. We walk farther down the path, to the display of butterflies that are just beginning to emerge from their pupae. Now they look like long-grain rice, that nutty dark stuff that used to be plentiful in organic stores when I was a child but is now nearly impossible to get.

"Mommy?"

"Yes, dear?"

"So then, where do they go?"

"Where does who go?"

"The souls of the deer. If Daddy doesn't use them and the sun doesn't take them, where do they go? Are they waiting to hurt me?"

There really isn't a concept of heaven anymore. The churches now teach very basic reincarnation, perhaps to help people accept the fact that their food is no longer organic and to encourage the byrotecnic farmers to recycle their metals. "You don't have to be afraid of the souls. They go—up into the night sky, where—where all the twinkling lights are. And they're very, very happy. There's no more pain, and no more sadness—"

"Daddy says they don't hurt. The animals."

"Sometimes, honey, they do. Like—like when you have a sunburn. When they twinkle in the night sky, they're twinkling because they don't have to be hurt anymore. They're twinkling with happiness, just like when Daddy winks at you."

He seems to accept this, and I want to be out of the heat. "Come on."

The Firefly Cave is welcome relief from the sun's watery eye and we descend into black lights and cool smells of green earth and moss. He leaps to grab the fireflies, and I just can't stop him. "We need to go." I finally say. "The zoo is closing in an hour."

"No."

"Yes, Nate."

"No."

"We can see these at home. You know the big tree that glows

at night? The big evergreen? We can go see them there. Every night for the rest of the summer."

It's too dark for me to see him thrust out his lower lip, but I know he's doing it. Then he slips his hand in mine and leads me to the gift shop, where he plunges his hands into a barrel of colorful projects that he can assemble and take apart, assemble and take apart: insect gliders crafted of metal with moving parts. "Please?" he begs. "I'm not going to take my lamp apart anymore. I understand, now."

I smile, thinking I will have to buy him a new lamp anyway—it's been through the wringer so many times it sits on his bedstand looking bashed up. "Okay." I buy him ten credits' worth of metal spiders, butterflies, bumblebees, fireflies and ants. We sit on the park benches and he's eager for me to open one of the packets and put it together. I tear open the red wax paper and empty a small body, black plastic head the size of a large blueberry, two curvy sprig-like antennae, and a set of wings. Slot A goes into Slot B goes into Slot C—much like the gliders I'd played with when I was a child, except a little more complicated and with batteries—and the butterfly is done. "Look, Punkin," I say, but he has not shown any interest in my putting it together. He takes the butterfly in his sticky hands, pulls wings from body from head from antennae, and thrusts it back in my lap.

"I could show you how to put it together," I say.

He shakes his head. "Can you do another one?"

So packet after packet I open: the indigo of the red-spotted purple, the blood red of the ladybug, the chocolate of the brown recluse, the fuzzy blinding yellow of the bumble bee, the putrescent green of the firefly. As I do each he takes it apart, and when he's done deconstructing every insect I've lovingly set up, I pile him in the truck for the long ride back across the state's waving grains and lavender sunsets.

"Mommy, can we put the bugs back together again when we get home?"

I want to answer that I think we've had enough of that for one day, but it's the first time he's shown an interest in actually assembling something on his own—shown an interest in rebuilding rather than dismantling, and I take this as a sign maybe he's growing out of his phase. At least I know he'll no longer be taking apart his lamp. "We'll see."

"I want you to show me how to put them together."

I smile and pat his bottom. "You want me to show you how?"

"Yeah." He peers back out the window, and I wonder if he sees things moving in the woods in the whorling dust; the wolves, maybe. The wolves that Jayce wished they hadn't forced him to make.

Nate falls quiet, and a few bumpy miles down the road, where it begins to turn to dirt and reach our farm, he is asleep.

The night is close and even sleeping without the sheet is like being cloistered in a warm bath; Jayce snores but it isn't the noise that keeps me awake. I roll over and look out the window, past sheer black curtains that flutter despite the lack of breeze, and there's the faint, green aura from the firefly tree a half-mile from the house. When we'd first bought the farm, back before Jayce had driven himself gray and little Nate was still a star in the sky, the tree had been by itself, standing, watching over us on summer nights; now, it's shrouded behind a decade or so of woods the boys planted.

I rise from bed and sneak into Nate's room, click on the lamp, and sidle up to him. "Punkin."

He opens his eyes, closes them, opens them again. "Mommy?"

"Come on. I want to show you something, something special." I set aside his yellow plastic screwdriver. "Put your boots on, and we have to be quiet. We don't want to wake your daddy."

He nods, folding back the pale green sheet and sitting up, letting his legs dangle over the floor. He studies the boards for a moment, then reaches out and turns off the lamp.

We creep down the hall like Jayce and I do on Yule Day at four a.m. when we're drunk and setting out the last of our son's gifts: toe by toe, hunch your back, avoid the third board from the wall on the right because it makes a pop-splinter sound. When we get to the bottom of the stairs, I unhitch the thick metal bolt on the door and set a hand on his back to usher him outside.

The lawn is quiet, and the corn rustles and everything is moving, alive, and breathing, and again I wonder why that could be when there's no breeze. The milk house light burns low, meaning the fire's last flames are licking themselves apart and the boys, I imagine, are passed out, Jigger's fleshy leg propped up on an old milk can.

"There." I point. "See the glow?"

"We're going to the firefly tree!"

"Yes."

"Really?" He tightens his grip on my hand.

"Yes, really. Now stick close to me." I step barefoot onto the pile of sand below the front step of the paint-hungry porch. I wonder if I should have consulted Jayce before doing this: we had decided that the day he was old enough to understand, we would take him to the tree to explain what had happened there. Neither of us had planned on tackling the subject without the other.

"I can't see, Mommy. Turn on the flashlight."

"Just give your eyes a minute to adjust. We don't want to frighten them." I crush blades of grass under my feet, and they prickle like pins. In the barn, the owl Jayce built for me last Valentine's Day hoots his awareness of something moving in the dark that shouldn't be. There is a distant clank of metal on metal, and I imagine Jigger knocking over his footrest.

The tree looms larger with every step, and then we're at the edge of the woods and I reach up to part the low-hanging branches of a pair of elms guarding the clearing. We step through, and I hear little Nate gasp as he becomes that topiary-still again. His face is illumed, a small pale-green moon, and he reaches to the tree to touch a branch.

The fireflies shimmy and part and spiral up and away into another section of the tree, and he runs in pursuit. I want to chase him, but am stopped when my toe stubs the bottle.

I bend down to pick it up; the label is still legible: *To Ilse. Tenth Anniversary Dandelion Wine. Jayce.* He'd vinted this himself, working on it for at least a year before the date; I probably hadn't noticed the collection of jugs, tubes, orange peels and lemons in the back corner of the lab because I'd been busy cooking up my own surprises: garlic cheese, pear preserves, ground wheat wafers.

Nate giggles and runs around the tree, tripping and getting caught in the tall weeds that have sprung up over the years; he falls and gets dirty, leaps into the air and swats the fireflies.

"Come here," I call. I set the bottle next to me and sit on the grass. He crawls into my lap and his breaths are quick and loud. "I just want you to look at them. Don't touch. Just look."

His hair tickles my chin.

"Why are they all here, Mommy?"

"Because this place is—natural. This place is where your soul came down from the sky." I can't tell him about that unusually warm first of May. The boys had been, for once, whooping it up somewhere else on account of the Spring Festival, and we'd come down to the tree, the two of us with our much-too-rich gifts to share. The fireflies hadn't been out yet, but we hadn't needed them, and when we'd finished—the last of the wine drained, the cheese gone, sticky dots of the pear preserves at the corners of our mouths—we'd set the bottle at the base of the tree in hopes it would bring good fortune. I wonder, now, if I were to put the empty bottle to my ear, would I hear the echoes of that night, the little wishes that had scaled the tree boughs to the heavens. "This," I say, rubbing his cheek, "this is where you were given to us."

"What does that mean?"

"Created. Made."

"Like Daddy does with the deers?"

"No, not like the deer. Daddy and Mommy made you together."

He squints. "Is that where I came from?"

"Yes. Your soul came down, and you went inside me, and I kept you safe and warm."

"Did you see what my soul looked like?"

"No. You can't really see a soul."

He is quiet for a long time and the crickets fill in the hole between us. Then he climbs off my lap and stands, stuffs his little-man hands into the pockets of his near-threadbare pajamas, and heaves a sigh. "Can we come back tomorrow?"

"We'll see, honey. Mommy has lots of chores."

"But Mommy, you said 'every night for the rest of the summer.' "

"We'll see."

I climb to my feet and take his hand to lead him back through the thicket and across the lawn to the house. He rushes a few steps ahead of me, head down, and for the first time I look at him and realize he may very well, indeed, grow up to be just like Jayce.

August is ebbing when the boys finally take those ghastly heads from the roof of the cold cellar; the days have pleasantly trundled by in a tumble of little Nate's deconstructing and assembling the animatronic bugs in his room. He doesn't follow Jigger out to call the cows in; he doesn't watch Hap dissecting car parts; he hasn't taken apart the new lamp I had Lair make for him. I'm overjoyed about all of these changes—I'm even happy to provide him with scissors and all the empty mason jars he wants "to keep the parts in," he says. However, he has been tired—the kind of tired where trying to rouse him from bed in the morning for breakfast or chores is a thirty-five minute affair. When I mention my concern to Jayce, of course he just answers, "Probably a growth spurt or something. He's eating, right?" in between his gulps of orange juice.

Sporting Day again, and the boys have killed off the last of Jayce's herd. They roar in on the truck and scream about eighteen-pointers and how *these are gonna be beauties*, and I resign to turn away from the scene and go right back to that apple pie I've been working on. I pick up the corer and set to work, thrusting the round instrument and listening to its blades cut through the flesh of each green fruit with a corporeal, wholesome *ffft*.

Nate comes down and runs to the decrepit window. He presses his fingers on the sill, resting his chin on the wrinkles of his joints. I hear the boys whooping and the *clang-clang* of metal legs and arms clattering against each other as they're all chucked onto the tarp.

"Would you like some apple?" I take three slices and put them in a bowl.

He turns from the window and walks to me and I see that his pale yellow shirt has some black smears on it. "Mommy, can you put my bugs back together?"

"You know how to put them back together." I pluck the seeds from the core and drop them into an aluminum pouch to save for the boys to plant. "You've been doing just fine the last few weeks. Eat your apple." I motion to the bowl. "There's even some cinnamon on there."

"No," he says, his blue eyes hot with defiance. He frowns and folds his arms in front of his chest.

"Don't tell me no." I finish peeling another apple; the peel falls into a spiral. "I'm sure you can do it. Why don't you get your tweezers and your jars and show me?" I wipe my sticky hands on my jeans and turn on the sink, and hear him tromping into his room, the boards beneath his feet whining like the shutters in a strong wind, that sound I sometimes hear at night when I know no one's awake and the shadows of the leaves on the trees spatter the walls in camouflage. Then there's silence.

I turn off the water.

A clunk, like a bag of beer bottles, and a *swoosh*. Silence. *Swoosh*. Silence. *Swoosh*.

I dry my hands on a towel and step to the base of the narrow, crooked stairs.

There is a sudden rush of hot air through the open window, and I hear Lair's laughter and Jigger's command to *cut that shit out let's go down the milk house*. Then I see little Nate at the top of the stairs, hauling with all his might a paper bag from a long-defunct department store. The bag slams against every step, foreshadowing disaster, and I think maybe I have been wrong, maybe he's been out in the milk house and the boys have convinced him to drink? Maybe that's why he's been so tired!

"See?" He gets to the bottom step, and the bag tips over and a few of my mason jars spill out, rolling like marbles across the warped floorboards.

I pick one up and peer inside. There's one of his father's razor blades and a pair of tweezers, and a pile of something that's like the wood dust at the bottoms of fireplaces in summers: black bodies shredded like mouse feces, wings splintered into fine gray powder, miniscule antennae crushed and cock-eyed. Fireflies. He's been going to the tree and getting real fireflies.

"I took the bugs apart like Daddy. I took them all apart and now they don't work anymore!" He pooches his lip out, like he's going to cry. "Where did they go?"

"Where did who go?"

"The souls! I couldn't find the souls! If you put the bugs back together they'll come back, right?"

I don't know what to say.

I look out the window and a river of light flows from the milk house down the drive. I hear Jigger and Hap and Lair, howling with laughter, louder than they've been in a while. I'm not sure what it is when I first hear the bang and the glass in the window shatters like so much rock candy. Then I see the gold sparks and the feathers, and I know the inside walls of the structure are tarred in downy flesh from the boys overheating another chicken.

HOW I STOPPED COMPLAINING AND LEARNED TO LOVE THE BUNNY

MY WIFE, BUNNY, falls in love with one of those hideous plastic lawn rabbits at Savers.

They're not around much anymore, but you've probably seen them—it's like one of the knee-high Santas with the hole in the middle of its back, just wide enough for one of those frosted Christmas bulbs. You plug it in, and Santa's cheeks glow peach-orange. Except this one's a bunny, so I guess it's for Easter, and when you plug it in the ears glow pig-pink. Noxious thought.

"Please?" she asks.

"You don't like rabbit." Once we went to a potluck game dinner, and she refused to taste the rabbit stew (we had contributed potato chips and corn on the cob).

"We had one just like it when I was a kid. Look." She touches the plastic that forms the bunny's blue coat. On the elbow, a small blur of white-yellow light bleeds through scratches. "Ours was even worn in the same spot!"

Her brown eyes sparkle and plead beneath the brim of her gray flannel cap, the one with the hugging penguins on it. "Come on! It's only fifty cents."

I have visions of it glowing as an embarrassing beacon of midwestern tack on our front stoop. But fifty cents it is, because she works at a zoo and loves animals, even plastic electric ones, and because it's my week to pay for our night out. Besides, maybe I'll get lucky, and the wiring'll fry out.

When she gets it home, she sets it on the kitchen counter next to the empty wine glasses from last night, a stack of plastic fish-shaped dishes and a spinach-encrusted pot from last week.

"I need to clean him up. He's pretty full of gunk." She puts the headset for her cordless phone on her ear and pushes buttons on the hand unit. "Could you get the rest of the stuff out of the car, honey?"

Like all the china dishes at a dime each, the fake Japanese black orchids in a pink vase, the scarf peppered with cartoon-style colonial men, the butterfly candelabra and other stuff that is far more interesting and didn't leer at me in the rearview mirror the entire ride home.

"Suzi! I have to tell you about what I just got!" she squeals into the phone. She pulls dirty dishes from one side of the sink and clanks them in the other side, then turns on the water.

After she cleans behind its ears with cotton swabs and shines it with glass cleaner so it looks as new as a thirty-year-old electric Easter Bunny can look, we start the ritual of finding the place he would work best with our décor. I had never thought of an Easter Bunny as a year-round thing, especially in rooms with gilded-edge mirrors and velvet couches, eggplant-colored walls and Canadian Goose bookends on mahogany shelves. But when I say, "I had thought we'd only leave him out a couple of weeks out of the year, at Easter," she gets that look on her face, the same one she got last year after the plumber gave her the estimate on repairing the upstairs john. And of course she wants my opinion on how it looks next to the leopard-print floor cushions or on the marble vanity in the guest bath.

I suggest the trash can, but she won't hear of that. The thing's sardonic grin brightens a little when she says, "Oh, don't you just have *such* a sense of humor?"

The project stops when she gets a phone call from her fashion-designer friend Avery. She sits on the bed with the phone on her ear and sips her wine like she always does, and I am glad to have a break from finding a home for Demon Bunny (that's what I've decided to call him).

I settle in the overstuffed leather chair and flip channels, and of course it's right there, next to me. Staring.

I hear the water in the kitchen sink running again, hear the bong-bang of heavy pots being pulled from their cabinets. Making dinner. She'll be awhile.

Classic movie channel.

Damn I wish that thing would take its blue plastic ass and walk away with disinterest—

—*Holiday Inn* with Bing Crosby. A rather strange choice for the beginning of August since everybody thinks this is a Christmas film, which it isn't really, and also because August doesn't have any holidays (well, at least not one Crosby would find worth singing about—who ever heard of United Nations Day)?

Astaire is doing that dance with the firecrackers. At least in the film it's July.

I glance at Demon Bunny. "You like this?" I settle back and put my feet up on the ottoman. I'm wearing flip-flops, but my bare heels stick to it. We should close the windows and put on the air conditioning. "It's called Fourth of July. Not one of the holidays with which you're familiar. You're away by then. This is when we eat lots of dead cows compressed into patties and pig guts crammed into long tubes."

Hissing from the kitchen. Obviously my wife is making something—oh, shit I hope it's not those veggie burgers. I'd rather eat a whole box of Steak-umms than those things.

Just when I think he should have a proper name—(Demon Bunny is too cliché, yet too strong, and it reminds me of movies and TV shows with talking dolls, killing dolls, possessed dolls)—that smile starts to unsettle me. I turn him to face the wall. I wonder if his grin is still there, or if it actually vanishes when people don't look at him . . . *snap-crackle-bang-bang.* Firecrackers . . . I'll just close my eyes for a minute and listen to this dance sequence . . . I've seen it a hundred times anyway and I've never seen the end of this movie but I've always gotten at least this far and I'd love to see what's on the other side of this number . . .

✻✲✺✲✻

The TV is off. The smell of stale grease hangs thick in the air, and I wish she would remember to put that heated oil air freshener in that makes the house smell like citrus.

I hear the gentle padding of her footsteps upstairs, and I envision her slipping off her bra, preparing for me, trying to make it different than it'd been last time. I climb the hall stairs and notice something's different about the cast of pale light on our wedding photo. Usually there's just the glow of her white veil and gown and both of our faces are dark. Tonight, I can see her smile, and there's an expression of plastered joy, like a shampoo model in a magazine ad: "If you *love* the scent of green apple, try this!"

Oh, the light *is* different on that picture. It's *not* just me.

I kick off my shoes up here now since we got the new Oriental rug. *"It's soft and reminds you of a lion's mane, doesn't it?" she'd asked. "I wouldn't know," I'd said.*

Our bedroom door. A crack open. That light. A swiss cheese wedge on the floor . . .

. . . I push it open. It cries . . .

Bunny. On the bed, her toes pointed, pig-pink light across her nipples . . .

—a pig-pink light.

Demon Bunny. In the corner. A salivating circus freak hungry for what lies beneath her silks—

"Won't he just be the coolest nightlight?"

"Not looking at us like that."

She recoils, motions with her hand. "What do you want me to do, turn him to the wall?"

"Yeah, maybe." Grin and watch me hump my wife. "Well, rabbits are symbolic of fertility, aren't they? Honey, that's the last thing we need."

I have to admit, the carpet brings out the color of his eyes.

❧❧❧

I sit down to dinner, and Bunny sets the cordless phone down beside her; I guess she's afraid it will ring and she'll miss a call. I would love it if she'd let us get caller ID like everyone else. Then maybe she'd be like my friends' wives: a little more fickle about who she talks to, and when.

She pushes the peas around on her plate. "You haven't said anything about the new dishes." She reaches for her can of Diet Coke.

I lift my slab of dried-out London broil and peek underneath. Oh, these *are* new dishes. Maroon stripes with yellow cornflowers spattered all over them. Like the artists had intended to draw imaginary spilled popcorn in the middle of them. "They're nice."

"You didn't even notice. I got them at Joe's estate sale, up the street."

"Joe?"

She scrapes some potatoes off her plate. "He died last year? You know, in that Ferris wheel accident at the fair when the bolts popped out?"

I remember something like that. I try to picture Joe. Sure, he was the one who was out watering his bright pink geraniums all the time in his socks and gray flannel shorts. He had three kids. Little girls, I think. They were loud, and he was always yelling at them to stop picking the forsythia. "Oh, yeah. I remember that."

Silence.

A crow caws outside.

We had agreed not to have children, but I look at the two empty red vinyl chairs on either side of us and the old pink serving platter full of steak between us, and I think maybe that is why couples start families. Because there isn't anything left to talk about except the fat neighbor and how he died.

I push myself back from the table. "You know what? I had a thought."

She just nods. She doesn't look up from her plate.

I climb the stairs and go into our bedroom, and there he is, Demon Bunny. "Hey, there," I say. I unplug him from the wall and lift him, noticing a swath of dust in the crook where his shoulder meets his neck, a spot Bunny missed. *We'll have to take care of that*, I think.

I walk into the kitchen and pull out the chair next to me.

Bunny drops her knife. "What are you doing?"

I lift him into the seat. "I just remembered—after dinner I have to go out and get him a new bulb, see if they make them anymore. We should have a spare in case he burns out. This should remind me to do it."

She seems satisfied with the answer.

"That's better." I settle back down and roll some peas onto my fork, slide them into my mouth. "Now I can eat."

Bunny puts her fork down and studies him a moment. "You know, maybe that's where we should put him. Right here, in the kitchen. We could get a baby chair or something from one of those piles downstairs. Isn't that a great idea? It would be like a whimsical kid-thing." She picks up her fork and knife and starts digging into her meat again. Then she gets up, still chewing. "Here. We might as well make it complete." She sets one of the new plates down in front of him. Then she pulls out another, smaller one from the stack. "Here's what the bread dish looks like. The set also came with a butter dish." She sets her hands on her hips, surveying her work. "I like these." She opens another can of Diet Coke. "Ever wonder what Joe and his kids ate on these plates? I wonder that sometimes about things. What they were in their past lives before they came here."

I shrug. "No, not really."

"Like, were they pasta people? Real pasta or Chef Boyardee? Were they meat and potatoes, or did they eat a lot of rice and beans? What kinds of things did they buy at the supermarket?" She sets her can down on the table and plays with her necklace, a gold American flag she probably picked up at Goodwill for a quarter.

I know I'm annoying her, because I'm chewing my steak noisily. I always have trouble chewing with my mouth closed, especially when it's a piece of London broil, all dried out and tough. I study Demon Bunny. He sits there, the empty plate in front of him, looking like the only reason he can't dig in is because I haven't given him any utensils. I stare at the grin on his face, imagining his lips morphing and moving, asking me where his portion is.

Bunny has almost finished her meal. I can tell she's hurrying. She probably wants to make a phone call.

I lean back and stretch. "Ever wonder if this bunny had a past life, huh? Sittin' on the front stoop, cryin' 'cause he couldn't run and catch the ice cream man like the other kids?"

She stops mid chew and furrows her brow. "He's an Easter decoration." She swallows. "He wouldn't be out on display in summer."

Then she gets up, turns, and puts her dish in the sink, knocks back the rest of her Diet Coke, and picks up her phone. I wonder if there are any peas left on the stove, and toy with the idea of giving some to Demon Bunny. You know—just a few.

She's on the phone again. This time she's talking about Hamster Face, the woman at her office who Bunny claims *had* to have gotten married in the dark because she's so ugly. It's probably true, of course. There are lots of ugly people in the world, but I do feel bad for Hamster Face. Like, does she *know* she's hamster-faced? If she does, and she grew up that way, is it a self-esteem obstacle she's had to overcome? Or is she simply ignorant? Does she think she's pretty?

Then I wonder what Bunny talks about all day at work. Does she discuss Hamster Face with anyone else?

When was the last time I had a conversation with her? A really great one, about the validity of short films and the lack of creativity in today's movie industry?

This is how marriages start to decline. Can't remember the last time I worried about or wanted to impress her. Like the refills on my aftershave. Let the last bottle shake empty, and now it sits there, collecting dust. Bunny dusts it because it has a ship on the bottle and it matches the bathroom. Although she likes to lay me and asks for it more than most women (at least according to my envious buds), she doesn't *listen*.

She *talks*.

I hear the monotone bell of the phone as she hits the *off* button on the keypad.

"Going out now," she says. I hear her disconnect the headset, cradling the cordless phone back on the unit. *Thud, thud, thud, thud* up the stairs. "I'll be back in a little while. You don't have to wait up."

What to do? Not like she and I had anything planned.

The piranha's tank needs a water change. Hanging out in the basement full of sheets and old board games—*Bonanza* (dusty) and *Battlestar Galactica* (dustier)—doesn't appeal to me right now. I was supposed to do it last night; what was I doing last night, anyway?

Oh, *Holiday Inn*. On the black-and-white movie channel. Hey, maybe they're running it again now and I can finally see the end.

I turn on the TV and take off my sneakers and socks; the backs of my feet stick to the ottoman again. Well, son of a bitch! It *is* on again! But we're back at Lincoln's Birthday, and how many holidays is *that* from July?

Quite a few.

Boring, so boring. I have to sit through this again. All I want to see is the end. I'd go out and rent it on video and watch it if we still had the VCR. Bunny took the old one away in a box, saying it was outdated. (We did buy it in 1985, but then the technology was new, buttons were buttons, and *solid state* was still the most important pair of words you could find stamped on the front of something.) So, I have to sit here and watch the movie through to the other side. Again. Alone.

Well, I'm not alone, actually. Not if I count Demon Bunny. As a person, sort of.

I tread up the stairs to the bedroom and unplug Demon Bunny, and for the first time wonder if we even *can* get a replacement bulb for him or even if the one in his back now is the original bulb. I'll have to check into it. It would be terrible if his light went out.

⁂

. . . spider. There's a spider on your arm . . .

. . . no, it's Bunny. Shaking me awake. Did I miss the rest of *Holiday Inn* again?

"Wake up," she says, and makes me sit up. I don't even think to click off the TV or Demon Bunny, just follow her upstairs and lay down in our bed. She settles next to me, smooths the sheets.

The TV is still playing downstairs, the sounds very faint. I wonder what the movie channel has on now.

"I'm pregnant."

This means the illegal piranha will have to go. I can't take the risk of little squid-like fingers getting in there. What about softball? What's that coaching thing I'll have to do now? What is that called? "I thought we agreed not to have children."

"*We* did, yes."

"I thought you were on the pill."

She sits up.

"Brad, listen. It's—complicated."

Something tells me there's a third party involved in this, and it isn't the piranha.

"What's his name?" The sound of someone slamming a front door across the street carries through the open screen.

"It's David."

It's hot up here. Maybe we should get the fan down. "The guy at work you told me was gay?"

"Yeah."

Duped? Is that why I'm mad?

Not really. It's more that I feel bad for the guy. Has she been telling *everybody* he's gay? The shadows from the leaves on the trees outside scurry across the ceiling like bird feet.

"Do you know whose it is? The kid?"

A car breezes by on the street. It reminds me of this movie I saw that took place in Queens or somewhere in the city, but all of the houses had little lawns and porches, and I had thought that was very strange.

⁂

The next day Manzino comes over. He's a train enthusiast; I met him at a workshop on track design once at the Railway Museum. We've been friends ever since. I have an electric train set in the basement, so every year for Christmas he buys me another addition to the small universe I'm building. I'm trying to make a university in the middle of summer. Or maybe a big aquarium or a recreation of Coney Island. I'm not interested in classic towns. Everybody does those.

"So, you're sure?" Manzino asks.

"I'm sure," I say. The water level in the piranha's tank is almost down to half. He's a beautiful red-bellied, and his red bottom sparkles like the shimmer of an elegant cocktail dress under dim lighting on New Year's Eve, that gauzy stuff. Bunny has a dress made out of that material.

Click, whir. Manzino plays with my train set. "Oh, come on. What do you really need a wife for anyway?" he asks. He always sounds like he's trying to sell me a washing machine. "Did you know the little light on your caboose is out?" The whirring stops. I think I would like to feed the piranha a live frog today. There's a bowl in the corner with the usual stock of goldfish, but I'm in the mood to watch something a little more interesting.

"I mean, all she does is talk all the time, anyway, right? Oh, by the way, the glowing Easter Bunny in the living room is pretty cool, you know? I had one when I was a kid. Had the Santa too."

I glance over my shoulder at him, careful to have my fingers and everything clear of the tank. He's toying with my caboose. I notice the back of his deep maroon cardigan sweater has a threadbare hole in it. Maybe his cat slept on it. "I didn't like it at first," I say, "but now I'm used to it. Except she keeps it in the bedroom."

"That's kinky. Why is it in the living room?"

"I dunno. Watching *Holiday Inn*, I guess."

"See, companions that don't talk. Good idea." The whirring starts again. "I think I fixed this light." *Whir, whir.* "I really think animals already went through a talking phase, and they figured out it doesn't make any difference. It only adds to confusion. So they decided not to talk anymore. They figured they were better off. So they run around naked with their tongues hanging out all day. But if you look at their faces and into their eyes, they have a real Old World look about them, like they're very wise."

"Manzino?"

"Yeah?"

I want to say, "It's okay. I've actually come to think of the little guy as my friend." Instead, I say, "He's plastic."

"Even better," Manzino says. "Plastic doesn't crap."

When Bunny moves out, I don't let her take Demon Bunny. I offer her a dollar—twice what I paid for it—to let me keep him. She just looks at me funny, and says, "Keep your dollar, you want him that bad. You bought him anyway."

She closes the hatchback on the old station wagon and pulls out of the driveway, and the porch light on the house across the street goes out.

I could turn on the TV and probably try to catch the end of *Holiday Inn*, but then I decide I'm tired. I go up to our bedroom, and there's Demon Bunny, sitting in the corner, smiling at me as I climb into bed and pull the sheets over my body.

I stare at the ceiling. Something's wrong. Something's—someone's—missing. Demon Bunny's not turned on.

I toss back the sheets and heft myself over to the corner, bend down and dig my fingers into the hole in the back to flip the switch. He lights up; I go back to bed. I lay there, still, and look at him. "Goodnight," I whisper.

He just grins.

ATTEMPTED DELIVERY

A WHISPER COMES from the package intended for my neighbor.

I'm Margolynn Jameson and I live at 53 Morgan Avenue, Mystic, Connecticut; the neighbor, Marilyn Jensen, is at 53 Morgan Avenue Extension. Occasionally, that's where my Amazon Pantry boxes get delivered—my phone often notifies me that my item has been *left on the porch*. I don't have a porch, so I cut through the woods, descend the embankment, and navigate the rickety wooden steps that parallel her steep driveway to get the parcel.

Marilyn and I haven't met. She's never home, no matter what time of day or night it is. My girlfriend Suzanne, who met her once, claims Marilyn works for a museum, and that she's probably always traveling to exotic places. Suzanne, though, has a talent for romanticizing. I didn't take her seriously until the first time I stood on Marilyn's porch amidst Tiki statues, wind chimes made of bones, and shrunken heads.

It's creepy, and I'm an anxious person. It's only my need for eyeliner and tampons that keeps me going back. But this is the first time one of *her* deliveries has ended up at *my* place, and it's only right to go drop it off.

I'm about to pick up the box when I hear the whisper: *broken lobster*.

What the hell was that?

I look to see if anyone's around. There isn't.

Broken lobster. What the hell does that *mean*, anyway?

I'm supposed to take Suzanne to Red Lobster for her birthday, and that's been on my mind because it's her favorite place and I'm not really a fan of seafood. That's probably it.

Broken lobster. There it is again.

I'm afraid to touch the box. It didn't come from Amazon—in fact, the return and shipping addresses are the same: Marilyn Jensen, 53 Morgan Avenue Extension. *Someone* was desperate to make sure this got to the right place. Then I think: *she won't be home, and what if the thing inside is alive?* It shouldn't be left outside in the cold—it's the first week in April, but the nights are still dipping below freezing on occasion, and the pouring rains we've had for the past two days don't make anything more hospitable. What if what's in there dies of exposure? What if it's—

Broken lobster.

I lift it; it's light. When I shake it, something rattles, but it feels like it's in one piece.

Maybe it's another one of those weird bone things that're hanging all around Marilyn's porch.

I put my ear to the box.

This time, louder: *Broken lobster!*

Startled, I drop it on the ceramic tile of my foyer floor.

Shit. Shitshitshit, what if it's broken?

Open it, I tell myself. *Just check it out and make sure it's intact, whatever it is.*

The problem is it's wrapped completely in what looks like butcher shop paper. If I tear into it, there's no way I'll be able to hide the evidence that it's been opened.

BROKEN LOBSTER!

That's it. I have to do it.

I get a knife—one of the joys of living alone, no one yells at you for using one of the good steak knives to open your mail—and plan my strategy. Every seam and flap is plastered in tape. It's a struggle not only to get the knife in, but also to keep from stabbing myself.

At last I'm through. The knife, now covered in sticky residue, is probably ruined. I toss it in the sink, where it lands on a precariously stacked pile of the Pier 1 dishes my last girlfriend left here.

I sincerely hope I broke at least one of them.

I work the box free of the paper and pull off the lid, inhaling a waft of something that smells like rotting leaves and bourbon. Once it passes, I take a peek.

Inside is an intact, petrified fish—what kind I have no idea, but the protruding mouth armed with murderous teeth gives me chills. Its taut, grayish-tobacco skin—only slightly heartier than tissue and tackier than crepe paper—is worn in patches, revealing bones. Equally disturbing are dark brushstrokes marbling its rib cage: meticulously painted characters in a maroon ink that bleeds into hairline cracks in the bones, spreading like tree roots.

But it's the perfectly round, tenantless eye sockets that nail stalactites through my core.

They look angry.

Who would want this hideous, scary thing in her house?

I slam the box closed. *I'm dumping this back on her porch where it belongs.* Just as I start trying to patch what I've done, Suzanne texts that she's waiting for me out in front of Red Lobster—no time to drop it off now. I brush my teeth, freshen my makeup, and am about to get on the road when I realize I don't want that thing in my house either—not even for a few hours.

I carry it to the fiberboard shelf in the garage and ram it between rusty cans of WD-40 and quarts of paint.

Broken lobster. It haunts me through the mojitos. *Broken lobster.* It haunts me through the cheddar biscuits. *BROKEN. LOBSTER!* I expect Suzanne will order her lobster with the shell already split.

Instead, she breaks up with me.

When I get home, eyes burning from mascara fail, I rush to the shelf and take the lid off the box.

"What are you?" I whisper.

It doesn't answer. It just stares at me with those sinister, accusatory pits.

⁂

I've always been anxious, waiting for that shoe to drop. I don't enjoy the now because I'm not certain of the later: Will I have an argument with someone at work? Will a friend suddenly ditch me? Will I owe more on my taxes than I can pay?

For a while I was hooked on tarot cards, and although they gave me a heads-up on the daily, they couldn't foresee the long term: Will my latest relationship go *Beauty and the Beast*—or *Kramer vs. Kramer?* Will I get fired or laid off? Will a meticulously planned vacation suck? Will I die from an illness or in an accident? Whatifwhatifwhatif. Sometimes my stomach roils so badly I can't eat.

I didn't sleep last night. While I'm upset about Suzanne and aware there are lonely waters ahead (I'm a sucker for that high-school-bathroom wisdom *the time it takes to get over a relationship is equal to the time you were together*) that isn't why.

I didn't sleep because I was haunted by the grotesque thing in the garage.

Broken lobster broken lobster broken lobster . . . it was telling me we were going to break up over lobster. It *knew* what was going to happen.

Why wouldn't it just say, "Suzanne is breaking up with you?" Why the cryptics?

On the other hand, it's not like the tarot cards used to show pictures of fender benders and overdrawn checkbooks.

I sip my double-downed coffee—so strong it's thick—and notice that, mercifully, the torrential rains that have pounded us since yesterday have stopped. Over the loud ticking of the kitchen clock, I hear noise in the garage.

My back stiffens. I listen.

Hishhishhish.

I set my coffee on the counter, tighten the sash on my bathrobe, and step deliberately down the hall toward the waiting door to the garage.

I set my hand on the knob, press my ear to the hollow core woodgrain.

Leaf left.

An ensuing empty sound, like the ocean waves you supposedly hear in a conch.

Leaf left, it hisses again.

I think about *broken lobster*. I think about the pain in my heart.

Leaf left.

"I raked the leaves in the fall and carted 'em away. I don't know what you're talking about!" This is ridiculous. I'm having a conversation with a dead fish.

I hear something metal hit the concrete.

I yank open the door and go to the shelf. A rusting can of WD-40 bumps against my slipper.

The fish is no longer in the box. It's sitting next to one of the dusted-over bottles of ArmorAll, and if I didn't know better, I'd swear its insidious mouth is turned up at the corners, like it's smiling.

My stomach pits in fear. I flee the garage, slam the door behind me, and breathe. *Just get ready for work. Hop in the shower, do your makeup, prep your Swiss sandwich and chips for lunch. Just like normal. Dump that evil thing on her porch on the way.*

When I'm ready to leave I seize the corpse with a long-handled grabber I keep around and set it back in its carton. I secure it with a piece of tape, toss it on the passenger seat, and screech out of the garage.

To get to Marilyn's the quickest way and avoid being late for work, I have to make a right instead of my normal left, and I can't possibly drive fast enough. The only thing that slows me down is the blind corner two hundred feet from my driveway; if you don't hug that curve, you're liable to lane drift and smack into someone.

I skirt the corner and slam on the brakes.

The road is blocked by an overturned garbage truck, muddy water damming up behind it. Dark green and brown trash bags hunch on the road. Two men in reflective orange vests stand guard; one smokes a cigarette and has his hand up to stop traffic (as though there's room to go around); the other, cell phone pressed to one ear, finger stuck in the other, paces back and forth.

It must've tried to take the corner too fast.

I'm stuck. The road's too narrow for me to turn around.

I curse at myself. Why didn't I go the way I usually go? I could've still been able to get to Marilyn's driveway. It would have been several additional turns and a bit of backtracking. That's all.

But it would've made me late for work.

If I'd made a left out of my drive instead of a right, I would've missed this whole incident.

I slide a glance to the box on the passenger seat.

I remember this morning's message. The one that spooked me into this position in the first place.

Leaf left.

Oh my God.

The fish wasn't saying leaf left, it was saying *leave* left.

That creepy thing was trying to help me.

The thought gives me the shivers.

✴✦✴

I arrive at my desk thirty minutes late, and my boss Courtney has to walk past to get to her office. I drape my jacket over my chair and sit down right away so when she powers through here clutching her green tea I'll be working.

Kasey—who sits behind me—and I don't usually talk. We don't have to, because she's like a mosquito, always hovering and swapping inanities like the latest drama on *Beer Pong Wives* with the other office supply manager, who's over seventy and messes up so much my real job is correcting her errors.

"Are you okay?" she asks.

"Fine." What am I going to say?

"Today should be a heavy mail day." Kasey opens her desk drawer and takes out her Post-It-tongued planner. "Fridays always are."

That is one thing she always does—reminds me that Fridays are our heaviest mail day. I'm frequently overwhelmed by it to the point that sometimes I hide at least half in a bottom drawer where no one will find it, because Mondays we get nothing. It's my little secret that I've been keeping for years; the only time I was ever anxious about getting caught was when I was unexpectedly out with the flu for two weeks and I remembered I hadn't locked my drawers before I left. There were customers' checks that weren't deposited. I ended up coming back and secretly shredding them, claiming we simply hadn't received them when complaints came in: "You know how the post office can be sometimes," I'd told Courtney, who'd appeared to believe me, although I had flashbacks and panic attacks for weeks afterward.

Courtney appears at first to motor by without noticing me; then, she stops and presses her thighs against the edge of my desk, gripping her *Of course I talk to myself, sometimes I need expert advice* mug with both hands. She peers down at me over the steaming rim with a forced smile. "Good afternoon."

I avert my gaze and reach under my desk to boot up my computer. "There was an accident on my road."

"Yes, well." She nods. "Big mail day today. Sure you're up to it?"

I look at her, confused. "Um—yeah, sure."

"Good. Because I have a big project I want you to work on for me." She sips her tea. "When you're done, come see me."

She pivots and goes into her office and closes the door.

"Wow." Kasey says. "*That* sounds like a punishment."

The panic comes on strong: first as a little queasy, then full-on nauseated, then my heart pounds in my ears and my fingers quake. I haul myself up from my chair.

I hear Kasey ask me, "Where are you going?" almost dimly as I round the corner and head down the hall through the double doors to my favorite hideaway: the janitor's supply closet.

I shut myself in and sit on a milk crate and focus on my breathing. As I stare at the mop—it's always looked like it's seen better days but is now so ratty I feel pity for it—I wonder what the fish would tell me.

✧⋆⊱✦⊰⋆✧

It's the next morning and I'm in my kitchen.

"You're going to think I'm insane." With a grapefruit spoon, I grind the sugar cubes I've just dropped into my lifelong friend Juliane's coffee cup, Courtney's *big project*—alphabetizing files— done and forgotten. The sound is as toe-curling as nails on a chalkboard. "And I don't trust myself to know that I'm not, so I'm asking you to help me out here."

Juliane leans against my kitchen counter, arms folded across her chest. She's one of the few people—okay, maybe the only person—that I admit anything to. I know she's had a crush on me forever, and even though it's never worked out, she's always around, giving me backup when I need it.

Now, though, I can't read her expression. "What?"

She shrugs and shoves her hands in her pockets. "I was expecting the usual wailing and gnashing of teeth, Margie." Everyone else calls me Margo, but she's called me Margie since the day we met. "I'm a little feeling like a fish outta water here, 'cause I just blew sixty bucks on the post-breakup Patrón—are you sayin' it's goin' to waste?"

"Nah, we'll drink it." I hand her the cup. It says *Keep Austin Weird*—a leftover from Suzanne. I muse at how I usually would've already destroyed everything the heartbreaker left behind.

Maybe we won't be drinking that tequila after all?

She furrows her brow over the rim of the mug, and I notice she's wearing mascara, which is rare. She takes a hard swallow and grimaces. "Damn, that's hot." She sets it on the counter. "So, you gonna show me this thing, or what?"

Nothing I say to her ever sounds crazy, either. I used to think this was because she was secretly in love with me. This strange fish has made me think, though, that it's just because she has a head full of interesting folklore about the creatures in her care down at the Mystic aquarium—and she's always looking to add one more. She's not a fan of her job, and has always told me it's part of how she keeps herself entertained.

I go out to the garage and retrieve the box. When I come back, she's got a Dum Dum lollipop in her mouth; she claims they help her think, but it's the mystery flavor that's her favorite (how she could say that about something unidentifiable, I don't know. The very thought of grabbing a Dum Dum out of the bag and not having any idea what's underneath the wrapper is uncomfortable).

"Hnnnn." She holds the mummy up to the kitchen's fluorescent, a light I usually keep off because it reminds me of the ones I see in morgues on TV crime shows. "What you've got here is a piranha."

The word *is* comes out like *ish* as she manipulates the lollipop. She sets the fish gingerly back in the box. "No idea where it came from, huh?"

"Nope."

"And it actually says things."

I sip my coffee. "I know it's not the television or stuff coming through my non-existent baby monitor. I know what I heard."

"I'm not doubting you, you know that." She bites through the Dum Dum and puckers. "Ooh! There's sour apple in the middle of this one. And it's only the future, you're sure."

I reiterate the two warnings it's given me so far.

She tosses the lollipop stick in the trash. "But . . . it doesn't seem to say things like secrets people are keeping from you, or anything like that."

"No. Not yet, anyway."

"You know." She turns and faces me. Her nipples poke through the white tank top that has the word *Twister* written across it in ragged black letters. "You ever heard of Fordlandia?"

"No."

She sighs. "It's a history lesson, but I'll keep it short." She moves to the white wicker bar in the sun room and grabs a couple of shot glasses. "In the thirties, Henry Ford wanted cheaper rubber for his tires. So he built a city in the Amazon— and I mean, it was a *city*." She yanks the Patrón from a paper sack and works at the cork. "It had a school and a dance hall and a movie theater . . . like, the whole nine yards . . . for the workers."

"It sounds like paradise."

"It was a disaster." The top twists free and she pours. "The houses sucked for the environment, the food made people sick, the rubber trees wouldn't grow or just plain died of a strange blight. Then synthetic rubber was invented and it was all over. Here."

I look at the clock. It's only just past ten in the morning. "Isn't it a little early?"

"Where the hell are you going, anyway? It's Saturday. And you're gonna need it by the time I'm done tellin' ya this."

I take the shot from her. We knock them back. The liquid fire spooks the chill from my bones.

Juliane refills her glass. "They *say* Ford was warned . . . by a mummy piranha cursed with the gift of foresight. Nobody remembers what the natives called it in their language, but in the stories it's called *ver los dientes*—in Portuguese, that means *seeing teeth*." She knocks back a shot. "Want another one?"

She was right. This is getting creepier by the minute. "Sure, what the hell."

She takes my glass and refills. "This piranha, you see—when it was alive—supposedly ate the heart out of a bathing witch doctor."

I'm beginning to suspect this is one of those stories she uses to tame rowdy boy scouts at her overnight programs.

"They both died, and the soul of the witch inhabited the piranha. Teddy Roosevelt picked it up in the Amazon. Roosevelt passed it to Ford. Roosevelt and Ford had differences, especially over Fordlandia, so the reason Ford ignored the warnings was because he thought it was Roosevelt messing with him."

"You're telling me *that's* what this could be?"

"Cheers." She gives me the shot and knocks back her own. "God, that's fantastic stuff! Hell, it's the kind of legend that's been around forever, which means there might be a grain of truth in it someplace." She refills again. "You said your neighbor goes lots of exotic places, right?"

I admit it's starting to sound plausible, and it does make sense when I think about yesterday's *leaf left* message. "You *really* think this thing is real? That it can really predict the future?"

"We should test it out over the next few days and see." She slams back another shot.

Then it occurs to me, and that familiar panic knots my stomach. "What if Marilyn finds out?"

"Why would she?" She pours another. "Damn thing was coming all the way from South America, it easily could've been lost."

"But . . . technically, we're committing mail fraud." My head fills with visions of orange jumpsuits, bad meatloaf, and crapping where everyone can watch. "It's a federal offense."

"If this thing can do what I *think* it can do, it'll warn us first." She downs the silver liquid with an audible gulp. "Then we can quit our jobs and drink Patrón every day of the week on some nice beach in Tahiti where no one will ever find us."

In terms of clarity, the fish is no better than the tarot cards—which kinda rules out the idea of using it to win at the Kentucky Derby or the office Super Bowl pools. But Juliane, determined, has one of her Kokuyo notebooks she uses at work, and we sit at my driftwood table and start a glossary.

Leaf is the first thing we add to the language—it will probably prove itself to have more than one meaning, but for now we know one of those definitions is *leave*. We add broken lobster, too, although we know that the lobster part really isn't important, it's the *broken* part, and Juliane jokes, *If you'd been having barbecue, would it have said ribs?*

Juliane and I hole up for the next two weekends and sit completely still—no TV, no music—so we can be sure we hear every whisper the fish makes. Most of its messages aren't critical—it warns of a phone call from Juliane's parents, the coffee pot shorting out, and salmonella-infested cheese—and we don't figure them out until after they've happened. There's also no rhyme or reason to when it decides to release the information, either. It spews when it wants to—whether it's first thing in the morning or midnight.

The third week in, we've moved our operation to the sun porch. Juliane lounges on the wicker couch with the lighthouse cushions, and that leaves me the Swingasan, but I bought it more for looks; I don't trust it'll hold me. Anyway, being on the floor gives me a unique perspective on Juliane as her chestnut eyes drift over the Pier 1 catalogue with a little more, it seems, than just casual interest—sometimes I catch her looking at me, then averting her gaze back to the colorful pages of coastal cottage tablescapes. In those moments, her eyes betray her desire for me.

I can't say that there isn't something inside me that's warming up to the idea of going for it with her.

Then the risk, as it always does, presents itself: it won't end up like *The Little Mermaid* but *Fatal Attraction*, where my heart's so crushed it poisons my mind, makes me slash my wrists and boil rabbits. Worse, I won't have my best friend to turn to because she'll be gone.

"Why'd you spend six hundred bucks on that Swingasan if you're not going to sit in it?" She gnaws on yet another Dum Dum—her fourth today. I hear the distinct sound of her teeth crunching through the candy.

"I don't like the creaking sound it makes. It gives me the heebie-jeebies."

She slams the catalogue against her thighs and slides me a look. "You have a talking mummified piranha in your kitchen and that doesn't bother you, but the chair freaks you out."

"I'm thinkin', broken tailbone if it snaps and I land on the wrought iron stand."

She sighs, then cocks her head back and yells: "What do you think there, Perry?" That's the name she's given it—Perry. Perry the WonderPiranha. "*You* can tell us what's going to happen. If she sits on it, will it break?"

The thing doesn't respond.

She tosses the catalogue on the glass coffee table, chucks her crystal-speckled Dum Dum stick in the ashtray, and reaches for the almost-empty bottle of Patrón. "That's what really sucks." She pops the cork and fills a shot glass. "We have this awesome thing here that can warn us about the future, but we can't make it speak on demand, so what good is it? I mean, we gonna invite people to sit on your sun porch in silence and wait for the thing to talk? It reminds me of *Waiting for Godot*."

⚜

Easter Monday everything changes.

We're eating garlic and onion pizza from Angie's when the fish speaks: *Peepers stairs tree crush.*

Juliane and I scramble to figure out what it means; it's the most words the thing has spoken so far.

"Maybe." Juliane knocks back yet another shot of Patrón. "Maybe peepers means peep frogs."

I've honestly lost track of how many bottles we've—okay, *she's*—been through. She glances out the window, where a menace of swollen greenish-gray clouds trundles across the sea; a threatening rumble resonates in the distance. "There's a big storm coming in, maybe they're going to fall from the sky or something. You've heard of that, right?"

I dip a piece of crust into my tequila. A sliver of fresh garlic drifts to the bottom of my shot glass like an errant flake of skin. "That was at the end of some movie, right?"

"Shit, they went crazy on the garlic this time." She swallows. "*Magnolia*. But it really happens. Earliest reference we have of frogs falling from the sky is in some medieval manuscript, like, five or six hundred years ago? I used to know but I forgot." She takes another bite, chews. "People thought it was all supernatural, but now we know winds or twisters pick the things up and drop 'em elsewhere."

I look beyond the houses across the street. The ocean is obscured in fog—a sure sign this is going to be one of those violent spring clippers. There's a flash of lightning, and a spray of rain hits the windows.

Peepers stairs tree crush.

The rain gets louder, and the fish raises its voice.

Peepers stairs tree crush!

The wind hastens past the house with a haunting shriek, which I'm not unused to; here on the New England coast, the winds gusting off the sea are shrill as banshees, and they wail on and off through the day and night, *every* day and night. Eventually, it grates on your nerves to the point that even when there is a lull for a day or so, you swear you hear it: in your dreams, in the shower, at your job. If you've reached this state, you are what we call *wind crazy*.

Wind crazy is definitely not what we're suffering now as the wind suddenly increases and railroads into the house. In the kitchen, the windows shiver. Outside, on the back deck, a stack of plastic turquoise chairs tips over. Upstairs, glass breaks.

For a second I just sit, paralyzed.

Juliane's up and moving, and I'm on her heels, but I'm not fast enough to keep her from rushing upstairs to see what has happened . . .

There is a bang and a pop and the whole frame of the house shudders. "Juliane!" I scream at the base of the stairs.

She doesn't answer, and I'm about to start up the staircase when a massive tree crashes through the living room ceiling, missing me by inches. A sharp piece of wood would have impaled my chest had I remained where I was standing.

It feels like someone's sucked every breath out of my lungs.

Juliane screams, tumbles down the stairs, and lands at my feet.

I pull her clear of the bannister, which suddenly seems flimsy as cardboard.

"My leg," she says. "Ouch, God!"

"It's okay!" I press her against my chest. Cold sea-salted gusts whip our bodies and rain needles our faces. My hands are already raw.

"Jumpin' dart frogs!" Juliane struggles to catch her breath. "What the hell's gonna be next?"

Somehow, despite the noise, we hear the mummified piranha.

Money coming.

"Oh my God!" Juliane shrieks. "It answered!"

I'm confused. "What?"

"Ow!" She grimaces at the pain in her leg. "All this time we've been hoping to get the damn thing into some kind of pattern. It just answered. I asked it a question, and it answered!"

It says it again: *Money coming.*

Juliane beams. "What'd I tell ya, right? We're gonna be rich!"

And then she kisses me.

⁂

My crippling anxiety is rooted in a thwarted trip to Disney World.

It was a tenth birthday present from Auntie Ree, so I couldn't wait—we were even going on a plane. She'd brought me Viewmaster reels showing a sleek white train parking inside a cavernous hotel lobby, a submarine we could ride in in a sparkling lagoon, and men in grass skirts twirling fire batons.

The night before we were supposed to leave, an ambulance came, and they took Auntie Ree away. The plane left without us. For weeks I hoped she would show up at our house and say it had all been some kind of cruel joke. I had dreams about her walking into my room, telling me she'd called Mickey Mouse and he'd said everything was just fine, *you can still come, see ya real soon!*

But I never saw her again.

Although that's when anxiety took over my life, nothing has been as bad since then.

Until now.

While the lovemaking is amazing and I relish in having decisions made for me, Juliane's been my friend for so long, the stakes are high. Worse, crawling out from the rubble of the fallen tree means that I have no home—at least for a couple of months. I'm terrified of the commitment of living with Juliane, but Juliane, clearly, is ready to live with me.

We stand in her tiny apartment with the dark-paneled walls and colonial furniture that has been in her life since she was born. She has an interesting theme going on with a ship's wheel on her chimney, and in her fireplace, a giant fish tank teems with darting streaks of blue, yellow, pink, and green.

The fish sits on the mantel and stares at me. I wish I could just ask it now what was going to happen, and it would tell me.

"No worries, Margie. When this is all over, we're going to take our piles of cash and get a really nice place together!" She roots through a Costco-sized bag of Dum Dums, taking them out a handful at a time and picking up each to look at the wrappers. She squints. "Motherfucker, I'm getting old. I'm gonna have to buy cheaters to read these things."

"Five dollars, Christmas Tree Shops," I say.

"Pffft." She waves her hand in a dismissive motion. "You're not *that* much older than me."

But yes, yes I am when it comes to that magical moment when you suddenly can't read small print. We may have been best friends, but that's only because I was held back twice—the thought of advancing a grade, where I'd encounter new teachers, new classrooms, even a new school—was so petrifying I'd be nauseated for weeks just thinking about it, so there were two years in there where I so badly wanted to stay in my safe surroundings I just deliberately failed so I couldn't advance. Eventually, Juliane caught up with me and we were in the same grade, but I'm at least two years older than her.

What if she gets bored and leaves me? What if I wake up, roll over, and there's only a note?

Worse, what if there *is* a happily ever after? No, really, what if there is? She's not in the safest of jobs. She told me once that people in her field even joke about it.

We were having dinner at Go Fish, and she was busy wolfing down her mussels appetizer. "Listen, you can't be an aquarist and be 'in the club' unless three things have happened to you." She speared a squishy tan morsel on her appetizer fork and swirled it around in the pool of ale sauce in the bottom of the bowl before dipping it in parmesan cheese. "One, you gotta fall into a tank; two, something's gotta take a bite out of you, or, you have to have contracted some kind of weird illness or parasite from somehow getting fish shit germs into one of your orifices." She shoved the mussel in her mouth and chewed noisily. "Three, you gotta get electrocuted. God! I kinda feel bad eating these, but damn they're yummy."

I had found it cheeky and cute then, but now, not so much. What if they call me and say *she fell into the shark tank*? Or *she contracted a flesh-eating parasite*? Or *there she was, standing in a pool of water when somebody plugged something in*?

What if she dies on me?

"Oooh! Cherry!" She's been scrolling on her phone and manipulates the Dum Dum to one side of her mouth. "I've been looking at all these websites that tell fortunes—you know, tarot sites, psychic sites—did you know there's even a site that lets you play with a virtual Ouija board?—and you know what's *really* popular now is live-streaming . . . people can watch ol' Perry just do his thing, *live*."

The idea of actually taking this thing so public scares me. "Wait a minute—you're doing this *online*?"

Juliane blinks. "Well, yeah, how the hell else would we do it? Sit on street corners like panhandlers?"

"What if my neighbor sees it and finds out?"

"She's probably in places that don't have the internet, so don't worry." She tosses the phone aside, rises from the couch, and stands before me. She sets her hands on my shoulders, and the smell of the raw fish she cuts up every day to feed the animals at her job is obscured by the cloy of her cherry Dum Dum and her lavender hand cream.

"But we don't know when the thing is going to speak; we can't guarantee that."

She shakes me by the shoulders. "Easy! We go freemium—in other words, we lure them in. They can watch Perry right from our page for as long as they like."

I take a moment and try to figure out how that makes sense. "But how is that going to make us money if we're not charging? And there's no way to ensure that what it says is the message intended for a specific person."

"Ha! No." She bites through the Dum Dum with a mighty *crack*. "That's really not what we're selling. We're the ones with the dictionary, right? *We're going to sell them the translations.*"

She chews the Dum Dum and it sounds like she's grinding sand in her teeth.

For some reason this instills panic. "What if we're wrong? *Money coming* hasn't happened yet."

She thinks for a minute, then cups my face in her hands. They're rough and dry from having been *in salt water and fish shit all day*, as she likes to put it, but to me they feel like magic. "*Sure* it has, honey. The insurance company's paying for the damage to your house, right? Doesn't that count as money coming?"

"They're paying the contractors directly."

She sighs. "Well, then, it means Perry's going to bring it big time. We'll call the site 'The Mystic Mermaid'! What do you think?"

"Well—"

"You know the coat closet we've got in the front hall? It's perfect to set him up, and a camera on a desk, a microphone—all we need is some fun stuff to decorate the backdrop with. You know, some sea shells, lights—ooh! We can get one of those blue lights that spins around and puts fake waves on the walls! We have one of those in the jelly exhibit in the aquarium and it just creates the *best* atmosphere. Whaddaya think there, Perry, huh?" She yells in the direction of the mantel. "You wanna be the Mystic Mermaid and tell people what's comin' on down the creek so they're not up it without a paddle?"

The mummified thing is silent.

Juliane frowns and shrugs into her jean jacket, then grabs her leather shopper and swings it up on her shoulder. "Well, that's just great, wrinkly one, I don't really care what your opinion is when it comes to this, anyway. We're gonna go buy some equipment and craft shit and make it happen." She rams her cell phone in her pocket and starts heading for the door.

I hear it: *Sunset and smackers.*

Smackers? My God. What does *that* mean?

She turns, jangling her keys. "You coming, or what?"

"But—"

She blinks. "What?"

Sunset. Does he mean *tonight* sunset? "You *heard* what it said. Maybe—maybe we shouldn't go today."

For a moment, she looks slightly confused. "It's almost never literal. We'll figure it out later. Come on! The future awaits!"

⁂

It wasn't until years later that I found out what had doomed my aunt. Apparently, there had been an undetected brain tumor.

She had, for a year or so before that, told my other aunts that her eye had looked strange—*droopy* was the word she used—but only *she* ever saw it, I guess, because they'd tell her it was just in her imagination, that it was all just stemming from fear.

⚜

Several hours later, Juliane cleans out the coat closet. She takes a kitchen stool and drapes it in sparkling aqua cloth that I'm sure is a fave of dance moms everywhere, and across from it, on another stool, she sets up her laptop so the camera is centered.

The fish she's decked out in a tiny turban and a pair of fake earrings. "Can't go scaring the customers," she says, struggling to fit a mermaid tail she cut off a Disney Ariel doll over his ass end.

I almost feel bad for him.

"I've already put out the word on Facebook and I'm going to run ads," she says. "Check out this website!"

What she's done is equally absurd, the front page bordered in a wallpaper of the Amazon jungle.

Now you can harness the power of the Amazon basin's best kept secret . . . The Mystic Mermaid. Underneath that, a version of the story she'd told me what seems like a hundred years ago now appears.

Hit the PayPal button below, select your prediction package, and we'll take you to meet this Amazonian wonder.

Our expert translators will give you the message you've been waiting to hear!

"Expert translators?"

"Well, we *are*. We're the only ones that've figured out what things mean."

"Except for sunset and smackers."

She blinks. "I'm sure we'll figure that out."

The Mystic Mermaid knows all. You'll never be anxious again.

Bing! comes from her computer.

"That's it!" Juliane beams. "I bet that's our first customer!"

Money coming, the fish says.

"Don't worry, babe." She sets a hand on my arm. "This is going to be awesome."

⁂

It's midnight and I think it's Juliane's snoring that wakes me—she snores a lot, something I hadn't really recalled from when we were kids having sleepovers at each other's houses. I watch the sheer navy curtains flutter in the breeze from the heating vent beneath the window, and I can hear the whispering as the hot air is forced through.

Then I realize it couldn't have been Juliane's snoring that woke me, because she's not snoring at all at the moment.

I roll over and rest on my elbow to look at her. Her full lips are parted, and I can see her eyes flitting about beneath their lids; I remember that this means someone's dreaming. I wonder what she dreams about. If I'm in those dreams, and we're on the beach in Tahiti like she promised, or maybe we're on a vacation together, or maybe—

Sunset and smackers!

It was the fish. The *fish* woke me.

Juliane doesn't stir—and she's a light sleeper. I remember when we were kids and the sound of my mom's footsteps coming quietly down the hall would wake her.

Sunset and smackers!

It makes me uncomfortable that Juliane keeps blowing off figuring out what that means, and although we've barely started this little adventure, I already long for those days spent gnawing on Angie's pizza and sitting on my sun porch. Still, sunset today came and went. Maybe Juliane was right; it's not a literal sunset that it's talking about. And smackers—I try to avoid thinking it's something bad. Smackers could mean money, of course, but you could give someone a smack on the lips, right? So it could be kisses . . .

Fire safe not present!

I sit up.

Fire safe not present!

I carefully curl back the blankets, tiptoe to the foyer closet, and turn on the light.

The fish stares at me. Despite its ridiculous getup, it almost looks sinister.

Leaf alone!

"What. What is it?"

Deviant whispers.

"I don't know what that means!"

"Margie?"

I nearly jump out of my skin.

Juliane stands in the hall. The shadow behind her stretches out in a spindly, almost inhuman shape. "What are you doing?"

I rub my arms as a chill settles over me.

"It's talking."

She hesitates, then frowns. "I *missed* it?"

"Yeah."

"Tomorrow we'll get the dictionary and set our heads to it! Come back to bed."

She takes my hand, and I look at the fish one last time before snapping off the light. In its dark pits I could swear I see a flash of pity.

⚜

Juliane goes to work. A few hours later, the call comes.

She was crawling in the ceiling over a ten-foot-high tank that contained poisonous jellyfish—the kind people get rushed to the hospital for.

Fortunately, she didn't die, but she's laid up. Her leg is four times its size, and she's not getting around unless I carry her. For a while I sit with her on the couch and rest my head on her shoulder while she creates Facebook ads for the fish.

"I can take more time off work to stay home with you," I say.

No slack, says the fish.

"You need to go to work." She kisses the top of my head. "Absolutely."

"I just feel bad—"

"Are you kidding? Getting into a smack of jellies is the best thing that ever happened to—it's the best thing that ever happened to *us*!" She reaches into the bag for a Dum Dum and unwraps it, sticks it in her mouth. "Ew. Peach Mango and S'mores. Foul." She shifts the laptop and types. "I obviously can't go back to work right now, so I can spend all my time with Perry and make our new lives happen."

Smack. "What did you say?"

She pulls the lollipop from her mouth. "I said, 'I obviously can't go back to—"

"No, before that."

"Getting into a smack of jellies is the best thing that ever happened? Why?"

"Smack—what is that?"

She smiles. Her teeth look a little less white now that she's not wearing her usual raisin-colored lipstick. "A school of fish, a shoal of piranha, a smack of jellies."

"Smackers!" I say.

She pulls away from me. "What?"

"Sunset and *smackers*! The smackers were the jellyfish."

"Jellies," she corrects me. "They're not fish."

Another *bing* from her laptop. "Ooh! We have another customer." She pushes me aside. "You know we've made two hundred bucks in twenty-four hours? We get four people a day, that's six grand a month!" She looks at me and I'm hoping she's going to kiss me, but she doesn't. Instead, she slams the laptop closed. "Here, go set this up."

I take the laptop and set it on its stool in the closet.

No slack, it says. *Fire safe not present!*

I have no idea what no slack means, but I don't like the word fire, and once I get Juliane settled, I spend the afternoon checking all the plugs in the house and replacing the batteries in all of her smoke detectors.

When I arrive at work there's a strange bustling over at Kasey's desk. Several coworkers—including my boss—are huddled, whispering and giggling, in front of her computer.

Now, as I set my coffee down and drape my jacket over the back of the chair and realize there's no photo of me and Juliane yet on my desk, she shouts, "Margo! Have you heard about this thing? Come here—this is amazing!"

I'm a little nervous—I'm not included in anything that goes on here; most of the time, I keep my head down. For me, staying out of politics has always been the best way to hang on to what I've got.

"What do you suppose it means?" says Jeanne, who loves to share where to find the cheapest yarn. "I mean, *kick out the quiet?*"

Oh, no.

I swallow and creep over to the bunch, trying to sound natural and at ease when I ask, "What *is* that?"

Meghan—who's actually quiet, bookish and reads *National Geographic* when she's not answering phones, pins her golden hair up using a freshly-sharpened pencil. "It's this thing they found in the Amazon . . . it's a prognosticator." She briefly explains how it works.

I feign surprise and amazement.

Courtney stands up and straightens the flouncy neck scarf on her hot pink silk blouse, sighing. "Okay, everyone. This is really interesting, but we were supposed to start work five minutes ago." She eyes me. "Can I see you for a moment?"

The gaggle disperses. Kasey looks quickly away and shuffles papers.

Courtney closes the door and I sit down across from her.

"We know what you've been doing with the mail," she says, and fires me.

⁂

After an angst-ridden ride home, I turn into our condo complex and see there are people milling about in the parking lot—Mrs. G, the dog lady who lives two doors down from us; Pete, the hotel manager who helped me move a trunk of my things into Juliane's place just last week. The air is heavy with the smell of burning wood and some kind of chemical, and then I see her—Juliane. Juliane, sitting on someone's forlorn patio chair, watching our condo burn.

I leap from my Corolla with not a thought toward killing the engine and grabbing the keys, and I bang my thigh painfully on the door as I try to shove my way past the few people and leap over a fire hose to get to her.

She looks up at me, ashen, but doesn't move to embrace me.

I lean down and try to get my arms around her. "What happened?"

"I crawled my way to the door." Juliane coughs. "Thank God I was in the foyer closet, so the door was right there, and . . . thank God I got Perry out."

I realize why she hasn't hugged me.

She's clutching that damn fish.

Stop slack.

The checks. It was talking about my shoving the checks in the drawer . . . it was telling me to stop that.

Fire safe not present.

It was telling me there was going to be a fire but we'd all be safe and I wouldn't be home.

Everything about the old legend of this thing comes back to me: *It was a disaster . . . Ford was warned . . . by a mummy piranha cursed with the gift of foresight . . . seeing teeth . . . Ford ignored the warnings because he thought it was Roosevelt messing with him.*

This thing doesn't foretell the future.

It warns people.

I think how I'd been given warnings and didn't really understand them, didn't listen. But if I really did understand them, if I *did* listen—I'd never not know what was coming around the pike again, would I? I could always be prepared. And have no more anxiety.

And that means other people wouldn't, too.

This is a gift. This isn't something we should be charging for.

There's the sound of breaking glass; our bedroom window shatters.

"Juliane, I . . . "

"Yes?" She's petting the fish.

Then another warning hits me: *Leaf alone.*

If I say something, she'll leave me. Not just homeless at the moment, but jobless and penniless, too. "I'm thinking that maybe . . . " A fireman walks by us, carrying an ax.

Her back ramrods, and she gives me a hard expression. She's not even the person she was three weeks ago.

Leaf alone.

"Come on, Margie. What?"

I watch as another hose attacks the second floor window. "I got fired today."

She doesn't react at first, and seems to hold the fish closer. "See? Now you won't have to quit."

My house hasn't been repaired yet, so for now, it's a hotel. Not that money's a problem—Juliane was certainly right about that, we've got loads coming in. But the close quarters, something young lovers should absolutely adore, seems to make things worse.

For one, I'm increasingly uncomfortable with the idea that we're charging people, and she's incredibly secretive about what's in the bank account. Two, our room is a suite and has not one, but two closets—one large enough for The Mystic Mermaid operation. The walls are Kleenex and spit, but Juliane clearly doesn't want me to hear what she's up to all day. She staples padding to the walls and tells me she can't be interrupted, because the spirit inside the fish might get spooked and deliver the wrong message, if at all. She spends less time with me and more time with the fish.

The fish has had a new, strange message for me as well: *Tear it down.*

Tear it down. Tear what down? And that's not something I'd ever do, destroy anything, break anything—that's not me. *Not me.* I like to keep things the way they are. I don't like change. I can't have uncontrolled change.

Tear it down.

Something isn't right. Not about her, and not about any of this.

I stand at the door and press my ear to it and hear: "Leaf left."

But that's not the fish's voice. Not at all.

I feel like I've just been Steve Irwin'd.

It's Juliane's.

"Leaf left," she whispers.

And she's selling old predictions—that prediction was *mine*, the day I was going to drop the damn thing on Marilyn's porch.

I think about the way she told me I needed to be at work. The way she reacted to the fire.

Deviant whispers.

She's cheating these people.

I bang open the door; Juliane jumps. "What!"

"Hang up," I demand.

"Why . . . "

"Hang. Up!"

For the first time, I think I see something like fear in her eyes, and it hurts me, that—even if only for a second—she's afraid of me.

I glance at the mummy. It just looks sort of pathetic and sad, like an old woman in a pink housecoat and smeared lipstick. I feel pity for him, and so instead of continuing with Juliane, I go to the fish and take off the ridiculous turban, earrings and worst of all, the fish tail; I hold him in my arms and for one second I swear I hear him say *thank you.* "What have we become? Never mind that, what have *you* become?"

"Oh, come on. It doesn't really matter, does it?" She stands, reaching for the fish.

I don't let her have him, and the words are out of my mouth before I can stop them: "Yes, actually. Yes, it does."

Juliane straightens and cocks her head to the side, pulling back. She blinks at me for a second, as though she's completely surprised. "What?"

"I said, it *does* matter."

"We're giving people *hope.* What's the difference *how* they get hope, the important thing is that they *have* it."

This infuriates me. I know what it's like to have such anxieties, to look at those tarot cards and make my daily decisions based on what I see there, or in many cases what some other woman saw there, and she doesn't understand what she's doing?

Or maybe she does.

In this moment I do not see the Juliane with the full lips. I do not hear Juliane of the interesting folklore, I do not feel Juliane of the soft tender hands or magical kisses, or taste Juliane of the Patrón who fixes me when I am broken.

She has become a woman-thing I don't know.

Tear it down.

Now I know what the fish means.

I take a deep breath and say it. "I think you should go."

Juliane just stands and stares, and I see the little clock wheels turning in her head. Then she folds her arms across her chest and leans back a little. "What?"

"I said, I think you should go."

"I'm sorry, are you—you just want some space, I get it."

"No. Get out and don't come back."

Now there's a silence in the room that is heavy, heavier than the thing I carry in the pit of my stomach, that painful boulder that makes me want to run and hide beneath anything I can find. But it feels better because it's not inside my body; it's not. It's *outside*. It's outside, and it's between us, and it's all those unspoken things I could never say to anyone, all the disappointment and the stress and the loss. Nobody had ever asked me how I felt, or cared enough about me to tell me what I should do.

But the fish, the fish knows.

"Are you—are you breaking *up* with me?"

I heave a deep sigh.

Sixty-five over, says the fish.

It's clear she hasn't heard that.

Sixty-five over, it says again.

I make the mistake of eyeing the horrifying thing, and she looks at me quizzically, then turns, glances at the fish. "Oh, my God. That thing stopped talking to me, but it didn't stop talking to *you*, did it?" She whirls on me. "Is it telling *you* to break up with me? Is that what this is about? Because, you know, you . . ." her voice softens, and she unfolds her arms. "Listen, this isn't like you, and the fish—you know, Perry, he was really just here for us to get off to a great start." She approaches me. "It's our time now! We can go be together somewhere, just you and me, and I won't have to work, and we can just—do whatever we want, and I don't have to tell these ridiculous stories to slow-on-the-uptake brats who don't give a shit about anything except their phones anyway."

I take a step back.

She stiffens, widens her eyes in surprise. "Is this real? You're really going to do this to me?"

For a moment I think there's still time, still time to take it all back. But wouldn't I rather be alone than dealing with this?

You won't be alone. You'll have the fish.

When I go to answer her and say *Yes*, something like a croak comes out. I nod instead.

Her expression flares. "I just—I can't believe you're taking the word of that *thing* over me!" She marches to the couch to grab her jean jacket. "Seriously? Well, all that money we made? I'm keeping it. All of it!"

I'm surprised when I hear myself say, "Fine." It occurs to me at this moment that I don't give a shit about money and never have, and that this was really all her thing. That everybody I've always been with, I just go along with whatever they want. I've never made a decision for myself, ever. I realize I have no real personality. I have nothing that's my own. I just sort of morph and become whoever it is the person I'm with wants me to be.

Well, not today.

Today, I'm making a decision.

Tear it down.

She gets as far as the door and rests her hand on the knob. "You were always so timid and afraid, I never had to worry about you leaving. Like all the others did."

I stand there, waiting for her to say more.

She approaches me, sets her hands on Perry, and gives him a tug.

I don't budge and clutch him tighter.

She gives me a desperate look. "Margie, I . . . I've done all of this for you! For *us*!"

It's like I'm standing outside of my body when I say it: "There is no *us*."

"I just don't understand!"

"There is. No. Us." I turn and look at her. She was so beautiful to me once. Before that, she had the face of an angel, someone I'd trust with my life, someone I could always run to when my heart got broken. But now, she looks hard, angular, and—not pretty anymore. She's not pretty. All I see is the ugliness that she made choices for people that should have made their own—even if it was on the fish's *genuine* advice.

I stand there and wait for her to say more.

"Well."

Silence. Just the sound of her panicked—yes, panicked!— breathing.

She opens the door and walks out, slams it behind her.

Suddenly, I'm not afraid to be alone. I can do this. I can move back into my house—not only repaired, but completely refurbished—or I can just sell the damn thing, get out of here, and never have to deal with Juliane or anyone again.

Where would I go?

House mouse perfect fun, says the fish.

Of course!

Disney World.

And it will be just the way it was supposed to have been planned. Starting over again. Starting from where the whole disaster element came into my life, and picking up fresh.

I behold the hideous wrinkled thing. "What do you think?"

I'd swear he winks at me. *Fifty-nine over*, it says.

"That's right, Perry!" I say. "It's *over*."

And I realize, repairs completely finished or not, that I want to go home.

I put the fish in his box and do just that.

I open my front door and, despite the fact that the living room still needs some work and there's a film of construction dust over just about everything, nothing feels like it's changed.

In the sunroom, I see the pillow where Juliane left it; on the stairs, I feel that magical kiss. In the kitchen, I taste the post-break-up shots of Patrón—in fact, miraculously, it seems like there's still half a bottle on the wicker bar.

But *I'm* different. It all seems so distant now, like it's not my life, and I feel strong.

"It's just you and me, Perry," I say aloud.

There's a knock at the door, and I jump.

I set Perry, in his box, on the mantel.

On my porch stands a slight young woman a few inches shorter than me, her hair the color of leather. She takes a step back when I open the door, almost as though she's unsure about disturbing me. "I'm . . . I'm sorry." Her voice is rich and low, like one of those exotic beauties in a 1930s adventure film. "I . . . I'm Marilyn. Your neighbor."

So this is what she looks like! Her eyes are the blue of peacock feathers—I know they must be contacts, but it would be wonderful if they were real—and she has a long, thin face and a nose that turns up slightly.

She runs a hand through her hair. "I'm sorry to bother you, but . . . I just got home, I've been away for several months, and . . . a friend of mine said your packages tend to get delivered to my house, and so I was hoping maybe this one time you got mine."

It takes me a second to realize the friend she's referring to is Suzanne. Suzanne was the only one who'd supposedly met her who would know that.

I suddenly wonder if Suzanne broke up with me for reasons other than what she'd cited.

"So, I was wondering if you got any."

The smell of late June tiger lilies wafts through the house.

"It's really important," she says.

Yes, yes it is. I will always know what's coming down the road apiece. I will never have anxiety again.

Awkward moment. A car passes by.

Less than one over, Perry says.

She tilts her head a little to the left. "Did you hear that?"

"Hear what?"

Forty-five.

The blue eyes I once thought so heavenly now pierce through me.

She blinks. "You don't hear that."

"I have . . . I've got . . . Netflix on upstairs."

Twenty-three.

"Really?"

My nerves kick in. I try not to stutter and say the first thing that pops into my head—what the hell was that movie Juliane and I watched? "Yes. Yes—*Mascots*."

"*Mascots?*"

"Yeah—it's—" Who the hell directed that? "It's—you know, the guy who did *Waiting for Guffman*? This one's about sports team mascots. Competing for trophies."

Sixteen.

"They must be at the part where they're doing countdowns for the routines or something." I glance down at my feet, then back at her. "It's a great movie. You should watch it."

Marilyn is quiet.

Perry says nothing further.

Marilyn looks away, perhaps at the rose bush alongside my driveway. "It'll drive you crazy, you know. At first, you'll think it's the most amazing gift, that you know things, good, bad, indifferent." She turns and stares intently back at me. "Until it tells you something you really don't want to hear, so you ignore it."

There is another uncomfortable silence. Then, she sighs. "Well, okay then. If you see a package show up, would you let me know?"

I nod. "Absolutely. Sure."

I close the door. Through a sidelight, I watch her make her way down the porch, her batik skirt that seems a little too long for her billowing with each step.

In the silence, the fish whispers the clearest message it's ever uttered.

Give me back.

An excerpt from
the upcoming novella

Tidings

By Kristi Petersen
Schoonover

CHAPTER ONE

In the sunburnt Iowa cornfield, dead crows stretched from the tips of Reese's Old Gringos to a dilapidated barn at the edge of the horizon. She could have believed it was a gloss of licorice if it weren't for the smell, like skunk and rancid chopped meat; between that and the sweat snailing down her belly into the waistline of her skirt, it wasn't easy to quell the rising tide of ill.

"So." Her ex-husband, Mason, let the word hang in the breeze like an empty noose.

She couldn't blame his apprehension. Her inexplicable, partly psychic gift of interpreting bird language had put a wedge between them seventeen years ago, but at the moment, it had brought them back together. In the wake of flocks of birds dropping out of the sky on an almost daily basis—even WHISPers, the event reporting system, was overwhelmed—Mason could no longer be the USGS's senior ornithologist, reassuring the media, "This means nothing." *We don't think what it means is good news,* he'd told her. *You understand the birds. You can tell us what's happening.*

There was nothing to say, and there was everything to say.

He shoved his hands in the pockets of his cargo shorts. "This is the magnitude of what we've been seeing. They're all this bad."

Nausea hit her, hard, but she refused to buckle.

"Reese?"

She closed her eyes and took a deep breath.

"You okay?"

The shrilling of the year's just-emerged cicada brood drilled through her. "Yes."

"Do you feel anything?"

"Incredibly sad. Overwhelmed." She brushed a sweat-dampened curl from her forehead. "Jesus."

"No." He turned to face her. "Do you *feel* anything? Can you hear them?"

She was held by his eyes; deep and full of trust, so different from the days when he hadn't believed her, when he'd thought she was insane, when he'd been embarrassed by her going to people's houses and helping them solve their bird infestation problems. "I can only hear them if they're alive, Mason. Did you forget that?"

He held her gaze for a moment, then looked down at his work boots and back out at the field. "I've forgotten a lot of things."

There was an uncomfortable weight between them, and a hot wind whipped scorched grit into her eyes and did little to cool her down. Despite the cicadas, she could sense something out there: a whisper, a *hish*, a rustling. "I think there's a couple that survived the fall."

He looked at her. "You kidding?"

"No. There's one, maybe two. They'd be on top—they landed on those that fell before them." It made her sick to say it. "Like a cushion."

"So what *are* they saying?"

"I need to find them, Mason. I need to find at least one and hold it in my hands. It's too weak for me to hear."

Another leaden moment between them, and she could feel her heart pulsing in her ears. He kicked at the sand and a cloud of brown silt drifted toward the truck. "I'll see if I can find some sticks." He turned and walked parallel to a line of skeletal cornstalks.

"No, no." She rolled open the flap on her messenger bag. "We're good, I have medical gloves—"

"I'm not getting that close to them. You use the gloves. I'll use a stick, thanks."

"Would *you* want someone poking at you with a stick?"

He stopped and glared at her, and after a few moments she saw resignation in his eyes. He held out his hand. "Fine. Gimmie."

She passed him a pair of blue latex gloves and contemplated the first step, which would render her calf-deep in avian corpses. An apple-sized yellow bird with a black head hit her shoulder and plummeted to the ground.

An eastern goldfinch.

She crouched down to tend to it, but then something hit her back, knocking the breath from her lungs. Next came a hit to her head, plowing her over on her side onto the bed of bodies. She felt the sickly crunch of their wing bones and heard Mason yelling before suddenly he had her arm and she was being hauled—her feet barely touching the ground—behind him, back to the truck. It was raining birds and leaving marks that would become bruises and something sharp scored a hot streak down her cheek—

He shoved her in the truck and leapt in after her, slammed the door behind him, and gathered her underneath him as the bodies fell with the metallic *clonk* of hailstones. She inhaled and closed her eyes, comforted by that familiar Devil's Holiday tobacco and sailcloth smell of his and his breath on the back of her neck.

One last *ka-thunk* and it was over.

Silence for several moments; even the cicadas sang nothing.

Mason let go and sat up straight, brushing himself off. "Instinct. Sorry."

"It's okay." She was ashamed to admit she missed what he felt like, so she said nothing.

"Your cheek," he said.

She blinked, not understanding. He took her hand and set it against her face, where she now recognized a searing sensation.

Her fingers came away covered in blood.

He produced a grimy souvenir washcloth—*Don't mess with Texas*—from the door pocket and handed it to her. "We need to get you sewn up, I think." He reached for the ignition and they hauled onto the two-lane road.

She felt a thrumming at her thigh, and at first she thought it was the ridiculously loud engine. There was something else, though, a faint *pa-chip-chip-chip per-chick-a-ree*, and the thrumming grew stronger, into a pounding. She peered into her still-open messenger bag. There was a puffball of a goldfinch inside, and she was alive. "Oh my God."

"What?"

She reached in carefully and picked it up. Its wing was injured, and the bird was angry enough to snap its little beak at Reese, but she couldn't hear it over the engine. "It's one of the birds. Pull over."

"We need to get that looked at."

"Pull over. You wanted your answers. You're not going to get them if you don't stop the car."

He seemed to only go faster.

"Do it on the way."

"I can't hear it over your fucking engine! Pull over, *dammit!*"

He glanced at her, then back at the road for a long moment. Finally, he slowed down and pulled off the pavement into a dirt shoulder peppered with brown shrubs.

He turned off the truck.

The bird's feathers felt like warm silk pajamas, the goldfinch's heartbeat thready beneath Reese's thumb. Crows represented the crossing of souls to the underworld, and finches of any kind represented an awakening to nature. When Reese looked into the finch's eyes, it stopped snapping its beak, and Reese heard its soul say what she was sure the world wasn't going to want to hear.

ACKNOWLEDGMENTS

Heather, Meghan, and Nanette: you waste no time refilling my creative goblet when there are only drops left. Thank you!

I owe so much to the Crow's Nest Writer's Group—Lauren Baratz-Logsted, Greg Logsted, Jackie Logsted, Andrea Schicke-Hirsch, Lauren Simpson, Rob Mayette, and Bob Gulian—for making the stories in this book possible. The hours you spent lovingly critiquing these pieces made them what they are today.

A shout-out goes to my childhood friend Kristina Hals, who spent her time reading through a large portion of my body of work to help me decide what should be included in this collection. Thank you, and may our summers by Candlewood Lake never end.

I'm grateful, also, to Stacey Longo. Who knew one afternoon selling books together at a Zombie Walk for Hunger would last forever? It's been eight adventurous years of acceptances and rejections, parties and illnesses, write-a-holic retreats and escapist trips. I wouldn't trade a minute of it and I couldn't imagine life without you. Long live Kipling.

ABOUT THE AUTHOR

Kristi Petersen Schoonover has recently made peace with her most frightening shadows, although she still sleeps with the lights on.

She is the author of the collection *Skeletons in the Swimmin' Hole: Tales from Haunted Disney World*, the novel *Bad Apple*, the novelette *This Poisoned Ground*, and the novella "Splendid Chyna," which appears in The Terror Project's *Three on a Match*.

She curated the *Ink Stains* anthology Volume 7, served as co-editor for *Read Short Fiction*, and was the recipient of three Norman Mailer Writers Colony winter residencies.

She studied under Daniel Pearlman at the University of Rhode Island and holds an MFA in Creative Writing from Goddard College.

She serves as co-host of the *Dark Discussions* podcast, and lives in the Connecticut woods with her housemate, Charles, her husband, Nathan, and two cats. Follow her adventures at kristipetersenschoonover.com.